KRISSY BACCARO

Lies That Bind

Ella Perri Mysteries Book 3

First published by Krissy Baccaro 2023

Copyright © 2023 by Krissy Baccaro

All rights reserved. No part of this publication may be reproduced, stored or transmitted in any form or by any means, electronic, mechanical, photocopying, recording, scanning, or otherwise without written permission from the publisher. It is illegal to copy this book, post it to a website, or distribute it by any other means without permission.

This novel is entirely a work of fiction. The names, characters and incidents portrayed in it are the work of the author's imagination. Any resemblance to actual persons, living or dead, events or localities is entirely coincidental.

First edition

This book was professionally typeset on Reedsy.
Find out more at reedsy.com

FOR SARAH AND MICHAEL my heart
FOR JIMMY my soul

Contents

Acknowledgments   iii

I   And So It Begins…

CHAPTER ONE	3
CHAPTER TWO	12
CHAPTER THREE	19
CHAPTER FOUR	25
CHAPTER FIVE	32
CHAPTER SIX	38
CHAPTER SEVEN	43
CHAPTER EIGHT	48
CHAPTER NINE	54
CHAPTER TEN	60
CHAPTER ELEVEN	65
CHAPTER TWELVE	74
CHAPTER THIRTEEN	78
CHAPTER FOURTEEN	85
CHAPTER FIFTEEN	93
CHAPTER SIXTEEN	100
CHAPTER SEVENTEEN	104
CHAPTER EIGHTEEN	112
CHAPTER NINETEEN	119
CHAPTER TWENTY	126
CHAPTER TWENTY-ONE	130
CHAPTER TWENTY-TWO	137

CHAPTER TWENTY-THREE	141
CHAPTER TWENTY-FOUR	147
CHAPTER TWENTY-FIVE	154
CHAPTER TWENTY-SIX	158
CHAPTER TWENTY-SEVEN	168
CHAPTER TWENTY-EIGHT	175
CHAPTER TWENTY-NINE	180
CHAPTER THIRTY	188
CHAPTER THIRTY-ONE	192
CHAPTER THIRTY-TWO	196
CHAPTER THIRTY-THREE	200
CHAPTER THIRTY-FOUR	208
CHAPTER THIRTY-FIVE	214
CHAPTER THIRTY-SIX	221
CHAPTER THIRTY-SEVEN	228
CHAPTER THIRTY-EIGHT	233
CHAPTER THIRTY-NINE	237

II Sneak Peek: Moment of Truth Book 4

CHAPTER ONE	247
CHAPTER TWO	251
Would you recommend this book?	256
About the Author	257
Also by Krissy Baccaro	259

Acknowledgments

This book evolved from several readers asking the same question: how did Luca become the dark soul we came to know at the end of the first book, **Buried Secrets**? At the time, I was in the middle of telling the rest of the story in the second book, **One Last Secret**. Although I always knew Luca's story, writing this book allowed me to dive into his past and peel back the layers of his life and I'm glad I did. So, I'd like to thank those who wondered about Luca and asked that question.

I'm so thankful for those who have supported me through this book's journey and throughout the entire journey of the Ella Perri Mystery Series. I am ever so grateful to my friend and editor, Megan Basinger, to my writing community, my family, and my friends.

I am ever so grateful to my very first readers and cheerleaders of the earliest versions of my book, Yolanda and Dennis Parnell and Corrine and Gary Baccaro, whose love, support, feedback, and guidance have never failed to steer me in the right direction.

My deepest gratitude goes to my children, Sarah, and Michael, and to my husband, Jimmy, ready at a moment's notice to lend their opinions and insights for this book and push me forward every step of the way.

And of course, where would I be without you: my readers and fans of mysteries? Thank you for taking a chance with the Ella Perri Mysteries and with me.

I

And So It Begins…

CHAPTER ONE

I awaken to the branches scratching feverishly against the glass, a warning from the wind of an impending storm. I pull the covers to my chin and listen as their crooked hooks drag across the panes, an incessant tap-tap-scratch rhythm. A flash of light and then a smaller light near the curtains, like from a flashlight, stills my heart. I freeze and stare at the window as fear grips me.

Someone's out there.

My hand slides to the vacant side of the bed. The fluffed pillow confirms Salvatore stayed through the night working at the marina. Again.

I glance around me. Nothing has changed. The Veglia windup clock ticks on my bedside table—a makeup gift from Sal last year after a fight. The glint of the moon reveals the placement of the hands to read four fifty-two in the morning, much too late for Sal to still be at work. I blink my eyes a few times to make sure I'm reading it correctly.

A half-filled glass of water sits next to the clock as well as the headache powder I'd forgotten to take. Or had I taken it? I would remember placing the powder on my tongue and washing it down with water, wouldn't I? Two crumpled packets lay among the dusty film on the table, both empty, edges torn, so unlike me to leave them there.

My doctor had promised this medicine was all I needed to eliminate my headaches. Eventually, I got my hands on something more potent to ease my anxiety and silence the chaos in my mind, even if it did become a bad habit for a while, one I'm still dealing with. I'd hardly gotten it under control before the whole town knew about my problem. It was and still is an embarrassment to Sal.

Word travels fast in a small town—like the news about Julia Bernardi, taken from the street she lives on, not far from her house, two days ago. The expressions on Franco's and Luca's faces when we heard she was missing is ingrained in my mind. A parent's worst nightmare.

I shiver at the thought as I gather the packets and sweep the powdery residue with my fingers. I still don't recall having taken any, but that doesn't necessarily mean anything. I glance at the foot of my bed, the dresser, the door—everything is normal in my room. Is it my overactive imagination and too much powder? I don't think so. Tonight feels different. Tonight is real.

A loud creaking from the first floor echoes through the house. Familiar, like the rusty front door I'd reminded Sal over and over again to fix. The noise scares me, but not as much as the footsteps plodding through the living room below. Those are not the sound of Sal's sloppy, whiskey-induced gait I hear. They are different, pronounced . . . purposeful. Sober. They are real, not imagined.

I get to my knees on the bed and think again of Julia's kidnapper, whom they never caught. I squeeze tufts of the blanket in my hands at hearing not one but now two sets of footsteps. One leads and the other follows in a rhythmless dance.

Low, breathy voices float to my bedroom, mixing and folding into one another. A deep man's voice and a smaller one rise and fall in tandem. The small voice—is it a woman? A child? Fear creeps up my spine and I can't move. Of all nights for Sal not to be here. How will I protect the children?

The footsteps halt and a scuffle ensues. The smaller voice urges, whispers, pleads. I strain to hear it—a faint, muffled scream. And then a thud. Then silence. An ominous hum hangs in the air.

Horrible thoughts race through my mind. Another shady customer of Sal's or an old acquaintance? It could be someone Sal cheated who has come to harm our family and even the score. Someone who found out where we keep our marina profits. I deny what I really think, and a sinking feeling curls in my stomach, because what I fear the most is that the person downstairs is the one who snatched Julia Bernardi when no one was looking.

But then a fresh idea comes to me like a punch in the gut: Someone is seeking revenge for what happened years ago. What I failed to do. But I was young, inexperienced, and I let my fear stop me from doing what was right.

Panic forces me back beneath the covers. I don't want to know who is down there. I don't want to look. But the need to protect my children is stronger than my fear. I toss back the blankets, forcing myself from the safety of my warm bed. My shaky legs step into slippers and I throw on my robe, half-tying it at the waist.

In my mind, I picture the phone on the table at the bottom of the stairs, situated in a small alcove between the living room and the kitchen. How will I reach the phone without getting caught? Escape scenarios fly through my mind. I glance at the bedroom closet next to the door—a potential hiding spot. Camouflaged within the panels of the wall, an unsuspecting person would never notice. I'll get the boys from their rooms and bring them back. We'll hide together in the closet until the intruder leaves. We'll squeeze beside the packed suitcase on the floor . . . or sit on top of it. That might be better.

My heart pounds with every step toward my bedroom door. The small table lamp illuminated in the dusky hallway peeks through the opened crack. I put my face to the crack, glimpsing the newel post at the end.

I force myself from my room, treading cautiously down the hall, avoiding the noisy planks, stopping and listening between steps. I want to turn and run back, but not without my boys.

I can do this.

My hand grazes the crack in the wall from Salvatore's fist. I trace the fractured line with my fingers until they dip into the indentation where my head landed the night of our first fight.

Halfway there, the thought of being alone in this big house in the middle of the night with a stranger fills me with terror. No woman should be in her house all alone at night. What if he comes up the stairs?

I open Franco's door and quickly peek in, relieved he's still asleep. I do the same at Luca's door. They have no idea they are no longer safe. But instead of corralling them to hide in my closet, something pulls me to the top of the stairs, and I glimpse the phone at the bottom. So close yet miles away. A corner of the living room peeks from behind. I rest my hand on the loose newel post and squeeze. My heart beats so hard it might burst. My throat squeezes against my windpipe. I have to do this. I have to keep my family safe. Today I cannot hide.

Unrelenting dread forces me to listen to the eerie silence consuming the house. I step to the first stair, and my boys' faces flash through my mind. I step to the next but freeze at a loud noise in the kitchen. Stay calm. Quick movements will give me away.

A new sound arises, hard to identify at first, soft, continuous. Something soft like fabric dragging across the floor. My eyes are glued to the phone. Can I reach it? I descend the stairs quickly and stretch for the receiver. A scratching noise coming from the kitchen, near the old service door, stops me. How peculiar that it is coming from a door that is never used—not for hundreds of years, back when the servants of the house did.

Only wealthy homeowners and their guests were permitted to enter through the main door. Servants were only allowed to use this one, unadorned and tucked at the back. When we first moved in, Sal forbade anyone from using the servants' door. He had warned that if the door were to be opened, the lingering spirits of mistreated servants would be released, and they might seek revenge on us. That same night he'd bolted the door tight. His superstitious, paranoid behaviors seemed to peak at that time.

I glimpse the shed through the window next to the door, illuminated by the outside light. Its presence for some reason chills me.

The scratching continues and pulls me back. It's him. It has to be him.

Suddenly, the doorknob on the servants' door rattles and then stops abruptly. I grab the phone, but the receiver slips from my hand when the rattling continues. He's coming in. I retreat to a shadowed corner near the stairs and brace myself against the banister. I think of Julia Bernardi and glance upward, remembering my first thought to hide with the boys.

CHAPTER ONE

My foot catches on the hem of my robe as I step to the first stair, throwing off my balance. I grab at the wall, accidentally swiping the photograph of my parents, a gift they had given me right before they died. I see it fall to the floor, landing face down. I reach for it on instinct and tumble beside it. At the same time, the servants' door bursts wide open. I scream, sliding back against the wall as Salvatore steps through the doorway.

The chill night air rushes in, along with relief at seeing Sal and not a stranger. But relief is quickly replaced by dread and confusion. As I reason Sal's presence at this moment, at this door, another man steps into the entrance and stands behind him.

Sal scowls at me, lips turned down, eyes filled with disdain. He staggers forward, and a strong whiskey odor swirls around me. He gets in my face and snarls, "What the hell are you doing?"

I cough at his breath and grab the picture from the floor. I jump to my feet and back away, keeping my eyes on him, allowing space between us. He makes me skeptical, untrusting, even of myself. With trembling hands, I set the photograph on the counter, eyeing the hairline crack extending from one edge of the frame to the other. I lift my gaze to the bloodshot eyes of my husband. Don't let him throw you off. He stares at me as if thinking of what to say.

I tighten my robe around my waist, soften my eyes, and say weakly, "You used that door." I point as if he wouldn't have known which one I meant.

The stranger over Sal's shoulder studies me as I negotiate with my husband.

"Why did you use that door?" I hear the shrillness of my voice. I wait for the outburst. Even in his drunken stupor, his eyes have a way of cutting through me. I know better than to ask questions of a drunk man who doesn't even like to answer them sober. But a voice from deep down pushes me, breaking through my need for silence for the sake of peace. "I heard noises," I say, "near the living room at first. Someone opened the front door. Was it . . . did you open the door?" I quiet the question in my head asking why two grown men are wandering around outside at this time of morning.

"Do I look like I came through the front door? So many stupid questions." Sal puts great emphasis on each word, dragging them out one at a time.

An effort to not sound as drunk as he is. "This is my house," he throws his thumb to his chest, "and I'll use whatever door I want. It's no damn concern of yours. Go back to bed."

Nausea fills my stomach at the condescending way he speaks to me, especially in front of a stranger. He has no care for my feelings at all or for my well-being. I stare past him at the silent, dark stranger, still as a statue. Bright beams from an early sunrise stream behind him, revealing unruly hair beneath a dark-rimmed hat. A light-colored tie and a slim-fitting jacket. Dark pants, dark boots, and a dark presence. His eyes are on me in a way that makes me uncomfortable.

Something behind him moves.

"Someone's there!" I point and they turn.

The kidnapper.

Sal's arrival must have thwarted his earlier attempt at breaking in. He is back to continue where he left off.

Sal turns back to face me. "Do you hear me?" He circles his hands at his ears. "Are you deaf or something?"

I cringe at his tone, but I want him to take me seriously. "Just look out the door, Sal. Please," I say.

He quickly does so, with little effort, to placate me. He doesn't care about the kidnapper or anyone else. I don't push him further, not under the influence of Cutty Sark whiskey.

"Salvatore," I say calmly, for us both, "I'm being serious. There were noises earlier. Voices—"

"Voices," he mocks, rolling his eyes at the stranger. "She hears voices now." The stranger is motionless.

"Two voices," I say. I don't describe the voices, and I don't tell him about the flashlight. He doesn't ask. "But you're right. I couldn't have heard voices. It must have been the wind." I realize I'm cowering, but I have to give him an acceptable answer.

"Exactly," he says.

"Are you sure you didn't notice anything unusual outside?" I have to ask. "I was about to call the police before you walked in." That door.

CHAPTER ONE

His eyes blaze. "Have you looked around? No one's here! No one was here before, no one is here now!" He throws up his hands and staggers a bit. "If you call the police, you make things worse. Don't you understand anything? You've got no business doing that." He turns to the stranger. "Her medicine does this to her. She always takes too much."

Why would calling the police make things worse?

I ignore Sal and scan the kitchen for someone hiding in the dark corners. The living room now brightened by the sunrise has no hiding places. I'm certain I heard voices. Someone had been in this house and in our backyard. I stare at Sal again, my eyes hot and angry.

I step closer to Sal and the other man, tilting my head, trying to make sense of everything. Then I do something I haven't done in years. I speak to the stranger without Sal's permission. "I'm Salvatore's wife, Isabella," I say, my arm outstretched. "I don't think we've met."

Sal's body stiffens, and he clenches his jaw. "That's not your business."

The man steps from behind Sal and takes my hand firmly between his. I see him better now in the light—his smooth, tan complexion, his dark-brown eyes staring into mine. He appears younger than Sal, clean-shaven, and friendly. A trace of a smile creeps to his lips and spreads on his face. "So nice to see you again," he says.

Again? I don't recognize this man. Should I?

"I'm sorry," I say, "have we met?" As soon as I speak, I have a vague recollection of a party with some of Sal's work friends. I'd had too much to drink and dozed off in the middle of a conversation. This man had walked me to the car when Sal had refused to. For weeks I didn't hear the end of how badly I had embarrassed Sal. I was mortified. The next day I replaced my three-times-a-day wine meals with real medication and made an appointment with my doctor. And then, slowly, I started mixing the two.

"I'm Massimo," he reminds me.

Massimo. Yes. How could I forget his kindness that night?

"Oh, yes, great to see you." My face flushes. I glance away.

"Told him he could stay a few days," Sal grunts. Of course, the thought of consulting with me about this never crossed his mind.

"I might not need to, but I'll let you know soon," Massimo tells me apologetically.

"Mind your business," Sal says, shoving my arm. "Run along." He shoos me with his hands. Condescending arrogance. And right in front of Massimo. I swallow my anger, searching for the right response—words that won't offend or test or pry. I walk to the stairs, not in obedience but out of worry for my boys. What if the kidnapper had gotten in somehow and he's hiding in the house? He could have gone upstairs while we were distracted in the kitchen. What if he is in one of the boys' rooms now?

I draw in a breath and open my mouth. "Nice to see you, Massimo. You are welcome here anytime." I clench my teeth, force a smile, then take the stairs two at a time to the top.

At Franco's door, I stop and wipe my eyes. I open his door, relieved to see he's safely sleeping. He sleeps the same as he did when he was little, arm across his forehead, mouth open, covers on the floor. A hug for my heart.

But then I'm overcome with guilt. No fifteen-year-old should shoulder the burdens he's had to. Sal's fault, of course. And mine for not stepping in sooner.

Franco's books sit in a pile on his nightstand beside his most prized award from last year, the Perfect Attendance Award, 1934.

Satisfied, I close his door and go to Luca's. Another pang of guilt. Only a few years younger than Franco but somehow more worldly. I fear what he observes when he works with Sal at the marina. I have my doubts about what goes on there.

I open Luca's door to find his blankets are piled high, something he's done since he was three years old. I'll never understand how he breathes under there, but I learned early on not to bother removing them. I called him my fluffy little mole because he'd snuggle under anything he could burrow beneath.

I walk to his bed to check on him, and something is odd. I place my hand gently near his pillow, expecting the softness of his hair or the warmth coming off him, but his empty pillow is cold. I pull back the blankets slowly at first and then yank them all the way off when I realize what's there in

CHAPTER ONE

place of Luca: a crumpled pile of clothes strategically placed to mimic a body, then covered up to simulate someone sleeping. But Luca isn't sleeping in this bed. And he's not in his room.

Luca is gone.

CHAPTER TWO

I press the light switch, my gaze darting feverishly around the room looking for signs of Luca. Something to illuminate where he might be. His closet door isn't closed completely, so I push it open. Nothing unusual among the clothes on the hangers or clothes on the floor. Did he leave? Was he taken?

My first thought is to alert Sal that Luca isn't here—tell him that, while we were arguing about the state of my sanity, our child was taken and it's his fault it happened. But I know divulging this information would most definitely backfire.

Luca has been known to push the limits and sneak out of the house in the past, but what if this time is different?

Think.

Luca likes to sit at his desk and work on things: projects for school, projects with his friends . . . Always a project, and always at his desk. I pull out the chair and sit, trying to regain my composure. Trying to think like Luca. I slide my hands on the soft wood like it might reveal something.

The top right desk drawer is slightly ajar. I drag the drawer toward me all the way and begin to analyze its contents. Nothing appears out of place. His wallet and house keys are in their specific compartments on top of his school journals. Neat and tidy as usual. Wherever did he learn that trait?

A cool breeze lifts the edges of Luca's homework papers sticking out of a textbook on top of his desk. The hems of the curtains sway and bounce, and

CHAPTER TWO

I bolt to the window to find that it's propped open with a textbook, which tells me all I need and confirms I was right not to tell Sal.

Luca has wandered off again and plans to return the same way he left. My fear pulses through me, morphing into anger. This is the third time Luca has snuck out of the house in the past few months. I recall the first time we learned Luca no longer had a sleepwalking condition but that he'd been sneaking out at night pretending to be sleepwalking.

Luca's sleepwalking started when he was only three years old. His doctor said he'd grow out of it, and at some point he had grown out of it. But for almost a year, maybe longer, Luca had kept that part to himself. Pretending to sleepwalk allowed him to sneak out of the house without consequence. "That boy is clever," Sal had said. But I wondered if he was clever or just devious. I was haunted by that thought for weeks.

My children are good boys.

The first time he disappeared, I did what any decent mother would do: I immediately called Sal at work, and after we hung up I called the police and alerted the neighbors. Sal rushed home to be with me because I was so distraught. He paced miserably up and down the hallway, and I couldn't tell if he was worried about his missing son or inconvenienced for having to leave work so early. I later found out it was the latter of the two.

The police arrived a few hours later with Luca, who apparently had been hanging out with two friends in an old, run-down neighborhood about two blocks away. One of the boys had a small bottle of vodka on him and a pack of cigarettes. Luca said the boy had offered him some, but he had declined.

When the police left, Sal flew into a rage, spouting old Italian words I didn't recognize. He had a crazed look in his eyes as he tore off his belt and stepped toward Luca. I jumped between them as the belt buckle ripped through my cheek. I put my hand to my face and looked at Sal. Nothing existed behind his cold, empty eyes. I begged him to stop, to think about what he was doing. And with one hand he picked me up by the neck and threw me out of the room.

My skin prickles when I think of the sound of Sal's harsh voice yelling at Luca between strikes. "I told you not to go there again! I trusted you! How can you be so stupid? Just like your mother!" I remember thinking, Again? Did he know Luca had been there before and not told me? I was a helpless wreck on the other side of the door while my husband punished my son.

That was the last straw.

That night I came to a realization: Sal will always have a reason to hate and punish me. Not because I tried to leave him once before or because of the brief indiscretion between Giorgio and me. Or the fact that he hates my parents for fostering independence in me. He doesn't need a reason.

He will use my boys as ammunition and punish them to hurt me, but I made a vow to myself that I will no longer allow this to happen. I set a plan into action, and I will see my plan through. I will not be persuaded no matter how different he seems or how attentive and kind he appears to be, because those things will come and go. I've witnessed it.

He became sweet as can be right after the incident with Luca, and I thought maybe he'd realized what he'd done was wrong. Later I would discover I was wrong—that he appears nice for a while on purpose to throw me off, make me think everything is fine when nothing is fine.

I tried to leave Sal three separate times, but he was always a step ahead of me. He seemed to know every move I was about to make before I could make it, and he would thwart my plans and punish me severely. The last time I tried to leave, I thought he would actually kill me, and that finally opened my eyes. How can I protect my children if I'm dead? How can I make sure they don't follow in their father's footsteps if I'm not around? Who would raise them and love them?

From then on, I became more careful of everything I did or said.

I slip the book from the window so the sash slides down. What will Luca do if he can't get back in? Will he use the front door and risk the wrath of Sal? I slide the window up again and replace the book in its expected position. I'm aware I'm enabling him by doing this, but I have no other choice.

I scrutinize every detail in his room for something to tell me where he went or who he went to see, but nothing stands out. Nothing amiss among his neatly shelved books organized by author. Nothing out of place near the leather chair next to Luca's bed—a chair handed down for generations, holding many babies in many mothers' arms, most recently mine.

I recall sitting there not long ago, worried about where my youngest son had gone. I hold my stomach, remembering the nights I stayed up late, tiptoeing down the hall, peeking through the door, praying Luca was still in his bed. The familiar view from that doorway. The chair, the books, the bed. The first time he'd crawled through the window and saw me sitting at the edge of his bed waiting for him. The expression on his face when I asked him where he'd been.

I'll never forget the way his eyes widened but then relaxed, and something shifted in them, something like intrigue or satisfaction. I'd warned him that if he didn't stop sneaking out, the next time he did it I would have to tell his father. He looked at me as if I had already betrayed him, and although I never would have told Sal, I needed Luca to believe I would. I had to think of something to make him stop, and if fear of his father wouldn't, what would?

Luca's alarm clock reads six seventeen. A whole hour has passed already. Where are you, Luca? Fear returns, invading my anxious thoughts. The intruder, the kidnapper who took Julia Bernardi, is still out there. What would happen if their paths were to collide? What if Luca was the next intended victim?

Stop thinking the worst of Luca and find him.

Could that have been the scuffle downstairs? Was Luca's voice the higher, younger one? Perhaps he tried to return through the window but was caught by the kidnapper. The kidnapper was shining a flashlight on Luca as he was approaching the back of the house. The light I saw. Maybe Luca tried to use the front door to escape, and the kidnapper followed him inside.

The air is thick. I can't breathe.

I force in the good thoughts, peppered among terrible ones. Luca is out there, yes, but he's safe from the kidnapper. His disappearance is innocent—perhaps a quick getaway to be with a sweetheart. Like Giorgio did with me when we were young. Innocent flirting is all. Something we'll laugh at in ten years.

All at once, it's too quiet. Where is Sal? I stand near Luca's bedroom door and breathe easier at the faint voices of Sal and his friend coming from the kitchen. Right where I want them to be.

I turn back to the window, and there's a quick flash of light like before. My body tenses. I pray it's not the kidnapper, and if it is Luca, I pray Sal hasn't noticed.

I run to the window and glimpse a dark figure coming from the Russos' backyard next door. As the figure draws nearer, I recognize that the dark silhouette entering our yard is, in fact, Luca. Had he been visiting next door? A secret crush on one of the Russo girls? It seems odd, as they'd drifted apart over the last year; but then again, maybe I'm simply unaware of it.

I slide away from the window before he catches me. I look on from his desk as he removes the book, slides the window up, and carefully crawls through.

"What are you doing?" I say.

Luca's head snaps in my direction. "Mamá," he says breathlessly. How far had he run to get home?

"Where have you been? We've been worried sick about you! Why do you do this when you know it makes us worry?"

"We?"

"I," I correct. "Your father doesn't know. Yet."

His eyes widen and his forehead wrinkles. "I'm anxious, Mamá. I need to get out and breathe the fresh night air sometimes."

"In the middle of the night?" I whisper-yell. "There's a kidnapper out there and you're wandering around for fresh air in the middle of the night? Are you crazy, Luca?"

"My head is so much clearer when I do that." His tone softens, as do his eyes. "You believe it's good for me too. Don't be angry at me, Mamá."

"Luca, stop." I thrust my hand in front of him. "There are other ways to clear your head and you know it. What would your father say if he found out? You know what he would do. Do you want that again?"

"Mamá . . . please . . ." Luca glances at the door.

"Were you coming from the Russos' just now?"

"The Russos'? No, I was cutting through."

CHAPTER TWO

"Cutting through from where?" I ask.

"The other neighborhood. The one behind them."

"The same one as before—when the police found you?" My voice strains against a whisper.

"No, not that one," he says. "One more over."

"One more over? Luca, this isn't right. This has to stop—now. You will not continue to defy us and sneak out in the middle of the night. I don't know what it will take or what you're up to, but wherever you're going—"

"Nowhere, Mamá. Only walking."

"Are you sneaking out for a girl? Luca, be honest. Tell me the truth. I was young once."

"N—no." His eyes fly to the ceiling.

"This cannot continue. Something's going to happen to you—I can feel it. What if something happens and we aren't there to help you? You could have been taken tonight like Julia was. He's still out there, you know." I face him squarely, place my hands on his shoulders, and look him straight in his eyes. A flash of something familiar enters his pupils. Familiar and bad. Something I've seen in Sal's eyes. "Listen to me. If it does happen again, I will tell your father."

Luca's eyes widen and then he squints as if he's analyzing the validity of what I've said. Does he think I'm lying?

Part of me is lying, and I hate that I've said those words because I'm aware that, if Luca sneaks away again, I will have to be true to my word, even though love and stability only come from me. I'm the one true constant in my boys' lives. Protecting Luca and Franco is what I've always done. I know I can't shelter them from darkness forever, but while they're still young and living in my house, I have to try.

Sal won't do any of that. It's the manipulation I can't deal with. There's a fine balance between knowing how to protect them without being manipulated and taken advantage of in the process. They all take advantage of me, all three of them, and I've allowed them to. But if Luca calls my bluff tonight, I have to be true to my word. I just hope the fear of telling Sal is enough to dissuade Luca from sneaking out again, because I can't turn back now.

A creak in the staircase betrays Sal's presence. Luca and I freeze, our eyes locked in terror. He's coming up.

"Get in that bed right now and pretend you're asleep. This conversation is done for now."

Luca does what I say and yanks the covers over his head.

I peek out the door. I don't see Sal, but I hear him. I slip out the door in the opposite direction of the stairs, my feet gliding until I'm safely concealed at the bend in the hallway before he reaches the top.

I race to my bed, crawl under the covers, and like Luca I close my eyes and bring the covers to my head, feigning sleep. Sal's footsteps grow louder with each step, as does my heartbeat. I listen to the door squeak open and sense the weight of his presence. But then the door closes, and I wonder if he's standing near the bed staring at me again.

Soon his footsteps retreat down the hallway and fade away. I listen. I worry. I wait. But I can no longer fight the weight of my eyelids, and I surrender to sleep.

CHAPTER THREE

Morning sun pierces the crack in the curtains, awakening me. An eerie hum of quiet lingers in the house, filling it like the calm before a deadly tornado. Such loud silence hurts my ears. Fragmented memories from last night play in my mind like a bad dream. I rub the thickness from my eyes; my head lies heavy on the pillow. The pieces join together: sounds from the kitchen, Sal's drunkenness, the pills I had or hadn't taken, Massimo, Luca.

The more I remember, the more anxious I become. I sit in the middle of the bed and draw my knees to my chest, afraid to go downstairs. Afraid to encounter the truth about last night and another confrontation with Sal. Afraid that Massimo will stare through me again.

At the bathroom sink, I splash cool water on my face and examine myself in the mirror. Water drips around my features, cascading into the fine crevices in my skin. I trace a finger at my eye's flared edge. When did those get there? At only thirty-three, I feel old and, I'm starting to look old. I examine my eyebrows, thankful for their natural shape and dark color. I run my fingers through my hair; at least no grays are hiding in the strands. My body grasps at youth while fighting the dark, heavy prisoner inside.

I force myself out the door to the hallway, strategically stepping on the quiet floorboards and holding my breath as if to make me weightless, stepping through the same motions as the night before. The phone rests on the table at the foot of the stairs, and a rush of panic surges through me. I get to the bottom and there's no one in the kitchen.

In the living room, I fully expect to find Sal and Massimo sprawled across the couches. But no one is there either. The furniture appears untouched, pillows perfectly placed on the sofa, and a white blanket draped over the arm of the chair. Perhaps Sal and Massimo sat at the kitchen table to smoke and drink before going back to the marina. But there are no drink glasses on the counter, no cigarette butts in the ashtray, no sign they'd been here at all.

Am I losing my mind?

I recall how, last night, I'd waited for Luca to return home and vividly remember the talk we had. I go to the front door and open it, cringing at the obnoxious squeak in the hinges just as I'd heard it last night.

Then I turn back toward the kitchen, toward the servants' door where Sal entered with Massimo. When Sal walked in, I was so caught off guard, so unprepared, and completely shocked. I remember falling and knocking over the photograph. It is now on the shelf, not on the counter where I'd placed it. How did the photograph get there? Sal certainly wouldn't have set it nicely on the shelf. He'd have left it on the counter, maybe even thrown it out.

I pick up the frame and turn it over in my hands as if to confirm this is indeed my most treasured photograph of my parents. I run my finger over the glass, looking for the scratch or crack from hitting the floor, but there's nothing visible. Could I have imagined seeing the crack? It was dark, so perhaps I'd seen something that resembled a scratch when it was only dust or hair.

The morning sun, high in the sky, illuminates the front window. I sweep the curtains back and am met with a picturesque view of our property. Beautiful, rolling, green hills stretch far past the plantation. Sal could be working in the fields.

His father taught him that with hard work and determination he could cultivate something both beautiful and prosperous. Sal has made his father proud; his diligence and dedication to the bergamot plantation resulted in prosperity, even if he is a little obsessive about it.

Every day he brings friends and customers to see the plantation that locals refer to as "green gold." The sour, greenish-orange citrus fruit is used in flavors such as tea and in fine fragrances and essential oils as it has been for centuries. We harvest the fruit and sell it to companies. Our plantation is the start of this intricate production, and we're very proud of it.

I didn't mind at first when Sal would bring his customers, but some of them made me uncomfortable the way they strutted through the field as if they owned it, and the way they looked at me.

Eventually, many of Sal's meetings and business transactions resumed at the marina. Although the customers were kept away from our home, the marina is my family's inheritance, not a place for side business deals.

Sal said I can't have it both ways, that the bulk of his business deals would either have to be at his home office or at the marina. I once thought choosing the marina was the right thing to do, but I regret that now.

If Sal's father had stayed in America, we all might be in a better place. Our families had arranged for Sal and me to be married and, although I didn't want to, the prospect of living in America was intriguing, especially as a woman. American women in the 1920s had more opportunities than Italian women.

Arranged marriages even back then were becoming far less common, but some families like ours still practiced the ancient tradition of assigning their children to someone else for the rest of their lives. It was a business arrangement, but I'm beginning to suspect something beyond business tied our families together.

Before we were betrothed, Sal's father left for America fully intending to send for us once he became settled. But that's not what happened. Unexpectedly and without explanation, Sal's father returned to Italy stating that business in America wasn't going to work out for their family. A missed opportunity for everyone.

Then again, being stuck with Sal's Sicilian parents in a foreign country might have had its own challenges and consequences. His father wielded a fiery temper and had connections to the 'Ndrangheta, but his mother was the one I feared more. To outsiders, Sal's father had the upper hand, but inside the family circle, everyone knew his wife ruled the roost. Sal always sided with his mammina, and I don't think she ever liked me. Maybe I'm better off where I am now; at least I'm surrounded by friends who actually care about me.

I adore my beautiful country, but this land I love so much is changing in a way that scares me. What Italy needs more than anything right now is strong leadership. I shouldn't speak ill of our prime minister, Mussolini, but he has made us weaker, not stronger. His support of fascism and violence has ruined our country. Sal, of course, thinks he is the greatest leader we've ever had.

I draw the curtains from each window as my mind walks through the past. The bright sun pours in, warming me. Through the window on the opposite side of the room, I view the thick patch of cypress trees where Sal parks his Fiat. Except for the wheels, his car is hidden quite well from the house. I strain to find the shiny chrome of the rims normally peeking beneath the lowest branches. If the Fiat is gone, he must have left for work early.

The phone rings, nearly stopping my heart. Sal is on the other end, and I'm not hearing him right. He's apologizing for not coming home last night. He says he's still at work and won't be home for dinner. Every now and then he does apologize for his rudeness.

"What do you mean?" I say, thinking he's joking or testing me. "You came home in the middle of the night. Remember? You scared me when you came through the servants' door with Massimo."

He makes a grumbling noise. "Here we go again," he says. "This happens every time you drink wine and take that medicine. You never listen. Now you're scaring me."

"What? No, I didn't."

"Yes, you did, then you hallucinated or had a bad dream. I did not come home last night. That's why I'm calling you now." He clicks his tongue like he does when he's annoyed at my stupidity.

"But I saw you," I say. "I told you about the noises from inside the house. I

CHAPTER THREE

thought someone had broken in." I try to mask the uncertainty in my voice, but Sal doesn't relent.

"You sound insane. Again."

"I'm not insane. I saw you come in through the servants' door. I told you I thought it was strange that you didn't use the front door. You were very . . . drunk."

Sal is silent on the other end. He was obviously intoxicated and doesn't remember anything about last night.

"Isabella," he says condescendingly, "I've been at the marina since yesterday morning. You can ask anyone. What is wrong with you?"

"I—" I realize it's no use. I push away thoughts of my parents' picture with no scratch on the glass. I am not insane. He had been here and he had been drunk, but this is not worth the fight. I let him win. "Perhaps I was dreaming," I say. "It felt so real." I swallow the vomit rising to my throat.

"You need to stop taking that headache powder with your wine," he says. "You really sound crazy."

I clear my throat and redirect the conversation. "So, you're calling now to say you'll be late again tonight."

"Not again, and yes." He breathes heavily, putting enormous stress on the last word.

"Will you be coming home alone, or will Massimo be with you?"

A long pause again.

"I have to go," he says. "Tell Luca to make sure he's on time. He needs to be here at four o'clock sharp."

I'd forgotten Luca would be meeting Sal at the marina today to learn about the business. I'd been reluctant to let him go and told Sal he is too young and still needs to be in school. I said he should ask Franco instead, but Sal refused, saying he had his own reasons and didn't need to share them.

"Are you listening to what I said?" he growls.

"I'll tell him," I say, and he hangs up.

I'm not crazy. I remember everything from last night vividly and can recall each detail with ease. Sal's drinking has gotten way out of hand if he can't remember anything that happened.

I retrieve the photograph of my parents and study the glass. The light catches it just so, and I notice a faint scratch close to the edge and a small dent in the frame. I knew it. I am not insane. As unreal as it felt, I'm sure of what I saw last night. Salvatore was either drunk or lying.

I pour myself a strong cup of coffee and pick up the phone to dial the operator and ask her to connect me to a number I haven't called in months: Greta Russo, one of my closest friends and next-door neighbor. I need to find out if Greta saw Luca in her backyard last night.

CHAPTER FOUR

Greta picks up after two rings. At the sound of her voice, I'm brought back to another time. Her sultry, warm hello changes when she realizes it's me on the other end. A hesitation, a slight hiccup—perhaps she expected someone else to call. We awkwardly fill the air with trite conversation. As she speaks, I examine her mood in search of words or tones that might reveal she had seen Luca in her backyard. She quickly changes the subject, and I'm surprised at what she says.

"I know why you're calling me, Iz."

I'm delighted she used my nickname, but it's not enough to calm my nerves. Yes, Luca was in her backyard last night, but I can't bear to hear it from her.

"It's on all our minds right now."

All our minds? "What do you mean?"

She replies with two words: "Julia Bernardi."

I pause, not ready to reveal my true purpose for calling. Julia has been on my mind since she disappeared, and I can't get her out of my head. I decide we'll talk about Julia and then I'll ask her about Luca. "Y—yes, you're right," I say. "I did call to talk about her. This is so awful. I can't believe what's happened."

"Me too," she says. "I'm sick about it." Greta's sultry voice returns, and I detect no hesitation. "What are you doing today?"

"Nothing much," I say. "The usual."

"Why don't you come for lunch and we'll talk," she says. "Catch up a little.

How long has it been since we've had lunch together?"

"Too long," I say. "I'd love to." I smile, pleasantly surprised at her invitation. We agree I'll come over at eleven thirty, and after we hang up I'm lulled to the past once more, recalling fun memories shared over the years.

With Sal at work, I rest knowing I won't be under his watchful eye and I'll have some time to myself. I take a homemade loaf of bread from the bread box and put it on the counter next to the white linen towel I'll use to wrap it and take to Greta's. But the uncertainty of last night stays with me like a dark shadow as I hang the laundry and clean the house. It's right at my side until I'm ready to leave. It stays with me as I walk next door.

But the dark shadow is soon replaced with nostalgia and a touch of regret when my feet hit the short path between our houses. When had our friendship gone awry? When did our relationship change? When we broke the promise we'd made that if our children one day grew apart, we never would? What was once a friendly smile and kind greeting across the yards was replaced by side glances and awkward silence, and right when Sal's long hours at work stretched into the night when I needed my friend the most.

I suspect Sal is the cause. He has always ruined things for us. I reach for the door knocker, recalling Sal's behavior on one of our last nights together. Alcohol and hot-headed narcissism are a bad mix. We'd lost other friends to that as well. Eventually, they'd distance themselves until we no longer saw them at all. I thought things would be different with Greta and Rocco. I thought they simply needed a break from Sal, that they'd be back.

I grasp the knocker just as Greta opens the door. "I saw you coming," she says, smiling.

We awkwardly hug, and I feel what I've been missing all this time. I follow Greta to the kitchen.

"Is that your Mamá's recipe?" she asks, pointing to the bread.

"Yes," I say, handing it to Greta, who places the loaf inside the warm oven. Then she pours two glasses of lemonade, hands one to me, and motions for me to follow her. As the bread warms, we sit in our old spots overlooking the hills and streets. An almost magical feeling overcomes me as I wiggle

CHAPTER FOUR

into my chair. My chair. It's as if I'd just sat in it yesterday.

"It's been a long time, you know?" Greta says.

"Yes, I do know," I say. I want to ask her why we didn't keep our promise. Why did a kidnapping bring us together again?

Greta pulls out a cigarette and lights the end. "So, what have you heard about Julia?"

I'm taken aback by Greta's eagerness to talk about Julia before we have a chance to catch up with each other. I want to go back to what happened to our friendship, how life has changed but not for the better. How I miss my dear friend. But Greta's eyes blaze with her own agenda, her need to talk about Julia. Apparently catching up will come later.

"Not much more than what the reporters are saying," I say. "What about you?"

" I know they finally cleared the father," Greta says matter-of-factly.

"The father?"

"They investigate the family first," she explains. "Usually it's the men—husband, father, you know."

I nod.

Greta sips her lemonade. "There's another person of interest, but they're not saying who. Rocco told me. They'll be questioning her friends soon, all of them, so be prepared."

"Did Rocco tell you that too?" Like his father, Rocco joined the Royal Italian Army right out of high school.

"He's not supposed to say anything during the investigation, but sometimes he tells me a little."

I watch Greta. How much does she know but isn't saying?

"Why are you looking at me like that?" she says.

"It's terrifying," I say, not realizing the look on my face. "Julia is practically our kids' age. She's their classmate, their friend. This could happen to our children—to anyone."

Greta nods. "She was on her way to a friend's house when it happened. It makes me sick to think my girls do the same thing almost every day. They're always at their friends' houses when their friends aren't here. But no more."

She puffs on her cigarette, releasing smoke from her nose like a dragon. And I think how beautiful she is despite her dirty smoking habit. "I can't take that chance. You have boys, so it's not the same for you."

"How do you know who the kidnapper wants? I won't take a chance with my boys either," I say, a little offended.

"What about Giorgio?" she says.

"What about him?"

"He's a journalist. Doesn't he have connections? Maybe he knows something," she says.

"I haven't spoken with him," I say, "but I don't think he would share something he wasn't supposed to."

"As close as you are?" she prods. "Come on, Iz, you know if anyone could get his ear, it would be you."

"I don't think so," I say, although she's probably right. Giorgio and I are very close. We grew up together—best friends, kindred spirits. Someone I should be married to. I plan to talk with him, but not yet.

"Well, they need to catch the filthy person responsible for Julia before it happens to someone else. I lock my doors every day now. What is this world coming to?"

"I pray to God they find her soon," I agree.

"It's been a few days." Greta snuffs the butt of her cigarette on the porch floor. "The more time goes by the worse things look."

I sip my lemonade, return the glass to the table, and glance at Greta. "Greta, I need to talk to you about something that happened last night."

Her face is somber. She places her hand on my arm. "Oh no. What is it?"

I fumble over different versions of what I want to say without coming right out and mentioning Luca. "I know you're usually up much later than I am," I begin. "Did you . . . by chance . . . hear anything strange last night? Or perhaps see anything unusual?"

Greta tilts her head. "I don't think so. . . . What time?"

"It was very late—almost four in the morning."

"Not that I can think of," she says. "I was asleep at that time but in and out a lot. You know how I am—the slightest thing wakes me. Was there something specific you heard?"

"Yes," I nod. "Voices at first."

"Voices? Where? How many?"

"I think two. I'm not sure. It sounded like they were fighting or struggling or someone was getting hurt. It wasn't normal. And it was in my house."

"In your house? Did you call the police?"

"I tried to get to the phone, but it's hard to without being seen. When I got downstairs, no one was there. The voices must have been right outside the house."

"You went down to check? That's not like you," she says, which is true. "How can you be so calm about this?"

"I might look calm," I chuckle, "but inside I'm a raging lunatic."

Greta cracks a smile.

"Don't laugh! I was scared to death."

"I can't believe you did that . . . all by yourself," Greta says. "Very strong of you—"

"I can't believe it either, but Sal wasn't home, so I had no choice."

"Good for you, Iz."

We're quiet for a few seconds, and I wonder if she's analyzing me.

"I also thought I saw something outside," I say. It's time to find out if she saw Luca.

"My backyard too?"

"Well, since our yards are so close, he—or whatever it was—could have been in either one."

"You're scaring me," Greta says. "You're sure about this?"

"Yes," I say. "I definitely heard noises before Sal got home."

"Four in the morning? That's when Sal got home?"

"I know. His hours keep getting later and later."

"Do you suspect he's seeing someone?" Greta says. "Could those have been the voices you heard?"

"No, I don't think so," I say, relieved Greta hasn't mentioned seeing Luca darting across her backyard. The voices in my house must have been Sal's and Massimo's.

"Iz," Greta says, her lips tight, "I don't mean to scare you, but what if it was the kidnapper?"

"I thought of that, but why wouldn't he have taken me or one of the boys?" A twinge vibrates in my stomach. If the kidnapper were trying to take Luca, he wouldn't have found him in his bed.

"Something isn't right," Greta says. "A criminal is out there and he hasn't been caught. We need to be vigilant. We need to watch out for each other. It could be anyone."

It could be anyone. My skin crawls thinking why two family men would have been out at that hour.

Greta rises to retrieve the bread from the oven and comes back with several cuts of deli meat, some olives, and salad on a tray. Our conversation departs from last night, and once again we are two old friends talking about our children. I even share my disapproval of Sal's desire to arrange a marriage between Franco and Cecelia. Greta says the idea of arranging marriages is old-fashioned and shouldn't be continued.

"Take you and Sal for example," she says. "I don't mean to sound disrespectful, but that has never been good for you."

She's right. We never had a say in who we wanted to marry. We never got to fall in love. Greta and Rocco, on the other hand, found each other on their own, fell in love, and chose to marry. A perfect match as far as I can tell.

"If you'd had a say, you would have chosen Giorgio, wouldn't you?" she says.

"Oh, I don't know," I say, feeling my face flush.

"I always thought . . . oh, never mind."

"What? Tell me," I say.

Greta smiles. "Well, I always thought Franco and Gianna liked each other. They remind me so much of you and Giorgio at that age. Actually, I think both your boys like her." She winks.

"Really?" I say, although I've seen it too.

"It's too bad Franco won't be able to choose for himself. Wouldn't their courtship and marriage have been fun to witness?" Greta says. "What about

CHAPTER FOUR

Luca? Any plans for him?"

"No, nothing like that yet." I can't imagine Luca being mature enough to have a girlfriend let alone a wife. "He's been working a lot with Sal. Much more than Franco has."

"Isn't he too young for that?" she says.

"I think so, but you know Sal."

"Whatever Sal wants, Sal gets." Greta raises her eyes to the ceiling. "Why not Franco? He's the oldest. Doesn't that seem odd to you?"

"It doesn't matter what I think," I say. "Sal has his reasons, and I don't interfere with that. Besides, Franco's not interested in the marina. He wants to work on the plantation and concentrate on his studies. School has never been Luca's thing." Sadness spreads inside me at the reality that our families won't be tied together through our children. How perfect life could be for both families to be joined. How happy Franco could be.

Greta's mind must have read mine on some level. She claps her hands and says, "Let's all come together again! How long has it been since we've done that? It'll be like old times. Come to dinner next Friday. Please say yes!"

"We'd love to," I say, but it doesn't sit well inside. "I'll check with Sal to make sure he doesn't have to work late again, and if he doesn't, we'll come."

The rest of our time together is blissful; the hours slip by with ease. I don't remember the last time my heart felt so light. Spending time with Greta is good for my soul. How silly I am to let Sal's poor outlook and negativity about other people influence my choices. Greta is a good friend to me, and I need to hold onto her.

CHAPTER FIVE

On the path from Greta's house to mine, the shed peeks from behind the first row of citrus bergamot trees. Its presence has always made me uneasy. A few years after we moved in, Sal repurposed the shed to a home office, stating he needed additional space that the bergamot and marina businesses required.

Its location from the house provides adequate privacy while being close enough to keep watch on the property and me. It allows the secrecy and mystery he thrives on and craves, a lust for power I've seen in his eyes. When he first mentioned the shed, those eyes flashed an intensity that both dared me and lured me at the same time, coaxing me to ask one simple question: why? Why do you really need this extra space?

But I'd fought against my need for answers at the time. His temples bulged when I didn't ask. I did everything I could to remain strong at that moment. He'd stormed off with nothing more to say. That small victory gave me one slice of strength.

As I approach my house, I veer to the side toward the servants' entrance. I stand before the door like I'm seeing it for the first time. How silly not to use an entrance for the sake of ghosts. I imagine what it must have been like to be a servant here, coming and going from the side while everyone else used the front door. The thought of being a servant makes me sick. If their souls are restless and troubled as Sal says, then their lives here were not happy. What happened behind this door, behind these walls? How does

CHAPTER FIVE

Sal know?

I press my hand to the old mahogany door and sweep it over the warped, aged wood. A cool breeze swishes through my hair, and I'm suddenly unsteady. I shake it off and reach for the doorknob, taking a firm hold and shaking it the way it was shaken last night. It scarcely budges, locked with no keyhole. Impossible to open. But Sal had opened it last night.

Puzzled, I go inside the house and attempt to open the door from the other side. I grip the doorknob like before and twist. Again it's immovable. This door cannot be opened from either side.

Frustrated, I lean my head on the door, and something catches my eye. Something tiny and probably insignificant, but when I get to my knees and I'm at eye level, there's no doubt: fractured wood splayed at the door's edge near the catch and in the same location on the jamb. Small splinters scattered on the floor like crumbs finally settles the debate in my mind. This door was opened, and recently. But why would Sal use a door plagued with his own superstitions, and why had he lied about doing it? What was he really doing last night?

The clock on the wall reminds me that Franco will be home soon, and Luca will go straight to the marina from school, leaving me a small window of time alone in the house. An opportunity to attend to Luca's room.

On my way upstairs, something crawls under my skin when I pass our family portrait and see in our faces what people have said many times before—that Franco is the spitting image of his father and Luca is of me. But when it comes to our personalities and temperaments, those closest to us, like my sister, say the exact opposite. Franco has my drive and compassion, and Luca has his father's nose for business along with his temper. I pray every night that neither of my boys has an ounce of their father's personality. The thought consumes me sometimes. I look away and proceed up the stairs.

At the doorway to Luca's room, I don't know where to start. A perfect view of a seemingly perfect room, not typical of boys his age. His bed is made, covers neatly rolled down, pillow fluffed, clothes in the hamper, garbage in the can, dresser drawers pushed in, and a clean desktop. His room is impeccable, nothing out of place.

At the window, I have a clear view of what I couldn't see last night. I visualize Luca running through the Russos' backyard and then through ours. My eyes try to stretch beyond the area I'd spotted him and imagine where he might have come from, but my view is obstructed by the trees surrounding the plantation. I analyze my view from the window, the rows of trees, bergamot, citrus, and olive in one area, lined by cypress trees, the small farm, and the shed. What happened out there?

I turn to Luca's bed, pull his covers back, and lift his pillow. Nothing there. I bend to the floor and poke my head under his bed. Spotless; not even dust resides beneath it. But something appears strange and unusual further in. Something protrudes from one of the floorboards. I hope we hadn't gouged the wood when we moved his bed from the wall to its new location. I reach under to examine the spot but stop when I hear the phone faintly ringing downstairs.

"Hello?" I say when I reach it, out of breath.

"Isabella?"

"Greta," I chuckle. "Weren't we just together?"

"Yes," Greta laughs. "Sorry, am I interrupting something?"

"No, not at all. What's going on?"

"I don't mean to bother you, but when you asked me if I'd seen or heard anything last night, nothing stood out to me at the time," she says, "but after you left I started thinking, and you know what? I do remember something."

I sit in the chair beside the phone. "What do you remember?"

"I got up to use the toilet as I said. I remember I saw a light through the window, a small one, like from a lantern or something. I almost missed it. Nothing stood out at first with all the lightning, but when the lightning stopped a different light was still there. I was so tired, though, that I didn't think much of it and went back to bed. I didn't remember anything until after we saw each other. The more I thought about it the more I remembered."

I never told her about the light, I think curiously.

"And there's something else," she continues. "I don't want to scare you, but remember how my bathroom window angles toward your house so I can see the side pretty well?"

CHAPTER FIVE

"Yes."

"Now, maybe I'm imagining this, but I'm pretty sure someone was standing near that old side door. I thought I was dreaming at first, but now I realize that was not a dream."

Sal and Massimo? Luca? "Are you sure?"

"Yes," she says confidently. "You know sometimes when you think you see something but it's so dark you can't tell what it is, but something is absolutely there? Well, something was by the door. What if it was the kidnapper? I think you should tell the police."

Oh God, the kidnapper. My stomach is in knots. "Maybe I should," I say. "Is there anything else you remember?"

"No, just that."

"That's a lot," I say. "I appreciate you telling me, Greta. If anything else comes to mind, even if you think it's nothing, please tell me right away."

"I will," Greta says. "I promise. But there's one more thing I want to ask."

"Yes?"

"Are you okay? I mean, aside from all this?"

"Yes. Why do you ask?"

"I sense that something is off. I just want you to know I'm here if you need someone to talk to. You know that, right?"

"Yes, I do," I say, "and I'm okay. You don't have to worry about me, but thank you for saying that." I peer out the window like I'm searching for a place to hide, unsure if I'm hiding from myself or that ominous feeling that hangs over me. "Thank you for being a good friend to me."

"Of course," she says.

"I'll talk to Sal and let you know what he says about dinner." I place the phone on the receiver and a chill runs through me. I just want it all to go away.

Before I can return to investigate the floor under Luca's bed, something catches my eye at the bottom of the front door. A white envelope slides beneath the door, hitting the toe of my shoe. I pick it up and flip it over to find it sealed but not addressed to anyone. I dip my finger into a small, ripped edge, tear it open, and pull out the folded paper inside. I open the paper, revealing a neatly composed manuscript in black ink.

You need to keep your mouth shut, and your eyes open. You think you know what's going on, but you don't. Someone is watching you. I'm watching you. Don't let your guard down.

I lift my eyes from the paper and glance around me. I go to the door, open it slowly, and step onto the porch, scanning the grass, the trees, and the road. Is the sender watching me now? I back into the doorway, examining my view once more before I close the door. Sweat beads in the small of my back and runs down. I look at the note again, wondering if I am the intended recipient or someone else in my family. Is this a mistake? I unfold the paper again. No date, no greeting or closing, and no return address. The handwriting is not familiar. The sender doesn't want to be known.

The narrative in my head spins out of control, and I'm at a loss for what to think about anything—the kidnapping, the break-in, Sal's increasingly hostile attitude and paranoia; Luca's behavior; Franco's aloofness. Questions I hadn't asked myself in a while.

And now this note.

What had Anna said to me not long ago about Sal? She'd seen him out with a couple of men and a woman? The woman stood close to Sal; Sal was smiling. Smiling. I'd pushed it aside as two work associates.

And what is Sal's reason for choosing Luca to work with him over Franco? He doesn't think Franco wants his hands dirty? Franco would go to work with Sal even if he didn't want to, but Sal chose Luca. I start to wonder where he takes Luca when they leave the marina before coming home. What kinds of side jobs are they into?

Anna had been the one to question it while I'd been medicating myself with alcohol and adding my medication as I saw fit. I remember laughing in her face when she first raised the question. When she suggested Sal was a dangerous man. That people in the community feared him.

CHAPTER FIVE

Now, as I hold this note in my hand, I'm thinking of what else I've missed along the way. What have I turned my head to for the sake of keeping the peace? And whose peace was I trying to keep anyway—Sal's or mine?

CHAPTER SIX

I walk through the next two days in a dark, blurry tunnel, absorbed in worry. The contents of the anonymous note, concealed beneath my jewelry box, are fixed in my mind as I carry the warm torta next door to Greta's house. Greta answers the door. I smile, handing her the dessert, and tuck those thoughts at the back of my mind. The sugary-cinnamon mix of apple and pastry floats in the air as Greta puts it into the warm oven. Its sweetness is a stark contrast to the ugly worry that consumes me.

An hour later, Franco arrives. Sienna, Maria, and Gianna stand behind Greta as he enters. His cheeks flush when he sees Gianna. I watch as he follows them to the kitchen. It's not long before they slip into old, comfortable conversation, reminiscing of childhood memories.

Rocco enters from the living room and greets me with a warm hug. Greta sets four stemmed glasses on the counter and pours red wine into three.

"We'll do a toast when Sal and Luca arrive," Rocco says. "It's good to see you, Iz."

My heart warms when he calls me Iz. Like all is well again. "It's great to see you too," I say. I remember when the four of us would get together and talk long into the night. I loved when he'd speak candidly about his job. He'd describe fascinating stories about different criminals he'd encountered, but he never gave names or other personal details. I want to ask him so many questions about Julia Bernardi, but I know it's not the time or place. We'll have plenty of opportunities after today to talk.

CHAPTER SIX

Soon our conversations and interactions flow relaxed and easy, like slipping on a favorite dress, sliding into the contours as soft fabric cushions the skin like a warm hug. Laughter from Franco and the girls floats from the kitchen where they play cards. Other than an occasional glance at the front door, wondering when Sal and Luca will arrive, and a fleeting moment when I wanted medicine, I am content at this moment. Part of me doesn't want Sal to come at all.

Don't ruin this for me, Sal.

It's another forty-five minutes and a second glass of wine before there's a knock at the door. Greta rises to answer. Sal and Luca are impeccably dressed in clothes I've never seen before. A strong scent of cologne follows Sal as he presents Greta with a purple-and-white, robust bouquet of flowers like the ones in our garden by the back door. I don't recall the last time he wore cologne. He embraces Greta with a long hug and smiles warmly as they pull away. He's on his best behavior. Luca says hello to Greta and Rocco and joins the voices in the kitchen.

The fact that Sal dressed up and gathered flowers from our yard to bring to our friends is unusually kind, and I'm pleasantly surprised. Sal turns to me and plants a quick peck on my cheek and then we follow Greta into the living room. Rocco and Sal shake hands, and Rocco pours Sal a glass of wine, topping off the rest of ours.

"*Ai vecchi amici.* To old friends," Rocco says, raising his glass.

"*Ai vecchi amici,*" we repeat.

We finish our wine and follow Greta and Rocco to a beautifully set kitchen table, the purple-and-white flowers at its center. We talk throughout dinner about where our busy lives have taken us: how Rocco is looking to become chief of police in the next couple years; Sal briefly talks about the marina and how well it's doing; Rocco asks about the bergamot trees and the process of growing them; Greta and I weave in and out of their conversations. But mostly at this moment, I sit back and watch everyone, enjoying the sensation of the wine pulsing through my body, relaxing and kneading the tension away. I listen to the conversations at our end of the table and the ones of our children at the other end, like I'm enjoying a picture show.

Greta rises from the table to clear the dishes and puts her hand out as I stand to help. "You sit right there and relax," she says. "I'm only moving them to the counter. I'll clean them later."

I smile, easing back into my chair. It's nice to be waited on for a change. Appreciated.

Sal and Rocco take their glasses to continue a conversation in the living room. The hushed, muffled tones of their voices drift to the kitchen table. I consider joining them, but instead I close my eyes for a moment and enjoy the lulling sensation of the wine. When I open them again, I feel a shift in the room and wonder if I've dozed off more than a few seconds.

I listen for voices but pick up only those coming from our kids in the back room. I stand, taking in my surroundings, using the table to steady me. My body sways to the kitchen doorway. I'm about to call for Greta when Sal walks abruptly past me from the kitchen, head down, brow furrowed. When had he left the living room? It couldn't have been more than a few seconds. Greta is at the sink, her back to me. Something in her body language is off. She's rigid, a bit too purposeful, as she places the dishes into the water.

"You're sure you don't need any help?" I say, making her jump.

"Oh, Iz, you scared me," Greta says, still facing the sink. "I'll be right out."

"Are you okay?" I ask. "Did something happen?" Did Sal say something rude?

"No, no . . . everything is fine. I'll only be a second." The pitch of her voice rises.

I leave the kitchen, puzzled, and go back to the table, wondering why it feels as if I'm in a different home. Franco and Luca are in a steady conversation with Gianna, Maria, and Sienna in the other room as if they haven't skipped a beat, as if nothing has changed. But something has changed.

Sal is back in the living room talking with Rocco again. Greta carries a different look on her face as she brings the torta to the table. The brightness in her eyes has dulled, and the lines on her forehead are more pronounced—the same expression she had when she talked about Julia Bernardi.

The fragrant dessert pulls everyone to the table again. Rocco and Sal enter quietly, serious. Sal casts a fake smile around the room. Rocco takes a bite, giving the torta high praise, and, surprisingly, Sal agrees he likes it too. Greta acts timid and not her normal self. She asks for the recipe, a scant smile on her face.

Franco, Luca, and the girls take their plates to the other room, and it's just the four of us again. An unseen intrusion has disrupted our natural conversation, and the ease between us an hour ago is gone. Too much wine? When Sal finishes his dessert, he leaves the table to use the toilet. Rocco walks to the living room and Greta follows. Unspoken words tell me to wait at the table.

Greta and Rocco whisper closely. Rocco steps back, squaring his shoulders. Greta becomes animated as she continues to speak, her voice at times rising above a whisper. I don't know what they're saying, but I know it isn't good. The fact that I'm left at the table tells me it's either something about Julia Bernardi or something about Sal and me. But the way Greta is speaking to Rocco feels more personal.

Greta sees me watching as she heads back to the table with an unopened bottle of wine. Sal passes Greta on his way back into the room without a glance in her direction. Greta places the bottle on the table and opens it. She refills our glasses without eye contact.

"We won't be needing that," Sal says, his tone sharp and loud.

"What? Why not?" I stare at him.

Franco and Luca come into the room as if on cue.

"Boys, say your goodbyes," he says. "Isabella, let's go."

Franco starts to object, but one cold stare from Sal and they're both moving fast. At the door, they turn toward the girls who stare wide-eyed next to Greta.

I look from Sal and the boys in the doorway to Greta, Rocco, and the girls. "I don't understand. What just happened?" I stare, waiting, trying to read their expressions, trying to make sense of this. "Greta?"

Greta glances at Rocco and then away. He stands tall, arms folded.

"Will someone please tell me what is going on?"

Rocco and Greta stay silent, glaring at Sal who's glaring at me. Slowly I step away from the table, acutely aware of the sadness that makes its way back between us. I join my family at the door. Sal opens it and exits. Franco and Luca follow and then I step out. It's like the house has a sour taste in its mouth, spitting us out one by one.

I turn once and glimpse Greta closing the door, a blank stare on her face. Our home feels like miles, not steps, away. I replay in my mind what started as a perfect evening and ended tragically. We had gotten on famously, laughing, drinking, and talking about the world as if we hadn't skipped a beat. It was the same with our children, especially Franco and Gianna. When had it fallen apart?

Had Sal said something offensive to Rocco in the living room? Was it when he was in the kitchen with Greta? It must have been what Greta and Rocco were talking about in the living room. It was Sal. It had to be. It's always Sal.

The house is dark when we enter, but I don't need the light to get to the stairs. As the boys retreat to their bedrooms, Sal walks slowly past me with something in his hands toward the door. I know he's going to the shed. He stops as if he knows I want to say something, and I do want to say something, but it's impossible to breathe.

I want to tell him how much I hate him for taking away one more thing that could have made me happy. My lips part, ready to unleash the storm inside, but I slam them shut because I've finally figured out that it's my loss of control he wants, and I won't give it to him anymore. I don't ask him what happened or where he's going or what's in his hands.

He grins. I grin back. He leaves. A few seconds later, the light goes on in the shed.

I so badly want to call Greta, but I decide to wait until tomorrow when we can be alone. I'll tell her everything that's been going on. Everything. I think about the suitcase in my closet and the money hidden in the kitchen. I can't stand it any longer. We need to get away from Sal before he ruins one more thing.

CHAPTER SEVEN

Morning comes fast after a restless night. Disturbing thoughts and unanswered questions of those final moments at the Russos linger in my mind. I turn my head at the vacant pillow and rise with a sick feeling in my stomach. I drag myself to the window and look out at the Russos' house buttoned up under thick, gray clouds that match my mood.

I knock on Franco's and then Luca's bedroom doors, a reminder to meet me in the kitchen for breakfast before they go to school. I wonder how they processed what happened last night or if they said anything to each other about it. I wonder what the Russos are thinking. Greta. Rocco. What happened?

I pause briefly at the foot of the stairs and glance at the phone, wishing I could call Greta and make things right again. At the kitchen sink, I glimpse the shed.

Franco's voice makes me jump.

"Mamá," he says, placing a hand on my shoulder.

"Franco!" I wrap my arms around him. At fifteen, he is already taller than me.

"What are you looking at?" he asks.

"The sky," I say. "Looks like rain today."

"I don't think they're up yet," he says. "The Russos."

Of course, he's thinking of them. He probably didn't sleep well last night either. "No, I don't think they are," I say.

"Did Papá leave for work?"

I see the empty hem of the cypress trees. "I think so."

"Mamá," he says, turning toward me, "it was wrong . . . what Papá did last night."

"Franco—" I stop myself from an unhealthy habit of defending my husband.

"He doesn't respect you," he continues, "or anyone. You need to—"

"Careful what you say." I glance around. "These walls have ears." Paranoia bubbles beneath my skin. Somehow Sal always knows when he's the topic of conversation, often accusing me of plotting against him. "Let's talk later," I say. Then I have an idea. "How about you go next door and see if the girls want to walk to school with you and Luca."

Franco flashes a smile as the phone rings. I'm pleasantly surprised at hearing Greta's voice on the other end. Franco sits at the table to eat breakfast, and Luca joins him.

"Greta," I gasp, "I'm so glad you called. I was going to call you later to—"

"They found her," Greta interrupts, her voice uneven. "Julia Bernardi."

I cup my hand to my mouth. Franco lifts his eyes to mine, mirroring my expression. I wave for him to continue eating and walk away as far as the cord allows.

"Oh my God. Is she okay?"

"No, she's not okay," Greta says. "They found her in the water, not far from the marina."

"She . . . drowned?" I say.

"Yes," she says solemnly, "but it's not an accident. She . . . someone . . . she was . . . murdered." Her voice collapses on that final word. Its heaviness shrinks the room.

I sit on the floor. "Murdered?" Near the marina?

"I shouldn't be calling," she says, "but we talked about it yesterday, and our kids know her, so . . ."

I swallow the lump in my throat. "How do they know it's not an accident?"

"The way she was found," she whispers. "Don't tell anyone I told you."

CHAPTER SEVEN

"Of course not," I say.

"There's one more thing," she says. "They found her jacket in the shrubs near the water, and there was something in one of the pockets—a note or a picture. They think it was from a friend or classmate."

"A classmate," I echo, lowering my voice.

"I tried to find out more, but Rocco couldn't tell me anything else."

"What if it's from—"

"I know—one of our kids," she says. "I was thinking the same. What if they're somehow blamed for this? What if they know something?"

She says what's on my mind. My stomach is in knots.

"Listen, I don't want you asking the boys about it yet. Don't say anything, please. Not yet," Greta says, desperation clinging to every word. "You can let them know she was found and how, but nothing else. Promise me that. I shouldn't even be calling you, but you need to know."

"I promise," I say. "I can't believe this has happened. That poor girl. Her parents . . ."

"They're devastated," Greta says.

"I can't imagine." A long pause follows. "Greta?"

"Yes?"

"When you say you shouldn't be calling me, is it because of the investigation?"

"Mostly." Silence hangs between us. "Iz, I think it's best if we don't see each other for a while, like you said, with the investigation and all."

"Tell me what happened last night, Greta. Please. I have no idea. Everything was perfect until . . ." I stop. I want her to tell me.

She sighs as if she's struggling to say the words, but finally she does. She says one word: "Sal."

My heart sinks. I knew it.

"What did he do?" I dread the answer.

"Iz, it's just—I—can't."

"Can't or won't?" I say. "Greta, please, I won't tell him you told me."

Mumblings come from her end of the phone, but they sound muffled like she is covering the receiver. "Hold on," Greta says, followed by, "Yes, it's the school." Then she says to me, "I have to go."

"Greta—"

In a low murmur, she blurts, "It's not merely what Sal did but what he does." She makes a tutting noise with her tongue. "You're protecting him, aren't you?"

"Protecting him from what?"

"I have to go," she says again.

"No, don't go," I plead. "I'm not protecting him. I don't know what you're talking about."

"If you don't know," she whispers, "if you're telling me the truth, then, Iz . . . you're not safe."

The person she was speaking to before returns.

"Greta?"

I'm met with empty static. She doesn't trust me enough to tell me. Or she's afraid.

Rocco inevitably knows what happened with Sal last night. The tension oozed from his eyes as we walked out the door. But if Sal did something, why wouldn't Rocco have defended Greta at that moment? Or had that happened while I was dozing?

If Greta thinks I'd protect Sal, then she doesn't know me like I thought she did. My fault for pretending my life with Sal is normal when it's anything but normal. How could I expect her to know?

Something from within takes over, and I spring into action. I head to the kitchen to talk with Franco and Luca in the few minutes before they leave. I want them to find out about Julia from me before anyone tells them at school. I want them to be prepared. I'll tell them they can stay home from school if they're too upset to go. I wonder if they're aware of what was in her pocket.

When I tell them—when I actually sit down and tell Franco and Luca what I've learned about Julia—I'm not surprised at their reaction, and it kills me to see it. Life and hope drain from their skin. Slouched shoulders, sorrowful eyes. Heartbroken.

What does surprise me is how quickly Luca's face brightens as he scoops up his books and says, "Ready, Franco?" just two minutes after I'd told them their friend had been found dead.

Franco, a little less animated, grabs his books and follows Luca to the door.

"Bye, Mamá," they say, but neither one turns to look at me.

Am I expecting something different? At least they can carry their sadness out the door with them. Maybe they don't want me to worry about them, and that's why they perked up so quickly. I watch as they go to the Russos' house, and about a minute later the Russo girls follow them off the porch and down the road. Good kids.

I can't imagine seeing the police at my door and hearing them say the words no parent wants to hear, that their child has been found but not alive. Nothing can prepare a a mother for that kind of news. How does a person accept those words? My heart aches for Mrs. Bernardi—her grief, her pain, her loss.

About an hour later, the phone rings again. I run to answer, hoping it's Greta. But it's Anna telling me she's heard about Julia and that she and a few parents in the neighborhood have planned a candlelight service tonight on the beach not far from where Julia was found. I tell her I'll come and I'll bring something to share. She doesn't say anything about her oldest son, Peter, and I don't ask. Peter recently asked Julia to go steady. I'm sure he's not taking this news well. Anna stays on the line long enough to share information about the service, but she's rushed, frantic, and tells me she has to go and call others.

When we hang up, I ponder what might have been in Julia's pocket, and then I realize whatever was in there more than likely had to have come from Peter. Relief from this notion is fast replaced by guilt. I don't want that item connected to any of our kids.

I take a deep breath and prepare to make my sweet roll recipe. The knot in my stomach twists with each kneading of the dough.

CHAPTER EIGHT

Flickering lights dance against a dark sky like lucciola, fireflies congregating and flashing in unison. I light my lantern and join the waves of light dotting the coast of the Tyrrhenian Sea. Only a week ago many came together, sifting through the streets where Julia lived and was last seen for a different purpose: the hope of finding her alive or a clue to where she could be. Never knowing she'd be found floating in the beautiful, teal-blue sea, now marred by the dirty hands of a killer.

Familiar faces mix with strangers converging as close as possible to where they found Julia's body, about a mile south of our marina. My heart races when I see Rocco and several police officers standing together at the front. Part of me wants to talk to him, and part of me hopes he doesn't see me. Behind them, in smaller clusters, a few teachers huddle together, and several churchgoers, neighbors, and others from town contribute to an expanding, luminous glow honoring Julia. Quiet gestures, grim faces. No one wants to be here. Not for this reason.

Franco and Luca walk beside me but veer off to greet friends I've never met, two girls and three boys roughly the same age as my boys. When I approach them, they stop talking and lay eyes on me.

"Mamá," Franco says, pointing toward his friends, "this is Gia and Tara. And this is Carlos, John, and Stephano."

The girls have long, dark hair that falls below their shoulders. They are dressed nicely and smile when they're introduced. Carlos has a brooding

CHAPTER EIGHT

sort of guise and greets me with a nod. Stephano and John offer their hands to shake. John is outgoing and polite, even removing his hat to greet me. My first impression of Gia and Tara is that they're sweet and a little shy, but Carlos and Stephano are harder to read.

"Very nice to meet you all," I say, smiling. "I'm very sorry for your loss. How kind of you to come and support your friend tonight. You're all welcome to our home anytime." They nod and smile awkwardly. "I'll let you get back to your conversation," I say, stepping away to give them space.

A little farther down, a woman waves at me. I wave back and realize it is Anna. As we're waving to each other, I think I spot Sal not far from her, and it seems strange that he'd come to something like this. If that is him, he must have left work early. He waves, too, but not at me. Then he stops to speak to another man. Could that be Massimo?

I wave my arms over my head, hoping to catch his attention, but it's no use; he is engaged in conversation with the man who looks like Massimo. I lose sight of him as the crowd thickens between us. As Anna and I move toward the middle, I scan the crowd looking for Sal again but don't see him anywhere.

Anna embraces me in a tight hug. I step back, sensing something is off. Something resides in her warm, brown eyes—a weary face of fear. I'd know it anywhere. She could never keep things from me when we were face to face, not since we were little. She and Giorgio were my first friends—my best friends. Other friends have come and gone; not them. Even Sal can't push them away.

Giorgio . . . I need to see him.

"You could always tell when something was off," she says.

"What's going on?" I say.

She motions toward Julia's mother, Layla. "Nothing compared to what she's going through, but it's still bad."

"What?"

Anna glances over her shoulder and pulls me close. "It's Peter," she says. "He's not dealing well with this. You knew they were dating, right?"

"Yes, I remember. Poor Peter. Hard enough to grasp all this as an adult; I can't imagine being a young man. Where is he? Is he here?"

"He's coming," Anna says, then she leans in close. "It's not only that, Iz. I heard the police want to talk to him. They'll want to talk to all his friends." She glances toward Luca and Franco.

"Why?"

"That's what they do," she says. "They have to find out if they know anything." She hugs me again. "I've missed you so much." She links her arm in mine and we walk to a small table set with pictures and other mementos of Julia.

"Whoever did this to Julia is probably here right now," I say, remembering some of Rocco's other cases. Rocco is probably watching the crowd closely tonight.

Anna's eyes widen. "Wouldn't they be afraid of being caught?"

"No. They like the intrigue," I say. "They'll blend in with the crowd. They might even offer to help."

"Wouldn't that be risky?" she says. "Wouldn't that draw attention to them?"

"Rocco says it's their way of manipulating the situation," I say. "They think they have control because they can blend into the crowd, weave their way in, listen to what people are saying, and get information. Rocco says people like this take pride in what they've done. They'll even visit the crime scene more than once." I'm saddened to think I might never listen to another story from Rocco.

"That's sickening," Anna says. "Is Rocco investigating this case?"

"No, he said he's still working on another one."

"How are they—Rocco and Greta?" Anna says. "I haven't seen them in a while."

"They're fine," I lie.

Anna looks away wistfully. "I just can't believe this has happened. Did you know she had marks on her neck . . . like she was strangled?"

I shudder at the thought. "Who would do this?" I say. "This kind of thing doesn't happen here."

"I don't know, but my girls will be locked inside until they catch him."

I nod, observing Franco, Luca, and their friends across the street approach-

CHAPTER EIGHT

ing Julia's family. Luca and Carlos stand next to Gia and Tara. Franco, Stephano, and John move to the display table of memorabilia. Julia's mother, Layla, joins them at the table and others follow with their lanterns, forming a semi-circle of light around her. Layla looks as if she's about to say something.

I motion to Anna, and we too join the gathering crowd. Dotted arcs of light extend like rippling waves of water as others join. Julia's father stands next to Layla, his eyes to the ground, his hand resting on her back as she speaks.

"Thank you all for coming tonight," she begins with a crackly voice. "We are overwhelmed by your love and care. We have no idea how we will manage through this, but we want to thank you . . ." She trails off.

Her husband's head pops up and he clears his throat. "We're thankful for the police and everyone who helped search for our Julia—" His voice catches and he stops for a moment. He turns to Rocco and the other officers. "Please don't stop looking for the person who did this. We must find justice for Julia and protect others from this monster."

Layla turns and nestles her head into his shoulder.

We lift our lanterns. Some shout, "Amen!" and others clap their hands.

I examine the illuminated faces in the crowd for the one who might be the killer. Is he among us, taking advantage of this opportunity to hunt his next victim? Will he look different? Seem different? I wait for an altered expression to befall an unassuming face—a shift of the eye, a crack on the lips. Is that what the police are looking for? My body shivers.

I scan the crowd again for Greta and the girls but don't see them anywhere. Surely Gianna, Maria, and Sienna would have found Franco and Luca by now. I'm surprised they're not here. I observe my boys interacting with their friends and I'm proud they're here to support the Bernardis in this tragedy. How respectful and attentive they were when the Bernardis were speaking.

Now Luca stands with Carlos, intensely watching them as if they might say something, but they never do.

"Are the girls here?" I ask Anna.

"They're home with Beppe," she says. "They're not handling this well at all."

Did you know I actually found Samantha locked in her closet this afternoon? I'm worried about them. I'm worried about all our kids. I'm glad the police are here."

"Oh my. Poor Samantha," I say. "Yes, our community needs their presence here. We need to know we're protected."

About half an hour later, Peter arrives, eyes red and swollen. He hugs Anna and then spots Franco waving, so he leaves us to be with his friends.

"Do you see how they stare at him?" Anna motions toward the crowd. "Already they are judging him."

"I don't see it, but perhaps I'm not looking for it. To me, everyone's face is blank," I say as we near the displayed memorabilia.

A poster sits in the middle of the table. A young girl's life unfolds in captured moments of precious time. I rest my eyes on a recent school picture of Julia—the way she smiles, her long hair pinned to each side with beautiful blue-floral barrettes, the pretty dress she chose to wear for picture day. I dab my eyes, absorbing the sadness of her family and the people here.

Little by little the crowd dwindles, scant lights fading as they go. Franco approaches us. "You don't have to stay, Mamá," he says. "We'll be okay here. I'll walk home with Luca."

"Bring your friends back to the house for a bit," I say.

He rolls his eyes. "Papá won't like it."

"I like it, and it's my house too," I wink.

Franco screws up his face as if I've lost my mind. I can't believe I said it either. I picture myself on our front porch, suitcase in hand, boys at my side, stepping off into a new life and never looking back. Soon.

"He'll say it's too late."

"I'll remind him that this is an exception," I say. "He'll understand."

He won't understand, but I'll spin it to Sal that if Franco and Luca have their friends over, they won't be away from home as much and we can keep an eye on them. They'll be safer with us than out on the streets. It'll give us an opportunity to get to know their friends better. And I'll get to see Franco and Luca in a different light as well. What could be the harm in that?

"You're sure, Mamá?"

CHAPTER EIGHT

"I'll put out some cake and cookies and you can visit for a while. Go ask them," I say, indicating his friends.

I watch as Franco suggests my idea to his friends. Luca's face is the only one objecting. Franco gives me a thumbs-up. I point to Luca to see if he's coming too, and Franco nods. He tells me not to wait, that they'll be right behind us. Anna and I walk together until we get to the end of the street, then she goes one way toward her house and I go the opposite direction toward mine.

Eventually, I hear several footsteps plodding behind me. I peek over my shoulder to confirm it's Franco, Luca, and their friends, but they're not directly behind me. Someone else is between us, but the darkness won't give away who it is. I see a dark hat, a long coat, and the self-assured gait of a man. I snap my head to the road ahead, caught off guard and anxious. When I turn around again, he's gone. The kids are closer. I stop and wait for them.

"Did any of you see that man walking in front of you just now?" I say, slightly out of breath.

"I didn't see anyone," Franco says. "Did you?" he asks his friends.

Everyone says no, they hadn't seen anyone either. Probably too busy talking to each other to notice. But I know what I saw, and I feel his eyes on me all the way to my house.

CHAPTER NINE

A faint, flickering light by the front door provides scant illumination of the porch floor. The shadowy blackness of night winds through the houses on our street, making me keenly aware of my vulnerability. I stay close to Franco, Luca, and their friends, thankful we live a relatively short distance from the coast. I'm surprised so many houses have already turned off their porch lights.

Every step I take, even in the company of others, and even in the safety of my short driveway, feels long and treacherous. I don't know who was behind me on the road or if he's still lurking in the shadows. And if he didn't already know where I live, he does now.

I enter a dark, quiet house, but the lamp glowing at the base of the stairs tells me Sal is home and in bed. The first one to bed turns on the lamp—that's always been our routine. Retiring this early means he's either getting an early start at the marina tomorrow or he's avoiding me. So, it wasn't him I saw at the service tonight, but I'm not sure whether to be relieved or on edge.

I quickly place a plate of cookies and the remaining half of last night's cake on the table for Franco, Luca, and their friends. Luca and Gia come to the table together. They're smiling at each other, standing close. I'm pleasantly surprised at the natural, genuine smile on Luca's face. I can't remember the last time I saw him smile like that.

"Thank you, Signora Perri," Gia says. She pushes her glossy dark hair over

CHAPTER NINE

her shoulder and takes a bite of a cookie. "These are delicious." Her eyes are as blue as the sea. She is confident and polite, possibly a good influence on Luca. I like her immediately.

"You're very welcome," I say. My eyes dart between Gia and Luca. I see the way Luca gazes at her, like he's mesmerized by everything she says.

"Your house is so pretty," Gia says. "I've never seen a kitchen so neat and clean."

"Thank you, Gia," I say, "that's very kind of you." I too am mesmerized by her confidence. She reminds me of how I used to be.

Franco and the others join them.

"It's just a kitchen," Carlos says to Gia. "What's so great about it?"

His rudeness surprises me. He flashes Gia a smile, and it's obvious he's trying to impress her. Luca notices and moves closer to her. Carlos glares at Luca but then quickly switches to a fake smile, as if he remembers where he is and who's watching him. He transforms right in front of me. The muscles near his jaw twitch and tighten and then his chin drops, and his lips form a shiny smile. I know this transition. I live it every day. He's no good, and I don't want him around Luca or Franco.

Tara and John share a piece of cake and converse mostly with Franco. So gentle, so quiet.

Sometimes it's the quiet ones.

"Help yourselves to as much as you want," I say as I leave the kitchen to read a book in the living room. The voices of Franco, Luca, and their friends talking to each other in our kitchen fills my home, and it's instantly warmer. Brief happiness and fullness in my heart.

* * *

I awaken with a start, and it's so dark I can scarcely see my hand in front of my face. As if the sky swallowed the moon and all the stars. Sal is snoring next to me, his head cradled in his downy pillow. The curtain hems bounce against the wall, and I'm met with a cool breeze. I go to the window and look out.

The darkened mounds of rolling hills are barely visible, but I know they're there. A noise coming from outside shifts my attention in the direction of the shed. My heart stops when I see a thin line of light below the door, something I would have noticed when I returned from the candlelight service. Had Sal gone to the shed while I was asleep and forgotten to turn off the light? It's not the kind of thing Sal would do. But Something's happening in there. I nudge the window slightly higher and listen. Luca better not have snuck out again. Even if he did, he'd have no reason to go to the shed.

I glance at Sal, still in the same position. If we were a normal couple, I'd wake him and ask him to investigate, but we're not normal, and I'm not about to wake a sleeping bear. So, instead of crawling back under the covers and pretending nothing is wrong, I grab my robe and see for myself. On my way down, I quickly check on the boys, happy to find them both in their beds and asleep. When I peek in on Luca, I'm reminded of the strange floorboard beneath his bed and make a quick mental note to check it later.

Before leaving the house, I go to the kitchen and open the knife drawer. I reach for the biggest one, pulling it out slowly as if I'm unsheathing a sword. Holding it firmly against my leg, I slip out the front door, keeping low and hoping to blend into the darkness. The crunching of dry grass under my feet echoes in the night. Not even the soothing sounds of the crickets can calm me now.

I hold my breath, fearful of being discovered. Fearful of going inside. But I have to know what's going on. I could never put a finger on why the shed has always made me uncomfortable. Greta's words ring in my head: "It's not merely what he did, it's what he does. Are you protecting him?"

The closer I get, the less I breathe. My legs shake with each step, and I almost drop when I see a darkened silhouette heading in the same direction I am. I stop. And I watch, my eyes confirming that it is indeed a person at the door of the shed. They seem to be fiddling with the lock. Who has a key besides Sal? What do they need from the shed at this hour?

I've only ever seen the inside of the shed twice: once when we first moved

CHAPTER NINE

in, and once right after Sal moved his things inside and made it his home office. I chastise my old self for not being brazen enough to ask him what was in the shed, or even just to see it completed. Once he was fully moved in, I was kept out. At the time, I was fine with the arrangement because I really didn't care. I was used to looking the other way. But I feel differently now. And something is different about that shed.

I scan the open space behind me and the unknown territory ahead as a terrible thought comes to mind: What if I've been lured here? Could others be waiting for me? Is it the man who was walking behind me from the candlelight service? The person who wrote the anonymous note? The kidnapper? All of this makes me intensely afraid to keep going yet compelled to. I'm captivated, spellbound.

The lock clicks, and the person at the door goes into the shed, probably unaware that the door didn't close completely behind him. A chill slithers up my spine as I reach the end of the fence near the bergamot trees. I squat low to the ground, only steps from the door. Doubts litter my mind, and I question what I know is true. I know what I saw.

I grip the knife's handle and step forward. I see that the lock is undone and the door opened a crack. My body trembles. I reach for the door and feel it move slightly at my touch. My heart races, my body stiffens. I use the sharp tip of the knife to nudge the door further, but it's not enough. Holding the knife in one hand, I push the door open with the other until I'm standing in the doorway.

I'm met with a strange combination of the sweet smell of hay and the dankness of dirt. A reception-like desk is centered in front of a wall in the brightly lit room, a door on either side of the desk.

I gravitate first to the door on the left. I go to it and open it slowly. It is dark on the other side, but I can make out a table roughly the size of our kitchen table but more substantial, and some chairs around it. This must be where he meets with clients. Bookshelves line the whole back wall, but it's hard to see clearly. I know from before that there's a window somewhere on the back wall as well. There is not much to see here. I quietly leave that room and go to the other one.

My hand hesitates on the doorknob. I twist and push it open a few inches. As soon as I do, I'm hit with a stronger scent of the smell upon first entering the shed, and I know it originates from here. This room is unfinished and appears to be used for storage. I can make out a stack of boxes on the righthand side. On the left side are shovels and garden tools leaning against the wall.

All of a sudden, something in the corner beyond the shovels moves and stills my heart. I raise the knife, my legs stiff and heavy, and brace myself for the worst. If I run, I'll never escape fast enough. Sweat stings my eyes and runs down my back. I feel like I might burst.

My words fly from my mouth fast. "Whoever's in here, I've got a gun and I'll use it!" Nothing happens. "The police are on their way!" My whole body shakes, and suddenly a rat scampers over my feet. I scream and cup my hand to my mouth. It was only a rat. I wait, and two more follow.

I hold the knife in front of me and walk to the corner. A sheet is strewn across the floor where the rats had been. With the tip of the knife, I reach for the sheet, pulling it closer to me. Another rat skitters by. Where did the person I was following go? Using the tip of the knife again, I scoop the sheet, lifting it into the air. As I do, something falls to the floor, something that was tangled in the sheet. I jump, ready for another rat, but it's not a rat. I move closer until I'm directly over it the object.

It's a white-and-gray lace-up shoe, something a girl would wear.

Frantically, I search the rest of the room but come up empty. But further back within the wall, I think I see the outline of a door. It must be where the person I followed had exited without me seeing them. I run to the door but don't open it, fearing the person waiting on the other side.

I turn and run out of the room and out of the shed as fast as I can with the knife held firmly in front and the shoe tucked beneath my arm. I run straight through the yard, my breath ragged, my legs rubbery, all the way to the house, not once looking back. When I'm inside, locking the doors, I still don't look.

I put down the knife and pace frantically in the living room, wracking my brains about what to do next. I examine the shoe. What does it mean?

CHAPTER NINE

Reason and logic escape me. Perhaps a transient found a way inside and stayed there for a night's sleep. Maybe that's who I followed, and when they saw me they took what they could carry and left through the back door, leaving behind a shoe. But transients aren't usually girls.

In the kitchen, I examine the sole of the shoe, which tells me it hasn't been worn much—the stitching at the sides and the smell of new leather. It's fairly new. Feminine design and colors, definitely belonging to a female. But what does it mean? Why was it in Sal's office?

I place the shoe in a special box at the back of my cupboard behind the flour and other baking ingredients. I call it my "hope box" that will someday set me free. Each week I add a small morsel of money to the box after skimming a very meager amount from the marina profits. I started doing this after that horrible encounter between Sal and Luca. That marina is mine, too, and without me, Sal wouldn't have any of the profits. If I didn't do this, I'd never have a penny.

I place the shoe inside my hope box until I can figure out what to do with it. I return the box to its spot, close the cupboard, and stand in front like a guard.

No longer sleepy, my mind races wildly. I open another cupboard door and retrieve my medicine. I twist the lid and upturn the bottle over my tongue, but instead of shaking out my medicine, I put the lid back on and put the bottle away. I have to be sharp. I have to tell someone about what just happened—Greta, Anna, or Giorgio. They'll know what to do.

I check the time. Everyone is asleep. It will have to wait until daytime.

I need to get back into bed so Sal has no idea I ever left; then he can't ask me where I've been. Before I slip under the covers, I peer out the window again at the shed. It's too far back, and I haven't got a clue if the door closed behind me or remained open. But I can't worry about that now. Whoever was in the shed must have seen me coming or they wouldn't have left. I recall the faded details of the unfinished side of Sal's office and the smell. I slide my cold body into the bed and relish the warmth, but it does little to calm my nerves.

CHAPTER TEN

I am alone in the comfort and privacy of my kitchen. The contents of the cupboard behind me give me strength. Except for one item: the shoe. Sal works in the shed and the boys work the plantation. I knead the prepared dough, folding, flipping, and pressing. My thoughts are lost in the stretchy substance that sticks to my fingers. I separate like amounts to form twelve rolls for dinner. A soft, light hum floats above me. Something nudges my shoulder.

"Mamá, do you hear me?" Franco says, his face serious. His voice snaps me back.

"Franco . . . were you talking to me?" I stop kneading. "You look upset. What's wrong?"

"The Russos!" he says.

"What about the Russos?" I pull clumps of dough from my fingers. "What?"

Franco's face is grave. "They're—"

"What? Say it!"

"They're gone!" he says, his eyes filling.

"What do you mean, 'gone'?" I say. "I'm sure they'll be back, Franco, calm down."

"No, Mamá, they are all gone."

How unusual to go on vacation during the school term.

Franco takes my hand and leads me to the Russos' house. He glimpses Sal's office and maneuvers to the left, probably to move us out of his father's

CHAPTER TEN

line of sight.

We climb the same porch steps we'd regretfully left two nights ago. My legs are rubbery as I follow Franco to the window. We peer through the glass at the dusky, empty house. A stream of light from the back window pierces the darkness enough to reveal the truth.

Everything inside the house that provided peace and comfort—the furniture and beautiful decorations, the painting of the sea that stood above the sofa, the soft, handmade rug, and, yes, the Russo family—are all gone. Gone. The word is obtrusive, heavy like a thick, wet blanket. Gone.

Franco goes to the front door and tries to open it, but it's locked. I follow him like a lost puppy to the window that looks into the kitchen. I see the cupboards and the sink where Greta stood with her back to me. I recall how she'd turned and insisted everything was fine when I knew it was a lie. I relive that night all over again—fierce happiness, sharp pain. Where had my friends gone, and why didn't they tell me? I feel as empty as the house.

I turn to Franco. "Did the girls tell you they were leaving? Did they say anything about moving?"

"No," he says. "We walked to school together yesterday, but we walked home alone. Sometimes they stay after to help clean."

"How did you figure out they were gone?"

"I came here to talk to Gianna just now, and that's when I found out."

"There's got to be an explanation," I say. But what? There's no way to get a hold of Greta. It's like she simply disappeared.

Franco's eyes fill. He catches a tear on his cheek and pretends he's batting at something. I hand him a handkerchief. He turns away and dabs his eyes.

"We need to get home before your father realizes we're missing. We have to act like we know nothing about this. We'll figure this out, I promise."

"Why do we have to pretend to not know anything?" Franco asks. "Because of Papá? Because of how we left their house? Why do we have to be so careful around him all the time?"

"It's just better this way," I say.

"I think we should tell him they're gone," he says angrily. "Or maybe he already knows, and he's the reason they left." He glares at me with resentful eyes.

"Franco, don't say that. Come on, we need to go."

He's probably right, although I don't want him to be. Franco is smart, observant. He reads people well and figures them out fast. I put my arm around his shoulders. "I promise you we'll find out where the Russos went."

On the short walk back to our house, I'm confused and overwhelmed, concerned about the sudden disappearance of the entire Russo family and all their belongings. As if they disappeared in the middle of the night, without a sound, without a trace. If only I could get inside the house, maybe I'd find something that would lead me to them.

My thoughts are cut short when I notice two policemen standing at our front door talking to each other. One is tall and thin, his arms folded. The other is short; he stands wide, hands on hips, wearing a thick mustache. They turn when they see Franco and me coming to the door.

"Hello, officers," I say.

"Good morning, Signora Perri," says the short one. "Sorry to bother you. We're conducting interviews for our investigation of the Julia Bernardi case. We wondered if we could speak to your sons for a few minutes."

"Why my sons?" I say, hoping to sound naive.

"We're talking to everyone who was in Julia's inner circle," the tall one interjects. "Her closest friends, family."

"Oh, well," I stumble over my words, "I don't think they knew her well enough..."

"It's all right, Mamá," Franco says.

I look at him.

"Thank you, son," the short officer says. "We'll talk with you first, and then you can send in your brother."

"Would you like to come inside?" I say.

"That won't be necessary," the short officer replies. "We'll sit out here if you don't mind."

"Of course," I say.

Both officers scrutinize me. "We'll tell you when we're done." A subtle hint that I'm not welcome to say and listen.

CHAPTER TEN

I pace inside by the door, listening to the voices on the front porch, unable to decipher their words. It's driving me crazy wondering what they're talking about and what kinds of questions they might be asking. Do my boys know what was found in Julia's pocket?

After about fifteen minutes, Franco leaves the porch to get Luca. I'm waiting for the moment when Sal discovers that two police officers are talking to his sons without his permission. The officers keep Luca on the porch a bit longer than Franco. I go back and forth watching the shed door through the kitchen window and listening by the front door to catch anything they might be saying. I'm partly tempted to tell them about the anonymous note I received but decide not to.

When they're finished, the officers knock on my door to tell me they're done for now but might be back again if necessary.

Before Franco and Luca return to their weekend chores, I ask them what they talked about.

"Nothing much," Franco says. "They only wanted to know how well we knew Julia, what she was like, when we met—stuff like that."

"Anything else?" Did they mention the pocket?

"Like what?" Franco says.

"I don't know," I say. "Maybe something else . . . something you weren't expecting?"

"It was fine," Luca says. "Nothing to worry about."

His reply seems dismissive. I give him a cautionary glance.

Sal is still in the shed, so he must not have seen the officers. Because he wouldn't have stayed in the shed if he had seen them. He wouldn't have avoided them, right?

"It's not what he did, it's what he does."

I hear the phone ringing through the open window, so I run inside to answer. When I hold the receiver to my ear, I'm met with a long tone. I hang up, and a minute later the phone rings again. I pick up. "Hello?" Nothing; no tone at all. Empty air like someone's there but not saying anything. "Hello?" I say again, louder this time. Then a click. They're gone. The third time the phone rings, I'm ready. "Who is this?"

"Oh my gosh, Iz, please say you can talk right now." It's Anna, and her voice is shaky.

"Yes. What's wrong?"

She talks so fast her words run into each other, hard to understand.

"Slow down," I say. "It's okay. Take your time."

"I can't—can't breathe," she says.

"Is Giuseppe home?" I say. "Are you alone? Should I come over?"

"H—he didn't do it!" she cries.

"Who do you mean? Giuseppe?"

Anna whimpers into the phone.

"I'm coming over. Can I come over right now?"

"Okay, yes," she whispers.

"Everything will be okay. Just hold tight."

As soon as we hang up, I call Giorgio to see if he can take me to Anna's. If he's able to come now, it will be much faster than walking. I only hope Sal continues to stay in the shed long enough.

CHAPTER ELEVEN

Leaving the house without telling Sal, especially with Giorgio, would send Sal into a rage, so I walk to the end of the road heading east toward town and meet Giorgio on his way to pick me up. When I get into his car, I'm overwhelmed by his presence. He exudes warmth, comfort, and a connection to the past I long for. I look at him and he smiles; it's enough to make my heart burst. I want to hug him and cry, let it all out.

"Thank you for coming on short notice," I say.

He smiles. "Good to see you, Iz."

My heart flips and I think he sees it. I brief him on Anna's frantic call and what's been happening lately.

He places his hand on mine. "You're a good friend," he says.

Gravel crumbles beneath the wheels as we climb the hill to Anna's house. She stands in the doorway waiting for me, her face distraught. Giorgio agrees to wait in the car. I get out quickly and run to her. As we hug, her body slackens. I walk her to the kitchen table and pull out a chair. While I get her a glass of water, I scan the house. She appears to be alone.

"Take a sip," I say, handing her the glass. "Take your time."

Anna drinks the water and looks at me, her eyes red and wet. "You haven't heard, have you?"

"Heard what?" I say.

Anna lifts her head, the life in her eyes depleted. "Peter," she cries. "The police took him."

"Took him? Why?"

"They think he knows what happened to Julia," she says. "They think he's involved." Anna cries into her hands.

"That's ridiculous," I say. "There must be some kind of misunderstanding." I wrap my arms around her. "Peter is a good boy. He'd never harm anyone. The police will see that."

It's true—Peter is good. He works hard, dresses well, he's helpful and kind and is loved by everyone. It was only recently that Peter started to rebel against his strict parents, but that's not uncommon for boys his age. He's never shown a lack of respect for his friends or classmates. Never displayed a proclivity toward violence. He's never even raised his voice in all the years I've known him.

"Peter was the last one to see Julia before she disappeared," Anna says.

I step back. "Are you sure?"

"Yes," Anna says. "He went to her house to ask her to go with him to a dance. He was in love with her."

"You never mentioned that before," I say.

"We haven't talked in a while," Anna says.

It feels like a stab, her way of saying I haven't called her lately. She's just as busy as me but implies it's my fault we don't see each other enough.

"Where's Giuseppe?" I ask.

"He followed the police when they took Peter. Peter had nothing to do with Julia's murder! I know my son!" she says, hiccupping between words. "You know him," she says. "He didn't do this."

"Of course he didn't," I say.

"Franco and Luca were around her, too, the week before," she says.

"So were a lot of people," I say, not liking her tone or what she hints at. "What makes you think they were around her?"

"They all went to her house after school—Peter, Franco, and Luca. Peter told me."

"That doesn't mean anything," I say. "Did you see them there?"

"No," she says, dabbing her eyes with a tissue.

"Do you mind if I make a phone call?" I say. "I want to tell Franco and Luca about Peter." I pick up the phone and dial my number, praying Sal

CHAPTER ELEVEN

doesn't answer. I relay to Anna that my boys aren't aware of Peter going with the police.

"Oh, Iz," Anna says, "what do I do? What if they arrest him?"

"Don't say that," I say, although I'm worried about that too. "Franco said he and Luca will come by to be with the girls while we wait for news on Peter. Is that okay?"

"Yes, that would be very nice," she says.

Anna's oldest daughter, Samantha, is in Franco's class; her middle child, Jenna, is Luca's age; and her youngest, Theresa, is still in primary school. They're all close—not as close as the Russos, but still very close.

I swallow hard at the thought of the Russos.

As soon as the boys arrive, they follow Anna's daughters to the backyard. Anna paces in the living room, making me anxious. I go to the car and tell Giorgio we might be a little longer than I anticipated. He says he's fine waiting. Before I sit with Anna again, I go into the kitchen for something to drink. I hear muffled voices through the window over the kitchen sink: Franco and Luca talking with the girls in the yard. I turn off the faucet and listen to what they're saying.

"You were there too." Samantha's voice.

"No, he wasn't," Jenna says. "He was in the library with me."

"You're lying," Samantha says. "Why are you lying for him?"

Lying for who? Which one? Say a name!

"I'm not lying," Jenna says.

"You need to say something," Samantha says.

"What are you doing?" Anna's voice startles me.

"Nothing," I say, turning around. "I was just getting some water." I pick up my glass and head to the living room.

Anna follows me. "Giuseppe just called," she says. "He's on his way back with Peter."

"He called now? I didn't even hear the phone ring."

"I picked up quickly," she says. "We didn't talk long. He said it was awful the way they interrogated Peter. I need to make sure everything is calm when they come home."

"Do you want us to leave?" I ask.

She doesn't answer right away, but the look on her face is enough. "I feel bad. The kids just got here, but—"

"No need to explain," I say. "I just wanted to make sure you're okay. Call me when you find out what's going on with Peter." I call Franco and Luca inside, we say our goodbyes, and leave with Giorgio.

"Everything okay?" Giorgio asks.

"Yes," I say. "Giuseppe and Peter are on their way home. I suppose Anna will know more when she sees them."

"You okay?" he asks. "You seem . . . distracted."

"Yes, I'm okay, just worried about Peter." And about what Samantha and Jenna were saying.

***

When we arrive home, I thank Giorgio for taking us to Anna's but deny his wish to stay. The boys are quiet; the air in the house is tight. Heavy thoughts float in my mind: a little bit of guilt for sending Giorgio home after he selflessly stopped what he was doing to bring me to Anna's, and a lot of worry about my boys. Franco and Luca look as if they have something to say but not to me. If I ask what they were talking about with the girls, they'll realize I was eavesdropping.

Luca breaks the silence when he asks to go to Carlos's house. He says Carlos needs to talk to him right away. I can tell by his creased forehead that he's stressed and anxious.

"Luca, you know your father doesn't want you going anywhere, especially in light of what has happened," I say.

Luca rolls his eyes.

I glare at him. "Carlos will have to either come here or he'll have to wait.

CHAPTER ELEVEN

Besides, I want to talk with you and your brother for a few minutes."

"About what?" Luca says, concerned.

"I can't imagine what you're going through right now," I say, "having lost a friend. It's got to be very hard on both of you, and now with Peter . . ." Franco and Luca glance at each other. "You both know you can talk to me about anything, right? No matter how hard or even if you think I might become upset?" I look at both of them. "You know that, right?"

"We're fine, Mamá," Franco says.

But they're not fine. I can tell by their awkward stances and the way they can't sit still for more than a few seconds.

"I'll love you no matter how bad something might be. Do you understand me?"

"Do you think we're keeping something from you?" Luca asks.

I'm caught off guard by this remark. "Are you?"

"Of course," he says to Franco, "she thinks we did something wrong already!"

"That is not what I'm saying," I say. "You're dealing with a lot, and I just want to make sure you understand that if something does come up and you need someone to trust, you can trust me."

"We know," Franco says. "Thanks, Mamá." Luca just stares.

"Did you and the girls talk about what happened?"

"No," Luca says. Franco shoots him a look. "A little," he corrects. "There wasn't much time to talk. Not a lot to say."

"Did either of the girls say anything? They're probably so upset about Peter," I say.

"Nothing was said, Mamá," Luca says. "Let it go."

"Watch your tone, Luca. I'm only trying to help."

"You don't need to worry," he says. "We don't need help."

"I do need to worry," I say. "This is serious and scary. I worry about all of you, including your friends. You shouldn't be burdened about things like this at your age. I'm sure the girls appreciated that you stopped by to be with them at this terrible time in their lives, even if you didn't talk about anything." But I know you did.

"Peter can be a jerk sometimes," Luca says. "He's done some stupid things."

"What are you saying?" I say. "Are you talking about what happened at the Parinello farm last summer?"

"No, that wasn't Peter," Franco says. "He wouldn't harm a fly."

"But that incident happened during the time he was working there, right?" I ask, vaguely recalling a story about a burglary gone wrong and an injured family member at the farm.

"Yes, but that had nothing to do with Peter," Franco says. "He's not like that."

"If you say so," Luca says. "Can I go now?"

"Don't listen to him," Franco says to me.

"You may go for now," I say, "but I might want to talk more later."

I'm not sure what to think anymore. Anna said Peter hasn't been himself since the fall when he turned fifteen. He's more withdrawn, easy to anger, not present. I told her it's probably just hormones, but I'm not sure she agrees.

After Luca leaves the room, I lean toward Franco. "I want to ask you something, and I want you to be truthful."

Franco looks unsure. "Okay."

"What do you think of Carlos and that other boy, Stephano?"

"I don't really know them very well," he says. "Stephano is quiet, keeps to himself a lot. Carlos has always been fine with me. Seems okay, I guess. Gets in trouble sometimes for cutting school—nothing else really—but Carlos has had a rough life. His mamá left and—"

"She left? When?"

"Three years ago," he says. "It's been just him and his papá for a while. And his papá is always drunk, so . . ."

Practically an orphan. "No wonder he cuts school," I say.

"Yeah," he says. "I feel bad for him."

I think about what must have happened to make Carlos's mother decide that leaving her son with an alcoholic father was the only thing she could do. I reflect on my own fantasy of leaving Sal, but I would never go without my boys. I'd never leave them with Sal. Maybe Carlos's mother had no other option.

"Why are you asking about them?" Franco says.

"I'm worried about Luca and the friends he keeps lately. I didn't have any trouble with him before he started hanging around those boys, Peter included."

"I notice a difference too," Franco says, "but not because of his friends. Ever since he started working more with Papá I've seen a difference."

For some reason, hearing this is like a punch in my stomach. I gasp inside.

"We're not as close as we used to be," Franco continues. "He puts up a wall with me now."

Hearing him say this breaks my heart. "Please keep an eye on him," I say. "If you become aware of anything or witness something concerning, please tell me. I'll make sure he never finds out I heard it from you."

"Okay, Mamá."

"One last thing," I say, taking advantage of the moment. "Are you sure there is nothing you need to tell me about Julia? Nothing at all?" Franco's eyes lock with mine and I know he has something to say. "You can tell me."

He fidgets with his shirt. "Luca really liked Julia," he says, "even though she belonged to Peter."

Hearing the word "belonged" is like stepping on a nail. "No one belongs to anyone," I say sternly.

"You know, like a girlfriend—they were together."

"Go on," I say, intrigued.

"That's it. Luca liked Julia and was jealous of Peter. Carlos liked her too. Everyone did. That's all there is to it."

"Was Peter aware that Luca liked Julia?"

"Word travels fast, so, yes, he found out," he says.

"What happened?"

"Peter confronted Luca and Luca threatened him. They almost got in a fight."

"He threatened him?" I say. "Are you sure about that? Luca doesn't make threats."

"Mamá . . . don't be blind. He's even threatened me."

"For what?"

"One time Julia asked me a question about what I do on the plantation. She was really interested in the whole process of harvesting bergamot, so we talked for a while. Luca didn't like the fact that we talked. He told me later that if I continued to do that, he would spread a rumor around school about me."

My tongue feels so thick I can't reply. I'm at a loss for what to say or think. The person Franco is describing isn't Luca. Finally, I push through my shock. "Franco," I say, "let's not mention this to anyone—not Anna, the girls, and especially not your father, okay?"

He nods and then looks at me. "It's only a matter of time before Papá runs them out of town like he did the Russos."

"Don't say things like that."

"I'm stating the truth," he says. "You won't admit it, but something bad happened at the Russos' house that night after dinner. I'm sure of it. Everything changed so fast, it was obvious. And when Papá showed up at Anna and Giuseppe's house on his way home from work, drunk and yelling and—"

"Wait," I say, thrusting out my hand. "When did Papá go by Anna and Giuseppe's?"

"Night before last," he says.

"Why were you there?"

"I was talking with Samantha."

"I don't understand. Anna never said a word about this, not once."

As we're talking, something catches my attention out the window, movement of some sort in an upstairs window of the Russos' house. Is the sun's glare tricking my eyes? I stare hard at the dark glass and watch for it to happen again, but there's nothing more I can see from here.

"What are you looking at?" Franco says, following my gaze.

"I'm not sure," I say, keeping my eyes glued to the window. "I thought I saw something."

"Up there?" he says, indicating the window I'm watching. He moves in for a closer look. "I don't see anything at all."

CHAPTER ELEVEN

"It was probably nothing," I say. "Probably just shadows."

Franco shrugs his shoulders, then he scoops up his books from the table and looks at me.

I smile, releasing him from my interrogation. He heads upstairs to his room. I stare again at the upstairs window of the Russos' house and fully believe there's more than just shadows behind that glass.

CHAPTER TWELVE

White clouds hang low in the sky, knitted together like a downy blanket. Sal is already up filling the barrels with citrus and lemons to bring to town. Has he noticed the unlocked door to his office? I get out of bed, run a comb through my hair, and brush my teeth. I haphazardly slip my dress over my head and shoulders, smoothing out the wrinkles as it falls in place. I knock on Franco's and Luca's doors, pushing them open a crack. "Rise and shine boys! Time to get ready!" I say as I make my way downstairs to the kitchen, where I hastily prepare fried eggs and toast. Sal doesn't like to wait even a second more for the boys' help when we arrive home from church. With all the farm chores and preparations for town deliveries and an afternoon at the marina, Sundays are no longer rest days.

Luca and Franco descend the stairs in minutes. Luca pushes past Franco to be first at the table. I quickly assess the looks on their faces and discern the kind of day it will be.

When I join them outside, Sal is quieter than usual, which could mean a lot of things. A quiet Sal is easier in many ways than a loud-mouthed, belittling one. But the thoughts ruminating in his head and his locked-up emotions worry me the most, because when they're finally released they have terrible lasting effects on everyone around him. I look in his eyes for clues that he's discovered I've been to the shed, but they are empty.

CHAPTER TWELVE

***

While the boys and Sal set up in town, I shop for groceries and other items. As I approach a fruit vendor, I notice several women hovered in a corner hugging one another. One dabs her eyes with her shirt sleeve. They're standing close and whispering.

While I'm selecting apples, I listen to their conversation.

The vendor seems curious. "You know them?" he says.

"No," I say, embarrassed that I've been caught.

"Friends of the Lovallos," he says. "Their older daughter didn't come home last night."

"Oh no," I say.

"She just disappeared," he says. "They think she was taken like the other girl."

Taken like the other girl. Julia.

I observe them from afar, their eyes downcast, postures deflated, clinging to each other, clinging to hope. I need to call Anna. I wonder if she's heard about this.

As I depart from the table, Mr. Valentino, the principal at Franco's and Luca's school, crosses the street to another vendor's stand. I head over to say hello, and when I'm just a couple of feet from him, his eyes flick up at me and look away quickly. Maybe he doesn't recognize me.

"Signore Valentino!" I say, stepping closer. This time he has to acknowledge me. I press my hand to my chest. "Isabella Perri, Luca's mother."

His eyes convey annoyance. "Hello," he says robotically.

I try to make small talk but, from the unwelcome vibe he exudes, I'm stuck with nothing to say. "Is everything all right?" I finally manage.

"Are you referring to what happened?" he says.

"I don't understand what you mean," I say.

"Let me ask you something, Signora Perri," he says. "Do you make it a habit to throw away your children's notes from school and pretend nothing's wrong?"

"Throw away notes?" I say. "No, of course not."

"I spoke with Signore Perri yesterday about another incident and—"

"Another incident?"

"I'm well aware of how you like to pretend everything is fine, even when you know better. And really, Signora—stealing your husband's car so you can arrive at the school before him just to make everyone think you care!" His words flow smoothly in one breath, sliding off his tongue as they whip the air like a snake. "I'm also wise to your drug problem."

"What?" I say, confused. "I don't have a drug problem."

"He said you'd deny it. Don't worry, your husband and I have everything all worked out. I am to call him directly at work to notify him of any problems with Luca and he'll take care of it. At least someone will."

"I'm sorry, but I honestly have no idea what you're talking about," I say. "I haven't seen any notes. My husband never . . ." I stop when he rolls his eyes.

My body tenses; anger pulses through my blood. I want to explain. I want to throw my shopping bags at him. But his mind is made up. To argue will strengthen his opinion of the unstable image Sal has created of me. He believes Sal, and there's nothing I can do about it.

"Good day," he says, then turns and walks away.

I am dumbfounded by his treatment of me, confused at his accusations. Stealing Sal's car? Throwing away notes? What does Sal say about me to other people?

I walk through the rest of the morning in alternating states of confusion from Mr. Valentino and nausea at another missing girl. Whatever else I do the rest of the morning is smeared together in one big blur. Eventually, I finish shopping and wait at the car for Sal and the boys, grinding my teeth the entire time.

On the drive home I plan to keep my eyes straight and my answers brief, but it's no use—I can't hold back. "I saw Signore Valentino in town today," I say, forcing myself to stay strong.

All three of them look at me but say nothing. A quick exchange of glances

CHAPTER TWELVE

occurs between Sal and Luca.

"We talked about school and how quickly the year is going." I let that hang for a minute. Maybe Sal is wondering if Mr. Valentino said something to me.

Judging by Luca's expression, he assumes we talked about the notes. Luca attempts to change the subject, asking Sal about the marina, but I bring them back.

"Signore Valentino mentioned something about notes. Were you supposed to show me something?" I cannot believe I said that.

Sal looks at me and smiles. "I'm not aware of any notes, are you, Luca?"

Luca, of course, says no.

I don't take the fall and pretend to be mistaken. "So strange," I say. "I wonder what he meant. I'll have to take a look around the house. I must have missed something."

All eyes return to the road, and no one says a word until we're home again.

Just before Sal leaves for the marina with Luca, he approaches me, quick and close, throwing me off guard. "That's enough about the notes," he says. "Drop it or else." He walks off, not waiting for me to agree or disagree. In his mind, talking about notes is over. In my mind, they've just begun. There are too many unanswered questions.

And now another girl is missing.

CHAPTER THIRTEEN

The late-afternoon sun hovers high in the sky. I'm sitting on the porch waiting for Anna. The last time we spoke, I told her I was determined to break into the Russos' house. I have to find out if there's anything they left behind—a clue to confirm or reject Sal's influence in their leaving; any indication of where they might have gone.

My head swarms with ruminations of the past week. Giorgio tells me to be more mindful, that sometimes the answer is right in front of me. Anna and Greta have both encouraged me to think more in the present and less about the future. But I have to think about the future. I have to be ready for my next move, prepared for any number of scenarios that might play out with Sal. But they're all correct—I do need to be more present. And in the present moment, there is much to think about.

So many things.

I recall a recent night when Luca worked late with Sal. What awakened me out of a sound sleep wasn't noise but a presence, an awareness that someone was near and watching me, a sensation that made the hairs on my neck rise. I didn't want to open my eyes, and when I did, Luca was standing near my side of the bed, very still, tears falling down his cheeks.

I sat up but didn't want to scare him in case he was sleep-walking again, so I gently reassured him and steered him back to his room.

As I guided him into his bed, he resisted and then embraced me tightly. "I'm so sorry, Mamá. I'm so sorry, Mamá. I didn't know."

"It's okay, Luca," I said, thinking he was still asleep, but his arms stayed

CHAPTER THIRTEEN

locked around my waist. He wasn't sleeping. Why was he sorry?

I stood back and looked at him to determine if he was awake, and he was. "Did you have a bad dream?"

He let go and climbed into bed but didn't answer me. He just stared at me in a very sad, remorseful way.

"Everything will be okay, Luca. You just need to close your eyes and go back to sleep."

Luca turned to his side, facing away. I kissed his head, something I hadn't done in the longest time. "I didn't know," I thought I heard him say as I closed his door. I tried to think about what might have made him react that way—something at school perhaps related to my encounter with Mr. Valentino. But he hadn't seemed the least bit remorseful when I'd mentioned running into Mr. Valentino or when I'd asked him about the notes. He'd denied anything related to the notes. No, something must have happened while he was working with Sal.

The night of that strange encounter with Luca was the same night I'd found a long strand of hair on Sal's shirt and a similar one on Luca's. A long, wavy strand of hair, much darker than mine. In the light, a golden-auburn sheen came through. Instinctively, I brought Sal's shirt to my nose and inhaled a sweet, clean, floral scent, not mine but familiar. Later, I'd found another strand of hair on Luca's shirt just like the first, but his shirt just smelled like Luca. I'd taken the strands, wrapped them in a tissue, and hid them in my jewelry box with the anonymous note.

Now I'm wondering if Sal was having an affair and Luca found out. Was Luca with them? I'm beginning to wonder if I really know my family as well as I think I do. Be mindful. Be present.

Sal catches my eye, distracting my thoughts. He approaches the porch with something behind his back. Already I'm on edge. He extends his arms and offers a beautiful bouquet of spring flowers: peach-colored roses mixed with white peonies and lilies, my favorites.

"What are these for?" I say.

"For you," he says, "unless you don't want them." A poor attempt at a joke. "I'm not here to stay. I have to return to the marina, but I wanted to bring you these. I know how much you love flowers."

I want to hand them back, but I bring them close and sniff their sweet scent. I'm sure he's waiting for me to thank him and fall all over him.

"Thanks," I say, my tone disingenuous. He doesn't catch on or he ignores it. I take the flowers to the kitchen and put them in a vase, wondering what he'd done to be guilty enough that warranted flowers. Maybe he's trying to throw me off. Maybe he's seen the suitcase in my closet.

***

Anna is never late, and now thirty minutes have passed since she said she'd be here. A shiny black Fiat drives slowly by our house. As it turns around the bend, I catch a glimpse of the driver's dark, wavy hair. Massimo? I crane my neck for a better look, but the sun's reflection blocks my view, and now the Fiat is out of sight completely.

Seconds later, a police car pulls into the driveway, stopping halfway. It's the same two officers who had been here almost a week ago asking about Julia Bernardi. I greet them as they approach, trying to read their stoic expressions.

"I'm Detective D'Amico, and this is my partner, Detective Parnello."

"I remember," I say. "My husband is working right now, but you're welcome to come back later tonight."

"That's okay," Detective Parnello says. "We're here to talk with all the members of the household today. We can talk with Signore Perri later. Would you mind if we ask you and your boys a few questions?" He looks around.

CHAPTER THIRTEEN

"What is this about?" I say, surprised he remembers our name.

Detective D'Amico pulls a notepad from his jacket and starts to jot a few notes. "Has to do with the missing girl, Gia Lovallo. Just routine questioning of everyone in the neighborhood, especially her friends," he says. "Your sons wouldn't happen to be home, would they?"

"No, they're at our marina with their father," I say.

Detective D'Amico writes as I speak, then looks at his colleague. "We'll go there next." He turns back to me. "Signora Perri, how well do you know Gia Lovallo?"

"Not very well," I say. "I met her a few days ago at the candlelight service for Julia. Such a sweet girl. Do you . . . do you think she was kidnapped?"

"We can't discuss that," Detective Parnello says.

"Did you know anything at all about her? How close were your sons to Gia?" Detective D'Amico asks.

"No, I'm sorry, I don't," I say. "Like I said, we only just met. She was very polite and kind. I'm not sure how well my sons know her. I think they might have become friends recently. I wish I could be more helpful."

"You are being helpful," Detective Parnello says. "The candlelight service was the only time you saw Gia?"

"Yes," I say, "and right after, they came here for a bit." A quick glance between the detectives. "A few of Franco's and Luca's friends. They weren't here very long."

"A few friends," Detective D'Amico says, scribbling into his notepad.

"And what time was this, would you say?" Detective Parnello asks.

"Had to be around nine-thirty." I have to think for a minute. Yes, it was definitely before ten. I remember looking at the clock at nine forty-five when I went into the living room to read. "Yes, it was nine-thirty when they arrived."

"Who else was here besides Gia?" Detective Parnello asks. "Other than your sons?"

"Carlos," I say, recalling him the most. The other names aren't as fresh, but somehow I pull them out. "And Stephano, John, and Tara," I say. "I don't know their surnames."

"And where was your husband at the time?" Detective D'Amico asks.

"He was home, in bed." I bite my bottom lip.

Detective Parnello arches his brow. "You don't seem sure."

"I am." Am I?

"What did the kids do while they were here?" Detective D'Amico says.

"They had some snacks and talked for a bit in the kitchen."

"And where were you?" Detective D'Amico says, judging me already.

"I was in the kitchen, too, but then I went into the living room to read a book."

"So they were unsupervised," Detective Parnello says.

"I wouldn't say that, Detective. I was only in the next room." They look at me strangely. "They're not children. They don't need me to be right beside them every moment. I gave them a little bit of space, that's all. Would you like to come in and see where the kitchen is in relation to the living room?" Am I being interrogated?

"That won't be necessary," Detective D'Amico says. "What time did Gia leave?"

"Oh, almost ten thirty," I say. "I'm sure." I remember looking at the clock and telling Franco and Luca I'd be waiting for them. I expected them home by eleven. They might have been a little late, but not much.

"Did Gia leave by herself? How did she get home?" Detective Parnello asks.

Now my chest starts to tighten as I ascertain where they're going, and I'm leading them there. "They walked her home—my sons and the other kids walked both Gia and Tara home."

More scribbling in the notepad.

"So," Detective D'Amico says, referring to his notebook, "Franco, Luca, Carlos, Stephano, and John walked the girls home, correct?"

"Yes."

"Very chivalrous," Detective Parnello says, his tone cynical.

"And your sons returned right after?"

"Yes, right after."

"You're aware that Gia was declared missing the next day? The day after

CHAPTER THIRTEEN

the candlelight service for Julia?" Detective Parnello says.

A hevy weight pushes down on me as I recall the next morning in town. Hushed, consoling whispers at a vendor's table close by: Gia Lovallo was missing. I'm sickened by it now as I was then. "Yes," I reply.

"You've been very helpful, Signora," Detective Parnello says. "If we don't find your sons at the marina, we'll be back. Here's my information if you think of anything else that might be helpful." He tears a piece of paper from his notepad with both detectives' names and the number of the police station written at the top.

Before leaving, they take a look around the property, specifically the driveway and the road. When I think they're leaving, they turn around and walk back toward the house, eyeing the back of the property.

"What's in that shed?" Detective Parnello asks.

"The shed is my husband's office," I say.

"An office in a shed?" he says. "That's unusual."

"My husband wanted additional space for business meetings."

"Business meetings?"

"You'll have to talk with him about that," I say, annoyed. "He doesn't include me in his business."

"So, the shed is now used for business meetings," he confirms as Detective D'Amico adds this to his notepad.

"And storage for his tools and farm equipment," I say. Where I followed someone. Where I found a shoe belonging to a girl. I should tell them, but I don't. I can't yet. I'm afraid to say anything else right now.

"Does anyone else besides your husband have access to the shed—office?" Detective Parnello asks.

"Only Sal," I say. And the stranger, and who knows who else.

"Signora Perri," Detective Parnello flicks his eyes up at me, "does your husband have ties to the 'Ndrangheta?"

Detective D'Amico shoots him a warning look.

"The mafia? Heavens no," I say.

Something catches my eye at the end of the driveway. Anna has finally arrived.

"I'm sorry, Detectives," I say, "but my friend has arrived. I think I've told you all I can."

"Thank you for your time," Detective Parnello says. "You've been more helpful than you realize."

They tip their hats at Anna as they head to their car. Anna awkwardly smiles back.

"What took you so long?" I ask Anna.

"I'm sorry," she says. "I tried to call, but I couldn't get through."

"That's strange," I say. "I'm the only one home, and I haven't been on the phone. Maybe it's not hung up correctly." I go to the hall to check, and the phone is neatly cradled in its receiver. Could Sal have made a call when he went in for a moment before going back to work?

"Those were the same detectives who took Peter in for questioning," Anna says. "They came by this morning to ask about Gia. Did they talk to you about her, too?"

"Yes," I say.

"I can't believe this is happening again," Anna says. "Why haven't they caught him yet?" She looks at me. "You okay? Are you sure you want to do this today?"

I look to the Russos' abandoned house next door. Now is the time to find out what happened to them. "Yes, I'm ready," I say.

Anna's eyes widen. "Let's go, then."

CHAPTER FOURTEEN

Greta's house sits neglected like a slighted friend. As we draw near, it pulls me in, daring me to enter and unlock the secrets it keeps.

Anna goes to the window and cups her hand against the glass, peeking in. "How did they move everything out of the house without being noticed?" She looks at me. "You didn't hear anything?"

"Nothing," I say. "Must have happened when we weren't home, maybe while we were in town."

"What about the kids or the neighbors? Have they said anything?"

"Not a word," I say, moving to the back of the house, to the back door that Greta never locked. Anna follows. When I get to the door, it opens easily.

"How odd to lock the front door but not the back," Anna says.

"Greta says no one uses the back except her family . . . and ours a while back," I say. "She says she feels trapped with all the doors locked. That's just how she is." So unlike our house. Sal would put locks on the locks if he could.

We step inside the Russo home, and immediately it feels wrong. We shouldn't be here uninvited. But I'm instantly nostalgic at the familiar smell of their home, like the pages of a book mixed with rain. It's comforting. How many times had Sal and I sat here and enjoyed drinks and laughs while our children slept in the next room?

I scan the empty walls that once held memories wrapped in frames. I leave the living room and enter the space outside the kitchen where we'd just had a wonderful meal together, so at ease like old times. I peek in the kitchen doorway to the sink where Greta stood uneasy and distracted. How quickly everything had changed. And right in front of me.

Anna's voice echoes from behind. "Did you hear me?" she says. I look at her, having missed something again. "I checked the cupboards and drawers and found nothing."

"Let's go upstairs," I say.

Anna goes to the girls' bedrooms while I head across the hall to Greta and Rocco's. Surprisingly, the beds and dressers are still here. On Greta's dresser are her mirror, three necklaces, a bottle of perfume, and a hairbrush.

I glance at Anna when she walks in. "They left everything here, even these." I refer to the items on the dresser. "Why?" Even her drawers are filled with her clothes. I catch my reflection in the mirror behind the dresser. "Something's not right."

I examine the items on her dresser closely. When I lift the hairbrush, my pulse quickens. I hold the brush to the light coming from the window. The sun catches an auburn highlight on the dark hair wrapped around the bristles, and my pulse races.

"What are you doing?" Anna says, watching me free a hair from the brush. I don't answer because I'm too busy watching the strand dangle from my fingers, similar to one I've seen before.

I turn to the perfume. Don't do it. I pick it up, remove the top, and bring the bottle to my nose as its contents reveal a secret. No. Not you, Greta. I scream and throw the bottle against the wall. The glass shatters, and long legs of perfume run to the floor, filling the room with Greta's scent.

Anna looks at me like I'm crazy. "Why did you do that?" She comes to my side. "Iz, what's going on?"

I put my head into my hands. I can hardly speak. "Greta . . . Sal . . . ," I cry. Anna hugs me. I look at her. "I have so much to tell you."

"I'm so sorry," Anna says.

I wipe my eyes and do what I can to pull myself together, to obtain the answers I came for. I take a deep breath and shove this secret into the dark corners of my mind with the others. I'll come back for it later. "When we're done, I'll tell you everything."

CHAPTER FOURTEEN

Anna smiles. "Whenever you're ready."

I remember something and go to Rocco's dresser. In the second drawer beneath his shirts, my hand grazes the edges of what I'm thinking of: books. I take them out and hand them to Anna.

"These belong to Greta," I say. "I knew Rocco had them. He took them from her as soon as he found out they were banned."

Anna looks them over. All Quiet on the Western Front by Erich Maria Marque and A Farewell to Arms by Ernest Hemmingway. "I didn't realize these were banned," she says.

I remember when Sal came home with both books in a paper bag. He took them out and placed them on the counter and told me to look at them carefully. He said he wanted to make sure I knew exactly which books I wasn't allowed to read and then tossed them into the garbage.

While he was at work the next day, I took them out of the garbage and gave them to Greta so we could read them together while Sal was working. The Fascist party had banned anything, including books, that seemed antimilitary or that might portray Italy with any kind of weakness. But Greta and I knew better. We knew the evil that was unleashed in our country was because of the Fascist party, and we wanted nothing to do with it.

"Greta hid these for me," I say, "until they went missing. I always knew Rocco had them."

Anna goes to the bedroom window that overlooks my house. "Is this where you said you thought you saw something?"

"Yes," I say, joining her. I look out at the clear view of my house, particularly the front porch and the servants' door—a perfect view of where I stood when I'd spotted something moving in this very window. A chill runs through me. If someone was standing here, they would have seen me that night too.

I glance at Anna, who is intently staring into the hallway. I start to say something, but she shushes me, pointing. We get to the door and listen. Anna turns to me. "I'm seeing things now," she says. "There's nothing here, Iz. We should go."

At the bottom of the stairs, I catch a glimpse of something on the wall. A dark swish of color on the white paint. So unlike Greta to leave marks on her walls. The closer I am to the mark the more pronounced its matted maroon tint becomes.

"What can that be?" Anna asks.

"I can't be sure, but . . . do you think it could be blood?"

"Blood?" Anna says.

I point to a small teardrop of the same color. "Here's one, and another one." We examine the wall closely and find several small, maroon-tinted spots near the first one.

"Should we call the police?" Anna asks.

"We can't," I say, "We're not supposed to be here."

"We have to tell someone," she says. "What about Giorgio?"

"Yes, Giorgio. He'll know what to do."

"He'll do anything for you," she says.

I don't respond.

We snap our heads at a noise near the top of the stairs and catch the heel of someone heading to Greta's room.

"Who's there?" I yell.

We climb the steps fast but find no one at the top or anywhere in the narrow hallway. Anna and I glance at each other and cautiously proceed toward the closet. I open the door and swish my hand through the clothes, but no one is there either. Next, I walk to the bed. Anna's expression is strained as I bend to the floor and peek beneath. Fear-filled eyes under the bed meet mine: Maria's eyes.

"Maria?" I say to Greta's middle child. She doesn't answer. "Are you okay?" Silence. "I won't tell anyone you were here. I just want to make sure you're okay. Is your family okay? Please come out."

Maria is the quiet one of her three sisters, the middle child caught between wanting to be like her big sister, Sienna, but still young enough to relate to her little sister, Gianna. She can be jealous and rebellious when she can't have her way. I always thought she had a crush on Luca, but Luca paid her little attention. He was too busy trying to attain whatever Franco had.

Maria pushes against the floor and slides to the side. She stands, holding something in her hand, but doesn't give me eye contact. Her clothes hang

CHAPTER FOURTEEN

loosely on her small frame like they've been slept in.

"Does your family know you're here?" I say.

Maria replies with an empty stare.

"We've been worried about you—all of you. Where have you been?" I'm coming on too strong, expecting too much at once, but I can't stop myself. "Is everyone safe?"

She barely nods.

"You can trust me. You know that, right?"

Maria looks as if she wants to say something, but she's fighting whatever it is inside her head. She glances from me to Anna.

"You remember Signora Rossi," I say, extending my hand to Anna.

Maria steps back toward the window.

"Wait. Just talk to me."

"I can't," she blurts.

"Why? What happened?"

Maria looks back with uncertainty.

"I just need to know," I say. "I won't tell anyone I saw you." Silence. "Was that you in the window the other night?" Her eyes widen. "Maria, I just want to help."

"You can't," she says, her eyes filling. She inches closer to the window.

"At least tell me one thing if you can," I say. "Did your family leave because of Signore Perri?"

Her lips part and her fists tighten. She doesn't have to say a word; her eyes reveal what I'd suspected all along. And now the answer is confirmed, only details are lacking.

"Listen, Maria," I say. "I have a secret too. Signore Perri . . . he's a bad man and . . . I'm leaving him soon. I haven't told anyone this except for you. I trust you won't tell anyone, Maria. You can trust me too. You can tell me anything and I won't say a word to anyone outside these walls."

Anna's eyes dart from Maria to me and then back to Maria.

Conflict resides in Maria's eyes, weighing her decision.

"Listen, Maria, I believe you left because of Signore Perri," I continue, "but what did he do to make your whole family leave?" I realize that Maria might not even be aware of the real reason they left. She turns to the window. "I'll take you to wherever you need to go," I say. "You shouldn't be out there alone."

"You can't," she says, tears wetting her cheeks. "I have to go. Please don't follow me." She hoists herself through the window, and I want to pull her back. Keep her here. Make her tell me why they're hiding.

"Maria, wait," I say. "Why did you come back?"

Her eyes flick up at me. She stands and walks toward the sloped roof.

I'm about to lose her. "Tell your mother I miss her and love her."

Maria slides down the slope and jumps to the ground. I yell for Anna to keep watching as I descend the stairs three at a time and out the door. I catch a glimpse of Maria as she sails through the backyard to the streets that spill out to the sea.

Of course. She's using the private road to get to the marina. The Russos used to dock their boat there. She's taking their boat to wherever they are. I run as fast as I can but stop abruptly when I think I spot Sal's Fiat at the crest of the hill. I turn and run to my house, hoping Anna sees me and does the same.

Anna meets me at my door, and we run inside sweating, panting, and consumed with worry. Had Sal seen me? We dab sweat gathered at our necks and brows with kitchen towels. I grab a pitcher of lemonade and quickly fill two glasses, then we sit at the table, hearts racing, trying to look as natural as possible.

Through the window I watch Sal park the car, and Franco and Luca follow him to the plantation. I glance at Anna, breathing easier. "That was close," I say.

"Too close," she replies.

"What was Maria doing at the house?" I say.

"I have no idea, but she dropped this." Anna slides a piece of paper to me.

I take the paper and, at first, I have no idea what I'm looking at until I turn it once clockwise. And then it becomes obvious I'm looking at a hand-drawn map.

"Do you know what this map represents?" Anna asks.

CHAPTER FOURTEEN

I think I recognize the drawing, but I don't say anything until I'm sure, until I get my bearings. I search the map for a point of reference and, finally, I identify the school. I trace my finger along lines meant to be roads, and it becomes clear what I'm looking at. I follow a line that leads to Julia Bernardi's neighborhood, ending at her house. I look at Anna, and my stomach sickens.

"What is it?" she says. "You look like you've seen a ghost."

I shake the paper, horrified. "This is a map to Julia's house."

"What?" she gasps. "Let me see."

I turn the paper and show Anna the school and trace the path from the school to her house.

"What is she doing with this? Do you think that's why she came back? For this map?"

"She must have. And maybe something else," I say.

"Then she must be . . . involved?" Anna says.

I wonder the same.

"This doesn't make sense," I say. "How can she be involved in something like this? Unless she innocently came across the map. And the person who drew the map discovered Maria had it and was looking for her. Either that or Maria is holding onto the map, hiding it for someone." I shake my head. "How can any of this be true?"

"We should show the police," Anna says.

"Are you sure you want to do that right now?"

"Well, yes, to take the attention off Peter," she says.

"What if they think Peter drew the map?"

"There's no proof of that." Anna squints at me.

"There's no proof against that," I say. "I'm not saying I think Peter is guilty. I'm just thinking how Rocco used to think."

"Maybe Rocco's covering for her; maybe Maria's involved and he's keeping things quiet. He has the resources and ability to do that."

"I don't know what to think, Anna." I check the window to make sure I can still see Sal. "Follow me. I have something to show you."

Anna follows me to my bedroom. I open my jewelry box, remove the anonymous note I'd received a few days ago, and place the note on the dresser. I take the two strands of hair I'd wrapped in plastic and place them next to the note. Then I tell Anna almost everything since Julia Bernardi was found floating face down in the water.

CHAPTER FIFTEEN

A loud, robust knocking at the front door brings Anna and me back downstairs.

"Izzy! Open the door!" someone yells from the other side.

"Giuseppe?" Anna says, running with me to the door.

I swing it open, and Giuseppe stands in the doorway with panic strewn across his face, his breath ragged. His knees buckle, and he stumbles into Anna's arms.

"What's wrong?" she sounds desperate.

"Peter—they took him again."

"What?" Anna says.

"They have proof this time—for Julia and Gia."

"Gia . . . what do you mean, Gia? What proof?" Anna is coming apart.

"They found Gia!" he cries. "She's—" He shakes his head.

I can't believe what I'm hearing.

"No!" Anna yells. "No! No! No!"

"In the woods behind the school," he blurts, breaking down again.

"Oh my God," I say, pacing.

"Why Peter?" Anna cries. "Why do they think it's him? What proof do they think they have?"

"I don't know," he says, defeated. "They think we've been lying for him."

"I think I'm going to be sick." Anna cups her mouth and runs to the bathroom.

Giuseppe paces back and forth in the small hallway between the kitchen and the living room. "I don't know what to do, Iz," he says. "The police are corrupt."

"That's not true, Giuseppe," I say.

"They take bribes from the 'Ndrangheta," he says. "Everyone knows that."

"What would they gain from framing an innocent teenager?" I say.

"A distraction from the real killer. It doesn't matter," he says. "It's done."

Anna returns from the bathroom and stands beside Giuseppe.

"We need to find out what the police have on Peter," I say. "Then we'll at least have some idea where to start when we try to prove them wrong. You're his parents; you have a right to know."

Giuseppe and Anna nod, willing to listen to anyone who gives them a glimmer of hope. I offer to let their girls stay with me while they go to the precinct to see about Peter. Within seconds they're out the door and in the car. I follow them out and watch them drive away.

The air changes fast on my way back to my house. Low clouds huddle tightly together, squeezing out the sun. Three black crows land on a branch and caw loudly at nothing. Dark clouds roll in and small droplets scatter around me. I make a run for it, racing the rain to my door, and win just as the sky opens and lightning strikes the earth.

I'm surprised to find Giorgio waiting there for me. Where had he come from?

A gust of wind throws the rain sideways, and we're instantly drenched.

"Giorgio," I say as we duck through the door, "did you just get here? I didn't see you arrive. Did you drive?" I grab a few small hand towels and we dry ourselves off.

"No, I walked," he says, following me to the kitchen.

"Did you see me waving to Anna and Giuseppe in the driveway?" I say. "Gia was found—"

"I know."

"You do?" I look at him. "I don't understand. Are you here for Sal?"

"No, I was hoping to talk to you," he says. "I've been following the stories—Julia's and now Gia's. That's why I haven't been around much. I've been working and interviewing, preparing updates for the public, you know."

CHAPTER FIFTEEN

"Yes, I remember how important your journalism is to you, Giorgio," I say. "I understand completely why you've stayed away. The police have been asking about everyone's whereabouts, especially Julia's friends. Being around us could jeopardize the integrity of your reporting and writing. It's okay."

"Yes, but it's not that simple," he says.

"I don't think it's simple at all."

"Listen, Iz," he says, placing his hands on my shoulders and squaring himself as if he's about to say something very serious. "As I've been digging, interviewing, checking my facts to be as accurate as possible, I've found some things I wasn't expecting to find."

"What things?" I say, stepping back.

"Things that tell me you're not safe, and I don't mean just from Sal's temper. Something worse. Far worse."

"Giorgio, be straight with me. Stop talking in code and say what you want to say."

He runs his fingers through his wet hair, flipping it to the back exposing deep, serious eyes. "Let's sit," he motions toward the table. We sit and I'm instantly nauseous, anticipating the worst. "People are talking at the school about Luca being involved in Julia's murder."

"What? That's absurd," I say, ignoring the voice inside that questions this too.

"They say he—"

"The person. Don't refer to Luca without proof," I warn.

"The person who did this has something of Julia's."

"Something from her pocket?" I say.

"You knew about that?"

"Yes. Go on."

"It's not that, though," he says. "Something else of hers that he kept like a trophy or a prize."

I've heard of murderers doing that—keeping something from their victim as a trophy of sorts.

"Can you honestly picture Luca doing that?" I say. "Luca?"

95

Giorgio silently stares at me. Then, "I'm not supposed to tell you this, but Gia's fingernails had blood and skin under them."

"Peter had scratches on his face," I say. "That's probably why the police took him." Luca had one too.

"Could have gotten that scratch from the fight—Peter and Luca," he says.

"They had a fight? How do you know about this and I don't?"

"It's my job. I thought you knew."

"When did this fight happen?"

He looks at me sheepishly. "Around the time Gia went missing."

"When were they all together?" The night of the candlelight service when Franco and Luca walked her home? Did they meet Peter along the way? The scratch came after the service, but I don't remember the exact day.

"Peter went to Gia's," he says, "and Luca came over at some point. I only know because Camilla was home the day Luca was supposed to come over to work on a school project. Luca told Max he'd be late, which seemed odd for Luca. He's never late."

This is true. Max and Luca don't see each other as much as they did when they were little, but when Luca and Max plan to do something, nothing gets in the way. Luca has no trouble being late at home or school, but he is never late for Max. I admire their friendship. Max is honest and has a strong role model for a father. They're both a good influence on Luca.

Okay, so the fight happened after Luca and Franco walked Gia home. "Go on," I say.

"Luca said he was late because he went to Gia's first. He said Peter was there and he was not happy when Luca arrived. I guess one thing led to another, and Luca punched Peter in the face. Max says they fought over Gia."

"This might not even be true. You know how kids are." But I can tell he's got more to tell me by the way he's looking at me. "What?"

"They're saying Peter isn't the only one who should be questioned."

"Who's saying this?"

"People—classmates, some police."

"And what do you tell them?" I say. "Do you challenge what they're saying

CHAPTER FIFTEEN

or do you agree with them?"

He doesn't reply.

"Come on, Giorgio, you've known Luca his whole life. Luca wouldn't hurt anyone. I thought you were my friend." My eyes fill, and I blink the tears away.

Giorgio leans in close to my face. "Iz, I'm telling you this because I am your friend. You need to look carefully at the people closest to you."

"You always want me to live in the present," I say, repeating old advice. I slide my chair from the table, wishing I could go as far away as possible.

Giorgio comes closer and gently says, "This is hard to process, I know. Maybe everyone is wrong. Maybe Max has his facts all wrong. Kids make mistakes. I just don't think he is making one this time. And all I ask"—I put my hand up to shush him but he doesn't stop—"is just do one thing," he says. "One thing."

I drop my hand and look away.

"Just observe Luca for a couple days. Watch what he does, where he goes. Take notice when he goes to his room and for how long. Do the same with Sal and Franco."

"Franco?"

"Just watch them. Each of them," he says. "Don't dismiss anything, and don't let your guard down."

That phrase doesn't sit well. A similar message to the anonymous note. Maybe Giorgio wrote the note to warn me, and because I didn't act soon enough, he has to tell me face to face?

"When Luca goes to work with Sal, what does he do there?"

"He brings the boats in and sends them out. Sometimes he's inside working with customers there. I'm not aware of every single detail."

Giorgio looks doubtful. "And you really don't think anything else is going on that Luca might also become involved in? Come on, Iz, don't be naïve. You can't pretend not to know that Sal—"

Suddenly the front door bursts open, spitting Sal into the middle of the room. Franco and Luca enter behind him. A mix of wind and rain slice through the open door until Sal forces it closed, locking it. He tosses his saturated hat on the floor. I hand him and the boys each a hand towel as water pools at their feet.

"Thought you might be here," he says to Giorgio. Giorgio stiffens. "Couldn't wait any longer, could you?"

I turn to Giorgio. "What's he talking about?"

"I came to see if Izzy knew about Gia," Giorgio says, "and offer my support to her and the boys."

"I'll bet you did," Sal says, taking a beer from the fridge. He empties half into his mouth and slams the bottle on the table. "I saw you talking at the table."

Franco and Luca exchange glances.

"I was upset. He was being a good friend—comforting me," I say.

"Uh-huh." Sal glares at me through the wilting purple-and-white flowers in the middle of the table. He leans toward Giorgio. "Tell us what you're really doing here with my wife."

"Just what I said," Giorgio says. "Not at all what you think."

"What does he think?" I say as Sal's fist connects with Giorgio's jaw, knocking him off his chair. Giorgio, bigger and more muscular, jumps to his feet and lunges at Sal.

"Stop!" I scream.

Franco and Luca dive in. Franco restrains Sal as Giorgio shakes Luca off his back.

"Get the hell out of here," Sal yells, "or I'll more than fight you. You know I'll win." Sal looks at me and wriggles free from Franco. "It's fine," he says to Franco. "I'm going to my office. He better be gone when I get back . . . and I will be back." He shoots a look of disgust as he leaves.

I walk to the door with Giorgio. The wind is strong, but the rain has stopped. "I'm sorry," I say.

He turns to me. "Just remember what I said. You need to get out of here."

"I know," I say. "When the time is right."

"And when is that?"

"Soon," I say, "very soon."

He comes closer. I nervously step back. "Don't wait too long," he whispers,

CHAPTER FIFTEEN

and slips out the door.

With my back to the boys, I swallow a rising cry. When I feel ready, I turn around to face them.

CHAPTER SIXTEEN

The detention center where Peter is held is in a small city north of Scilla in Gioia Tauro. I agreed to go with Anna since Giuseppe is away on business. Anna keeps to herself, fiddling with her hands and picking her nails, occasionally gazing out the car window. I can imagine the torment in her mind. I'm anxiously watching her as Giorgio's visit replays in my head.

As soon as the detention center is visible, Anna starts to hyperventilate.

I park quickly and try to help her. "Breathe, Anna," I say. "Concentrate on your breathing."

Her eyes are wide and fearful as she tries to breathe slowly. Tears fall to her cheeks as her composure returns.

"I can't do this," she says. "I can't go in there."

"Yes, you can. We're doing this together. I'm right here," I say through my guilt from what Giorgio told me. Does she see it? "Take one more big breath and let's go."

A small, tan building sits alone on a dirt foundation; tufts of grass sprout in odd places. Crumbled stone walls are in desperate need of repair. I heard it was once an old jailhouse before becoming a detention center for adolescents. Anna and I hold hands until we reach the door.

Inside, we wait in a simple seating area with four chairs. An elderly man sits behind a small desk. "How may I help you?" he says, smiling.

CHAPTER SIXTEEN

When Anna doesn't answer, I say, "We're here for her son, Peter Rossi."

He looks at Anna for confirmation, and she nods. He refers to a clipboard and flips back two pages. "Peter Rossi, yes. I'll need you to sign and date right here." He points to the line next to Peter's name.

Minutes later, a portly woman enters from a narrow corridor behind the desk. "You're here for Peter?" she says, scarcely moving her lips, and turning back to the corridor. Anna and I look at each other, puzzled, and then follow the woman. Inside the building is just as bad as outside—chipped paint, worn-out floors.

We emerge into what appears to be a big, barren room, perhaps for large gatherings or family meetings. The woman turns and says, "Wait here." We stare at her as she disappears inside another dark corridor.

It feels like hours pass, waiting for her to return with Peter. We jump at the click of the door where they enter. Anna runs to Peter and embraces him.

"That's enough," the woman says. "You can sit there." She indicates a small table in front of a worn sofa and a chair. "I'll wait here until you're done."

I hug Peter before sitting in the chair across from them, shaking away the image of Luca being here instead.

Anna faces Peter and takes his hands in hers. Her eyes frantically search his face, probably for signs of abuse or neglect. She moves his hair to the side, exposing his eyes. "I'm so sorry you're here. We're doing everything we can to get you out."

Peter stares blankly.

"Are you hungry? Are they treating you okay? Where did that woman go to get you?"

"I'm fine, Mamá," he says, but his sad eyes tell a different story.

"You don't look fine," she says. "Are you sleeping at all? You smell like smoke."

"I'm sleeping fine." His voice is flat, deflated. "We were outside having a smoke break."

"Smoke break?" Anna says. "You don't smoke."

"Smoking is the only way I can get outside. If you don't smoke, you don't go out."

"You'll be out of here in no time," she says again. "I promise."

Peter glances at me and then at Anna. "Why is she here?"

"Peter, that's not polite," Anna says. "Isabella came with me for support, and for you."

"I don't need her here," he says.

Anna tilts her head. "Peter," she warns. She looks at me and I mouth, "It's okay."

Peter looks at me. "What? Does that offend you?"

"Not at all," I say. "I know it must be hard to be here, so don't—"

"Hard?" he interrupted. "You think it's just hard?"

"Peter!" Anna warns again.

"Hard is an understatement. It's hell. I shouldn't be here, and you know it," he says, still looking at me.

"You're right," I say. "You shouldn't be here, Peter."

"Peter, why are you talking like this to Isabella? That's not like you," Anna says. She looks at me. "He's never done this. I'm sorry."

"Don't be sorry, Mamá!" he yells. "She's not the friend you think she is!"

Anna's jaw drops. "Peter!"

"Don't let her fool you, Mamá."

All at once, I regret coming here with Anna.

"Ask her who should be here in my place," he says. "I wasn't the only one to see Gia and not the last."

The blood drains from my body.

"What are you talking about?" Anna says.

"Luca got to Gia's after me," he says, "and then Signore Perri came."

"Sal?" I say.

"You're surprised at hearing Sal but not Luca?" Anna says to me. "Did you know Luca was there and you didn't say anything?"

"I . . . just found out myself. I didn't think it was true. I really didn't." I feel dizzy and grip the table.

"Time's up!" the portly woman's voice echoes.

"We're not finished," I yell.

CHAPTER SIXTEEN

She lumbers toward us. "Rules are rules."

I stand in front of the woman. "We need more time."

"You don't have more time."

"Money? For an extra five minutes?"

"I don't take bribes," the woman says, unblinking. "I'll give you five minutes to say your goodbyes, then you're out."

I sit down and face Anna and Peter.

Anna looks at me. "You can go," she says.

"I'm not going. How will you get back?" I say.

"I'll find a way," Anna says.

"Anna, you have to believe me—this is all a big misunderstanding," I say. "We can talk about this on the way home."

Anna's eyes flit for a minute as if she's mulling it over. But then she shakes her head. "No, I can't. You'll have to go back alone."

We stare at each other for a few seconds. Anna turns and whispers to Peter. I wait in disbelief until the woman collects Peter and takes him out of the room. Anna remains seated, looking down at her feet. Reluctantly, I turn, leaving the detention center the same way I came, but alone.

CHAPTER SEVENTEEN

I return from the detention center conflicted and hurt from Peter's words and Anna's actions. How could Peter say I'm not the kind of friend Anna thinks I am? I am that friend. I consider calling Giorgio for support and advice but think better of it. He'd say to pay attention, stay in the present, and I can't do that right now.

From the kitchen cupboard, I remove the box behind the flour bag. I take off the lid and place my hand on the cool money. I need to feel its reassurance for my future. If I only stay in the present, I'll never get out of here. I can wait until this investigation is over. If I go now and take Franco and Luca, it might look like we're hiding something.

My pinky grazes the shoe and anchors me back to the present. This shoe belongs to someone who was in the shed.

A warm breeze sweeps through the room, catching the edges of something on the floor: a folded piece of paper like the one in my jewelry box. I scoop it up. Another note. Familiar jagged strokes, uneven and not all connecting, relaying a serious message. Is Giorgio doing this?

I read the note slowly, dissecting each word piece by piece.

I'm still watching. You're not listening. Time's almost up. Now I take matters into my own hands. I tried to warn you. I see you, even now.

The hairs on my arms raise and my skin prickles. I look over my shoulder. Where are you? Do I know you? I peek through the window. Are you out

CHAPTER SEVENTEEN

there? Is Greta trying to warn me?

A feeling of doom clings to me like a cold, wet blanket as I put away the box of money, the shoe, and both notes in my jewelry box. I can't shake it. It's all around me now, and I don't know what to do or who to trust.

Luca traipses through the door about half an hour later without Sal. How many times had I told Sal to bring Luca home himself, not pawn him off on someone else, especially someone Luca isn't familiar with? I glimpse the car through the window, but I can't identify the driver. I step outside as it speeds away.

"Who dropped you off?" I ask Luca.

"A friend of Papá's." He opens the fridge. "You don't know him."

"Were they smoking around you again?" I ask, smelling the stale smoke in Luca's hair.

"Yes, and it's no big deal."

Sal knows exactly what he's doing. He's fully aware that giving Luca responsibilities, even those he's not ready for, will endear Luca to him. Luca will feel independent, important, and grown up, which is exactly how he already views himself even at thirteen. Luca will do anything to please Sal, and that's what worries me.

"What did you help Papá with at the marina today?" I say, realizing I never ask him this question.

"Loading and unloading stuff," he says.

"Work materials?"

Luca nodded, "Yep," he says. "What can I eat?"

"Anything on the top shelf," I say. "What else? Are you able to work with a lot of people?"

"A few on busy days."

"What about getting boats for people, helping them dock—are you still doing that?"

"That's what I mostly do," he says, "and when work is slow, I help unload materials."

"What kinds of materials?" I can tell he's getting frustrated.

"Why are you asking me all these questions?" he says. "Don't you already know what Papá does at work and what materials he has?"

"Yes, of course," I say, "I just like when you tell me all the things you do to help."

"He does the paperwork and meetings, but I'll help him with that soon, too."

"And the other night when you came home late? Were you at the marina all that time, or did you go somewhere with Papá?"

Luca gives me a cold stare that makes my stomach flip. I've never seen such an intense stare from him before. He mumbles something under his breath. "Fattig gli affari toui."

"Mind my own business? Is that what you said?"

His eyes fall to the floor. "That's not what I meant."

I fold my arms across my chest. "I can't believe you said that to me. I know your father talks like that, and it's not okay. You might think I accept how he talks, but I don't. I'm very disappointed, Luca."

"I'm sorry, Mamá."

I try to soften my tone and my expression. "I think you should go to your room."

He goes without hesitation.

* * *

Saturdays are our busiest days, but no matter what we're doing, our family always comes together at dinner time. It's when we finally can relax together.

CHAPTER SEVENTEEN

I prepare all of Sal's favorite dishes. Dinner is set for four. Shiny white dishes glimmer under an amber light from the old chandelier. Sal hates the chandelier. He says its swoops and curves are too feminine, but the chandelier is one of my favorite items in this house. Its elegance makes me smile.

Franco comes to the table first, then Sal clomps in without a care in the world, a newspaper tucked in his arm, a cigar between his finger and thumb. He takes his seat without so much as a glance at me, never mind a greeting.

I remove the pesce spada, swordfish, from the oven and bring it to the table, taking my time in hopes that Luca will arrive before we begin. But he doesn't.

I look at Sal, blissfully absorbed in his own world, completely unaware of anything else going on around him. I sit and clear my throat. "Have either of you seen Luca?" I say, looking from Franco to Sal. Franco shakes his head and Sal continues reading the paper. I call Sal twice, and the second time he folds the paper harshly and puts it down.

"What?" he says, looking annoyed and surprised, as if realizing for the first time that other people are around him. "What are you yelling about?"

"I'm not yelling," I say. "I simply asked if you have seen Luca. Franco and I have not."

"Haven't seen him," he says, "but that boy better be home soon or he'll miss dinner. I'm not waiting any longer. Let's eat."

Sal prefers eating and getting on with his night over taking time to figure out where his son is. But after what's happened with Gia, I'm not okay with Luca being late.

Seconds later, he storms through the door and heads straight for the stairs, keeping his head low.

"Where do you think you're going?" Sal yells.

"Toilet," Luca yells back.

"Not so fast," Sal says.

Luca stops.

"Come here."

Luca turns slowly and approaches the table, his eyes at his feet.

"Closer," Sal says.

Luca comes closer and stops a few inches away.

I flinch as Sal reaches for him but only to lift his chin. Under the light, I see cuts and bruises on his face and near his jaw; his left eye is swollen shut.

"What happened?" I say, standing.

Sal puts out his hand out to indicate he's handling this and I should stay out of it.

"What the hell happened to you?" Sal says.

"Nothing," Luca says.

"I won't ask again," Sal says. "You'd better start talking."

I go to the kitchen to retrieve a wet towel and see to Luca's injuries. I can't believe what is happening and instantly feel bad for scolding Luca earlier.

Sal's face reddens and his temples bulge. He looks like he might explode. When Luca still doesn't answer, Sal slams his fist on the table.

"I got in a fight," Luca blurts.

"A fight?" I say. "With who?"

"He's okay, Isabella!" Sal says. "Enough." He stands and looks at Luca. "Let's go to the living room."

My muscles tighten and twitch. How dare he leave me out of this. Normally I'd walk away, but not tonight. I put the damp cloth on the table and follow them to the living room. I listen at the door to whispers I can't decipher. Then Sal says, "You can't keep doing this, Luca. I can't keep cov—"

"What?" I emerge from the doorway. "What can't you keep covering?" I go to Luca. "This?" I motion toward his face. "Is this a result of something you're covering? I've never seen this happen before, but it sounds like you have."

Both Luca's and Sal's jaws drop, and they stare at me like they've never seen me before, as if they're noticing me for the first time.

"Tell me," I say, growing bolder by the second. "Tell me what's going on. I'm his mother—I have a right to know."

I wait for an object to be hurled at me, but it doesn't happen. I prepare for a sharp lashing from Sal's angry tongue, but again, nothing. Not even a fabricated story from either of them. I stand, legs wide, my hands on my

CHAPTER SEVENTEEN

hips, and wait.

Surprisingly, Sal replies. "Luca and that Carlos kid can't get along. It's gotten out of hand. Luca prevailed. He's fine."

"Prevailed?" I say. "What do you mean, 'prevailed'? Are we supposed to be proud of that?" Questioning Sal's judgment is one of the worst things I can do, but I can't stop myself. "What happened to Carlos? Is he in as bad of shape as you?" I don't wait for answers. I know the next question will push Sal over the edge. "Why did you bring Luca in here to talk instead of staying in the kitchen?"

Sal's rage-filled eyes widen. He lunges at me, but I dip to the left.

"Papá!" Luca yells.

Sal stops and stares at Luca. Turning back to me, he says, "I'll be the one to take care of discipline around here." Spit flies from his lips as he yells. "Woman, you take care of things fit for a wife!"

My instincts tell me to avoid this moment that has the makings of a devastating storm. But if I continue to do what I've always done, nothing will change, and we'll be in this hell forever. So I don't stop poking him, and I don't walk away or let him have his way so he'll be quiet.

I muster all I can and release what's on my mind. "I have a right to know what's going on with my children, just as much as you do, including how they should be disciplined."

His chest rises and falls rapidly.

"And now, suddenly, you take it easy on Luca's punishments, but Franco still can't do anything right in your eyes because he reminds you of your father. I don't care anymore about all that. I only care about my boys." I'm shocked at the calm, confident voice coming out of my mouth, nothing like the scream inside.

He glares at me, his face twisted. "You lost that right, and you know when you lost it," he growls.

Don't let him weaken you. That was a long time ago. Nothing can excuse his behavior.

"Don't you tell me how to raise my sons!" The pitch of his voice is like cats fighting. His body stiffens; he's winding tighter. "Who the hell do you think you are, coming in here to tell me—"

I open my mouth and let out a raging scream that brings Franco into the room. Everyone stares at me.

What comes out next surprises me. "You sound exactly like—"

He cocks his head. "Say it. I dare you."

"Mamá!" Luca yells.

Franco comes closer.

But I can no longer stop what's rolling off my tongue. I fix my eyes on him, a burning stare into his dark eyes, and I delve into the blackness of his soul. "Like. Your. Father!"

I hardly release the words and he lunges at me again, pinning me to the wall. His fat, hot hand wraps around my neck and squeezes. I faintly hear the boys pleading. I struggle and wrestle with him, but he's too strong. Sounds begin to fade and black spots appear in my eyes. I'm slipping.

Don't let him do it.

Somehow, I find the strength to kick my leg as hard and as high as possible, and it connects squarely with his groin. His fingers loosen and he falls to the ground writhing in pain. I slide down the wall and hit the floor, gasping for air. Franco rushes to my side. Luca looks at Sal but then joins Franco and they both help me up. While Sal is doubled over, I snatch the keys from the table and run to the door. A fleeting thought to my suitcase and the money—this isn't what I planned! But he might kill me if I don't leave now!

"Let's go!" I yell to Franco and Luca, but they stare at me transfixed, frozen.

Sal gets to his knees.

"Run, Mamá!" Franco yells.

"Franco, Luca, hurry!" I scream.

Sal stands, slumped over, holding his groin.

Franco glances back at Sal and turns to me. "Go! Go! Go!"

"I'm coming back for you!" I scream, running to Sal's car.

I slide into the driver's seat, another nail in my coffin, and start the car, shoving the gear shifter into drive. I peel out of the driveway, not looking back, and drive to the only place I am safe.

The events of the last ten minutes echo in my mind, Franco's and Luca's

CHAPTER SEVENTEEN

faces as their shock morphed to utter fear. Watching me in the doorway as I waited for them. We've never been apart. Why didn't they come with me? What kind of hold does Sal have on them? I didn't leave you. I'm coming back. My stomach churns. I pull over, open the door, and vomit. *What have I done?*

I pull back onto the road and continue to drive in the direction I was headed, knowing my heart is behind me.

CHAPTER EIGHTEEN

Giorgio lives fifteen minutes away in a small farming community with his wife, Camilla, and their son, Max. Their two older children are grown and on their own, leaving an empty bedroom in their small home.

I never wanted to interrupt their lives in my plan to leave Sal.

I sit in the driveway and think of what I'll say when I go to the door. Part of me wants to turn back. I wish I had a way to tell Franco and Luca to meet me somewhere away from home so I can take them without Sal's knowledge. Going back now is the wrong thing to do. As if it isn't enough that I kicked Sal in his privates, then I went and took his other pride and joy, his car. And I left. It doesn't get much worse than that for Salvatore Perri.

I glance at the doorway where Giorgio is standing, arms folded, face inquisitive. Waiting for me. I put the keys in my pocket and approach him. As I draw closer, my knees buckle from the weight of what I've done, the reason I'm here. He must sense it, because he steps forward and opens his arms. I fall into them and release my sorrow. We stand that way for a while until Camilla comes to the door. I step back, wiping my eyes.

"What happened?" she says, coming outside.

"I'm sorry to barge in on you like this," I say. "I—I can't go home right now."

"Did Sal do something?" Giorgio says defensively.

"No," I glance up, "I did."

CHAPTER EIGHTEEN

"What did you do, Iz?" What is he getting at?

"Not that," I say. "I can't talk about it right now."

"Do I need to pick up the boys?" he says. "Where are they?"

I want that more than anything, but I can't send Giorgio. Not him. "It's not a good time for that."

"Are they okay?" Camilla asks.

"Yes, they're okay for now." I hope with all my might that it's the truth.

"I'll make a bed for you," she says.

"No, please don't bother," I say. "I just need to sit." I refer to the bench on the porch. "I don't want to come in and disrupt your family time. I just need a place to be for now."

"Nonsense," Camilla says. "I'll prepare the room. If you don't end up staying, that's okay." She hugs me and goes inside.

Giorgio looks over his shoulder, and when Camilla is gone he says, "What happened?"

"Oh, Giorgio, it's bad," I say, placing my hand on my neck. "Very bad. He came at my throat."

Giorgio moves my hand. "My God."

"I kept demanding answers from him and then I said he sounded like his father, which was a mistake. I shouldn't have—"

"This is not your fault," he says. "Not for one second is this your fault. Doesn't matter what you said or did; it's never okay for him to do this." He brushes his finger at the mark on my neck.

"I thought I was going to die—I was losing consciousness—so I kicked him . . . there . . . and he let go. That's the only reason I'm here right now."

His eyes water briefly and then a faint smile brushes his lips. "Good girl," he says, hugging me. "You finally did it."

"It's not how I planned, Giorgio. I've got a packed suitcase and money. I still need those. I can't stay here, and I can't be without the boys. They need me now more than ever. Everything is a mess."

"Not everything can be planned out. You did what you could. If you hadn't, you'd be—" He stops and looks away.

"I don't know what to do. I don't think I can stay here, not for long."

"What about your sister?" he says.

"Not now," I say, "not in the middle of this investigation. She lives too far from here. You even said Luca's name has come up. Maybe Franco's will too. They need me."

"If you go back, he might finish what he started."

"Maybe not if I pretend to be exactly what he wants me to be," I say, "if I go back to being silent and submissive. . . ."

"No, Iz."

"It would only be a ruse to make him feel content, make him think he's in charge again. And when all this is over, I'll be ready to leave with Franco and Luca for good. I can't be without them, Giorgio. I won't." I cry again in his arms.

"We'll figure this out," he says, caressing the back of my head.

Camilla steps out to the porch. "Everything is ready for you," she says.

I jump back, and she gives me a strange look. "Thank you, Camilla," I say.

We go inside the house together and sit at the kitchen table. Giorgio picks up the phone and tells the operator the number he'd like to connect with. I hear only his end of the conversation. He's asking someone to go to my house, pretend they're lost, and ask to use the phone. He says they need to spot two teenage boys, see if they're distressed or if they appear injured.

I stand to object, but he holds up a finger telling me to wait. Camilla puts her hands on her hips and stares at him crossly. After a few minutes, he hangs up and faces us.

"I've got a friend going to check on the boys—make sure they're okay," he says. "Someone Sal has never seen and would never suspect is connected to any of us. If possible, he'll give a note to one of the boys."

"What note?" I say.

"The one you're going to write to tell them you haven't abandoned them." He looks at Camilla who is standing with her hands on her hips. "She needs to know Franco and Luca are okay. They need to know their mother hasn't abandoned them and that she'll be back for them. Wouldn't you want that for Max if you were in this situation?"

"I wouldn't be in this situation," Camilla says. Giorgio shoots her a look.

CHAPTER EIGHTEEN

"I'm sorry. That's selfish of me. Yes, of course I would want the same for Max," she says, glancing at me with pity.

Giorgio hands me paper and a pen, and as I begin a short letter to my boys, my heart fills with remorse.

My dear Franco and Luca,

Whoever reads this first, please share it with your brother. I want you to know that I love you more than life and I have not abandoned you. As you witnessed, if I hadn't done what I did, I might not be alive to write this. I'm safe and only staying away briefly to give your father time to cool down. I have a plan to come back and another to leave again but with both of you this time. Be strong. It won't be long before I see you.

All my love,

Mamá

About an hour later, Giorgio receives a call confirming that the boys have been seen and they appear well. A young boy answered the door and said his father wasn't home and his brother was working on the plantation. The note was handed to the boy with specific directions to share it with only his brother and destroy it immediately. Giorgio asked the caller to describe the boy he spoke with. He said he had short brown hair, longer on top, parted at the side, and had a small mole near his lip. The caller confirmed seeing the other boy near the plantation as he left but didn't speak with him.

When Giorgio relays the message to both Camilla and me, I know at once the boy who answered the door was Luca. Relief pours over me, soothing my whole body and most of my mind. Franco and Luca are home and appear to be doing okay, but where is Sal?

"Giorgio, I can't thank you enough for sending your friend to check on the boys. I will not forget this."

"It's what friends do," he says. "You'd do the same."

He's right. I'd help Giorgio and his family in a heartbeat.

We sit and talk on the porch until the sun goes down. A surge of panic grips me as the last bits of yellow and orange disappear to the earth. The idea of sleeping in a bed and in a house that's not mine, with people who are not mine, is unnerving. I can't stop thinking about what's happening at my house. Is Sal home by now or has he left Franco in charge? What's he saying to the boys about me? What's he planning?

When my head hits the pillow, I think about Giorgio's friend who stopped by the house and spoke with Luca. Can I trust Luca to show Franco the note and then destroy it, or is there a chance he might show Sal to prove that he's useful to him?

* * *

I rise early with the birds, my body sore from a restless night's sleep in a strange bed. Downstairs, Giorgio is already up making coffee. He pours a cup and hands it to me. I join him at the table where a bouquet of peonies and lilies rests. Instantly I'm on edge.

"I won't ask how you slept," he says, "'cause if I know you, you didn't sleep."

"Not much. Maybe an hour," I say. "Where did those flowers come from?"

"Camilla found them on the porch this morning."

"On the porch?" I say.

"Yes. . . . What's wrong?"

"Was there a note or anything left with them?" I say, feeling the air leave the room.

"No note," he says. "It's probably one of the neighbors. We do that around

CHAPTER EIGHTEEN

here—help each other, send flowers, food . . ."

"Those are from Sal," I say.

"What makes you say that?"

"Peonies and lilies are my favorite flowers, and Sal knows that. He brought me a bouquet just like these a couple of weeks ago for no reason. He does that sometimes when he's feeling guilty or pretending to care. I know these are from Sal. This means he knows I'm here." I stand and pace across the kitchen floor, feeling myself coming undone. "I can't breathe."

Camilla enters the room, and both she and Giorgio are at my side trying to calm me.

"How does he know I'm here?" I say.

"Well, he knows you and Giorgio are close," Camilla answers. "He probably didn't have to think too hard about it." I think she means well, even if her tone sounds a little sarcastic. "He's probably trying to convince you to come home."

"He's messing with me—with all of us," I say. "He wants us to know he was here and that he can find me whenever he wants. He wants us to know he can do anything, and we'll have no idea until after it's done. Trust me, I know him well."

Camilla stares at Giorgio, her face covered in worry. She has to be thinking that my being here is a threat to their family. If Sal can be here undetected, he'll have no trouble doing it again. And next time he probably won't bring flowers.

I recognize what this means, and it takes a lot to convince Giorgio that my presence in their house places them all in danger—a danger I'm not willing to put them in any longer. Sal may have left me flowers in an attempt to bring me home again, and in some sick way he probably thinks it will change things. He might even be different for a while to keep me there. In his deranged mind, having a wife who leaves him exposes his vulnerabilities and lack of control over his family. So even though I've brought him to the edge and his anger almost killed me, ultimately, he doesn't want that.

But knowing I chose to go to Giorgio's for protection is a cut to his ego as a man. And even though Giorgio had no idea I would show up on his doorstep, it won't matter to Sal. They've always had a sort of rivalry between them, probably because I've grown up with Giorgio; therefore, to Sal, he's a threat.

And then there was that brief moment in Giorgio's arms when a comforting hug became a kiss right on our front porch. Neither of us expected it to happen, and I'd denied it, but Sal saw what he saw and made several false accusations as a result. Sal may give me a pass, but he won't do the same for Giorgio.

No, I can't stay here. I have to go before things get worse.

Before leaving, Giorgio and Camilla insist I stay for lunch. I only agree because, by the time we're finished, Sal should be at the marina and the boys at school. I'll enter an empty house. I'll be able to get my bearings and adjust my plan to leave for good without anyone interrupting or distracting me.

As I bring the dishes to the sink, Giorgio and Camilla are in a heated conversation. I step outside to give them space and wait by the car.

Giorgio comes out alone. He says he wants to go with me and hide in the house in case things go badly when Sal returns. I love that he wants to protect me, but I dread the potential outcome, and I can't take Giorgio from his own family. Nor can I risk losing the chance to leave in the way I planned to. We briefly argue our points and finally agree that it doesn't make sense for him to wait at my house for what could be hours before Sal gets home.

Instead, Giorgio will follow me home to make sure Sal isn't there and then he'll leave. When Sal arrives, I'll observe him closely and, if anything seems off, I'll call Giorgio but then I'll hang up. The phone's ringing will signify a problem and Giorgio will come. He makes me promise not to call the police for fear of their possible connections to Sal.

It's surreal pulling onto the road that leads me home. As if I'm an outsider visiting someone else. The wheels bounce as I drive, and it's like I'm floating away from myself, away from my life.

CHAPTER NINETEEN

The first thing I do when I'm inside the house is check the box to make sure it's still there, and thankfully it is. The money and the shoe are positioned exactly as I'd left them. Satisfied, I tuck them at the back of the cupboard behind the flour sack and drag the sugar and baking soda over for extra coverage. I scan the house looking for signs of anything suspicious purposely planted by Sal while also watching for him through the window.

The phone rings and stills my heart. I pick it up fast, but no one is on the other end, not even the operator. Just dead air and then a click. I'm left with an uneasy feeling, a reminder that things are not as they should be.

A quick trip to my bedroom confirms everything is the way it was when I left, including the suitcase in my closet. I push it further back behind the hanging clothes, obscuring it from view.

Time goes slowly with fleeting moments of relaxation squelched by a rush of panic. I'm always on edge, waiting for the sky to fall. The clock reminds me to look for Franco and Luca at the top of the hill. A rush of excitement and worry flies through me when I spot them both. Franco spots the Fiat and points it out to Luca, and their walk picks up speed, almost to a run.

I anxiously wait for them on the porch. When we spot each other we all run until we meet in a fierce embrace. I step back and look them over for signs of distress, physical or mental.

"Thank God," I say through my tears. "I'm so sorry I left. You know I had to, right?"

"I told you to go, Mamá," Franco says, "remember?"

"Thank you for reminding me." I look at Luca. "Luca, you know I'd never leave you and not come back for you, right?"

"Yes, Mamá," he says. "You had to do what you had to do. But you're back and that's what matters." The words are right, but the tone is off. Did Sal get to him already?

"It'll be okay, Mamá," Franco says, placing his hand on my back.

"I was so worried about you both," I say. "You got my note?"

"Yes," Luca says. "I showed Franco, and we threw it out."

"You threw out the note?" I say in a panic. "Did you rip it up before you threw it away?"

"No, but I crumpled it up," Luca says.

"Which garbage did you put it in? The kitchen?" I say, my voice thinning.

"Yes, in the kitchen, Mamá," he says.

"Your father doesn't know about it, right?" My eyes dart between them.

"No," Luca says, "and he never knew that Giorgio's friend delivered it, either."

"What makes you think Giorgio's friend delivered the note?" I say. "Because you're wrong. It wasn't Giorgio's friend."

Luca glances at Franco and then at me. "My mistake, Mamá. We're just glad you're home."

"Me too," I say.

"Does Papá know you're back?" he asks.

"Of course not," Franco says crossly.

"Did you get the flowers?" Luca asks as we walk toward the house.

"You knew about those?" I say. "How did you know about the flowers?"

He looks at me funny. "I brought them there," he says.

I glance at Franco who lifts his shoulders.

Franco looks at Luca. "You brought them on behalf of Papá? How did you know where to find her?"

"Not directly," Luca says, ignoring the second question. And then it clicks.

CHAPTER NINETEEN

Luca brought flowers to make me think they were from Sal so I'd come home. And it worked. I did come home. And Sal isn't expecting me to be here, not from any effort on his part. The air around me thickens.

"Luca," I say, slowly, "are you saying your father doesn't know a thing about the flowers and is probably not expecting me to be here?"

"It's okay, Mamá," Franco blurts. "You're here now. It'll be okay when Papá comes home. He'll be glad to see you."

I give Franco a questioning look, doubt creeping into every bone in my body.

When we're inside the house I consider calling Giorgio, but I freeze when Sal exits a car at the end of our driveway. He must have seen the Fiat. I have to think fast. If flowers didn't bring me home, what did? I'll have to pretend that I came to my senses, that I realized I needed to be home with my family.

The only reason I left was that I felt so terrible about what had happened and knew he needed time to cool off. Yes, I'll pretend I left for him. And kicking him in the groin was an accident, a reflex because I couldn't breathe. I'll have to convince him that he's the only one for me. I just pray he doesn't ask where I've been, but if Luca knew, he might too.

I take a deep breath as he steps to the porch and brace for the worst.

He enters with no emotion, his face an empty slate. My hands ball into fists at my sides and I wait. Slight movement near his mouth and a tiny line appears, splitting his face into a half grin. I can't assume anything good from this sudden shift in expression. It could still change in a flash. But it doesn't. His smile spreads, brightening his eyes, and then his whole face lights up. I jump when he comes at me but not with fists—with a hug.

My arms hang awkwardly, not knowing whether to break free or hug him back. I hug him back and we sway, like in a dance. Is this a trick? Am I being tested? Is he doing this to throw me off, make me even more vulnerable as I'm wrapped in this moment, then he'll swing when I least expect it? We're still swaying, and I am utterly confused.

He steps back and looks at me, still smiling. Then he pulls me into another warm embrace. He steps back again. "You came back," he says, still with a smile.

"Yes, of course," is all I say. My words must be chosen with such precision. I don't know whether to apologize and get it done or wait and respond to what he says. I choose the latter.

"I knew you'd be back," he says, but I don't like the sound of the word "be." It's almost too presumptuous. "You'd come back" would be better, but I go along.

"I was never planning on leaving," I say. "It was just in that moment—"

"Shh." He holds a finger to my mouth. "Don't say anything." His display of affection is so unusual it sickens me, and I don't trust him. "You're here now and that's all that matters. You would never leave me."

Please don't remind me of the reasons why. "Of course not," I say. "This is where I want to be." Lies, lies, lies.

"Seeing you here right now," he continues, "makes me not want to go back to work today. So, instead, I'll spend the rest of the afternoon at home with my family. Won't that be wonderful?"

"Yes, yes, that would be so wonderful," I say, forcing compassion and warmth into my voice. "I'll make a special dinner tonight."

He smiles again and sits at the table to read the newspaper.

I glance at the phone through the doorway, thinking of Giorgio, wondering what he's thinking.

Suddenly, the phone rings.

I prop the phone onto my shoulder and hold it with my chin, "Hello?"

The smooth voice of a woman replies. "Oh, I—I think I must have the wrong number."

"Who are you looking for?" I ask, but we're disconnected immediately, reminding me of the uncertainty and turmoil we're still in.

Franco comes into the kitchen. "Franco, were you expecting a call from someone? A girl, perhaps?"

"No," he says, blushing. "Maybe Luca is."

"She sounded older. Probably the wrong number," I say.

About half an hour later, I'm deep into dinner preparations and the phone rings again. I grab a towel to wipe my hands so I can answer it, but Sal's already got it in his hand. Could it be another wrong number? I listen to a

CHAPTER NINETEEN

conversation taking place in the distance. Then Sal takes the cord and goes further into the living room with the phone.

I move closer to listen.

"I told you not to call here," he says, his voice stern but quiet. He says something else I can't make out followed by, "I know, yes, I will. I promise." Then he hangs up and goes outside.

As I'm clearing things from the table, I see Luca's school bag on one of the chairs. It's strange that he didn't take this upstairs like he usually does.

I open it and look inside, and as I'm rummaging through, I notice two pieces of paper folded into thirds, like something official.

I open the first one: a detention slip dated yesterday, and at the bottom is an empty line where a parent's signature is supposed to go. My stomach sinks. If he's been suspended for a whole day, where has he been? The next paper is a note requiring a two-day suspension from school. Luca, what are you doing? I'll have to decide how to handle this. I also find three crumpled cigarettes—I knew I smelled smoke on him—a dirty sock, an overdue library book, and a girl's ring. It's odd finding a girl's ring in his bag, yet its familiarity makes me uneasy.

I'm just about to close everything up when I find a sealed white envelope. But even as I hold it up to the light, I can't decipher what's inside. Against my better judgment, I open the envelope and inside is a small piece of paper, with one name printed in the middle: Brianna. I don't put this back; I keep it for later.

I hear Luca's feet padding down the stairs, and I step away from the bag, but he looks at me strangely, almost like he knows. He grabs his bag and starts back up the stairs.

"How was school today, Luca?" I ask.

"Fine," he says.

"What did you learn?"

"Nothing new," he says.

"I guess not," I say. "I'm sure it's hard to learn something when you're not even there."

His jaw drops and he looks at me.

"You weren't at school today." He starts to talk but I cut him off. "You can stop pretending, Luca. I know you were suspended." A dead stare in his eyes. "But what I'm really curious about is if you weren't in school today, where were you?"

"I was at school," he says, looking away. "Why don't you believe me?"

"Do I need to give you proof?"

"Were you looking through my things?"

"Is there something in there I shouldn't see?" I say, then I soften my tone. "Luca, tell me what's going on with you. I can help you with anything. I want to help you if you need me."

Luca's expression changes. His eyes soften and his face relaxes, as if he's actually listening and contemplating whether or not to take me up on my offer and tell the truth. He looks as if he wants to say something. Maybe he's trying to get his words right. He tilts his head and squints like it's too painful to say but finally says, "It's—it's Peter. I've been trying to protect him."

"What do you mean you're trying to protect him? From what?"

"Mamá, you know how he is. He can be awkward sometimes and has trouble keeping friends."

I nod, acknowledging that Peter often did or said things that were easily misinterpreted. Even though he's a little bit older, he sometimes doesn't act his age, but he's also one of the kindest boys I know.

"So," he continues, "sometimes I'd . . ." He stops.

"You would what?"

"Take the blame."

This catches me off guard. I study my youngest son for a moment. Did we have him figured out all wrong? Is he finally putting forth the effort to think of others?

"What do you mean by that?" I say.

"I've been getting detention slips and not telling you," he says. "Not because I didn't want to tell you but because I didn't do those things that caused me to get detention. When they happened, I was with Peter. But it was Peter who was responsible."

CHAPTER NINETEEN

I come in closer to him so that we're face to face, eye to eye. "Luca, now is the time to be completely honest with me. No matter what the truth is, even if you are involved, even if something is all your fault, I can help you. But I can't help you if you're not being honest with me. That's all I ask for is the truth. Do you understand?"

He nods.

"You're telling me Peter is the one responsible for getting you in trouble?"

He nods again.

"Is he the one who hurt those girls? Is he responsible for that?"

"Yes, Mamá," he says. "I didn't want anyone to know. He's not tough like me. But now he's in jail, so I guess I didn't help that much."

I'm not sure why, but I don't reply to this. "I don't think you should have gotten suspended. Maybe I can call—"

"No, Mamá!" he says. "Please don't do that. I'll stop defending him. I'll stop taking the blame, I promise."

I'm conflicted and can't think straight. "I need to give this some thought," I say. "We'll talk more later." Then I reach for him and pull him into a hug. "I'm proud of you for wanting to protect your friends, Luca. Just promise me you won't do it if it's for something they shouldn't be doing."

"I promise," he says. Luca stays put for a moment and then quietly goes back to his room with his bag slung over his shoulder.

Although part of me questions Luca's story, another part that wants to accept what he says as the truth. All this time I'd been doubting Luca, accepting what Mr. Valentino said about him, accepting what the teachers were observing. Never once had I questioned their judgment. And after all this time, Luca was the one who had been good. He still needs guidance—he shouldn't be sneaking out at night and he shouldn't be taking the blame for others. Maybe I've been too hard on him. Maybe I need to trust him more as Sal does.

CHAPTER TWENTY

I awaken in the morning pleasantly surprised yet cautious of the seamless reunion yesterday with Sal and the boys. I'm alive and unharmed, which means another day to prepare for my true departure.

In the kitchen, a loud bang against the windowpane above the sink startles me, an impact so loud I expect to find shattered glass by the faucet, but there's only a mark on the glass.

I check the window on the outside and I'm caught off guard by what I see: feathers scattered on the grass and a small pheasant lying dead beneath the window. It must have flown right into the glass. What strikes me as strange is that the feathers are not from the pheasant but from a different kind of bird, longer, grayer in color, like that of a goose. I collect the feathers and quickly scoop up the bird before Sal discovers them.

He'll remind me of his mother's superstition about birds—that a bird or its feathers inside a house, or a bird found dead on your property, is a bad omen meaning grief and suffering will come to the family. I recall one time before we were married when I gave his mother a bowl with a beautiful peacock in the center and she wouldn't accept it. I couldn't understand why until Sal explained that the design on a peacock's feather is similar to the evil eye, which his family, as do many Italians, believes will bring bad luck.

Sal's mother demanded he take the beautiful bowl to the trash container outside the house. Then she performed a strange ceremony where she added oil to water to dispel the impending evil curse. When she finished, we returned to our normal conversation as if nothing ever happened.

I don't believe in superstitions, but I can't shake an eerie feeling I have,

CHAPTER TWENTY

which I believe is connected to this dead bird and the feathers.

On my way back to the house I see someone near the shed. I look for the Fiat's wheels to confirm Sal's presence, but they're not there, and they shouldn't be since he said he'd be at the marina today. When I squint my eyes, I realize there are two people near the shed. I sidestep to the house so I can get to the phone when the two faces look up at me . . . and it takes my breath away. They come closer as I near the door, their features sharpening until I realize it's Giuseppe and Massimo. An unexpected combination.

I wait for them on the porch next to the door.

"Good morning," I say. "What brings you here?"

Massimo removes his hat and says hello.

Giuseppe smiles. "Sorry to bother you, Iz. Sal asked us to come and check his office. I guess there have been a lot of burglaries in the neighborhood, and he asked us to look in and make sure it's still locked and undisturbed."

Or to check on me and make sure I haven't meddled with it.

"I haven't heard of any burglaries," I say, "but I suppose he just wants to be on the safe side. Does his office seem to have been disturbed?"

"We just arrived," Massimo says. "We haven't examined the inside yet."

I look to the driveway and the road for their cars but see none. "Did you walk here?"

They exchange glances. "Yes," Giuseppe says, "we walked from the marina. Sal asked us to make a few minor repairs inside, so we'll be a while—in case you hear or see us again."

"Repairs?" I say. "I didn't know his office needed any repairs."

"So good to see you," Massimo says, ignoring my statement, holding his gaze on me. And then he and Giuseppe turn and walk back to the shed.

Something doesn't sit right with me, so I wait until they're back near the shed and then I go there myself. As I come closer, I'm suddenly hit with a wall of something foul that stops me in my tracks. I cover my mouth at the fusty, malodorous cloud and look around expecting to see a dead animal carcass, but there's nothing in sight, and now I've lost sight of both Massimo and Giuseppe.

They must be inside the shed. Such an odd pair from very different walks of life together right now in our shed: Giuseppe, the average, law-abiding, working man, and Massimo, the mysterious businessman. Have they always known each other?

My thoughts go to Anna and our last uncomfortable encounter at the detention center. She undoubtedly needs a friend now more than ever, but she refuses to speak with me. I wonder if Giuseppe knows what happened between us at the detention center and if Anna knows Giuseppe is here right now in our shed with Massimo.

I continue toward the shed, my hand cupped tightly around my nose and mouth. Massimo's and Giuseppe's voices echo inside the shed. As I draw nearer, the heavy odor permeates through my hand, making it impossible to breathe. I can't stay any longer; I have to go back. I'll tell Sal about the smell later today. I'll tell him I caught a whiff of something coming from that area when I was on the porch, so he doesn't think I've been near his office. But what I want to know is what could smell so dreadful, and is it outside the shed or inside?

I'm not far from the house when Giorgio comes running up the driveway, picking up speed when he sees me. He hugs me tightly and then releases me.

"I had to make sure you're okay," he says breathlessly.

I look back toward the shed. "You shouldn't be here. Massimo and Giuseppe are in the shed."

"Why?" he says.

"Sal sent them to make sure it wasn't burglarized and to work on some repairs inside."

"They came together?" he says.

"Yes—so odd, right?"

"Very odd," he says. "I won't stay long. When I didn't hear from you, I assumed you were okay, but I just wanted to be sure." He looks me over. "You look okay. Are you?"

"Yes, and I wanted to call you, but there was never a good time. Sal was actually happy to see me. He hugged me and said he was glad I came back. It was shocking, really. I'm still a bit cautious."

"Don't let your guard down," he says. "Remember what I said about

CHAPTER TWENTY

watching each of them."

"I remember, and I will. I had an interesting talk with Luca, which I'll tell you about later. You really should go." I glance again at the shed to make sure the two men are still inside, hoping they haven't seen Giorgio. I shudder thinking of the last encounter between Sal and Giorgio. If Sal were to find him here again, that would be it. He'd be convinced something was going on between us.

"Thank you for coming to check on me and for being my friend," I say.

Giorgio's face lights up. "You never need to thank me for that. We're meant to be friends. I've known you my whole life. I'll always be here for you." He looks down at his feet and then up. "You're still going to leave him, right? You know you're never trapped in your life."

"I know," I say, "and yes, I am definitely leaving him. It's just complicated with the boys and with what's going on right now, but I am definitely leaving, and soon." I hug him tightly.

"You are never alone," he whispers. "Remember that." He smiles. "I'll see you soon." Then he turns and walks to his car at the end of the road, and I go back inside my house to watch the shed from the window above the sink.

CHAPTER TWENTY-ONE

Today I begin to take matters into my own hands. Sal denies any smell inside or outside the shed. To prove it, he brings me to the shed to see for myself. I prepare for the wall of filth to hit me, but it doesn't. Only hints of sulfur, nothing like before. At times, I catch a whiff of bleach or something clean, a puzzling combination.

Sal takes my hand and pulls me right up to the door. He lets go to unlock it as I wait behind him, wide-eyed, heart pumping, as he opens the door. We step inside but there is nothing amiss. I walk toward the storage door and he stops me.

"See?" he says. "Smells fine. Must have been a dead animal. Massimo and Giuseppe probably found it and cleaned it up. Satisfied? Now, let's go; Massimo will be here any minute." He leads me again by hand out of the shed. He doesn't mention a thing about what Massimo and Giuseppe were repairing inside.

Massimo arrives not five minutes later, and I'm crawling out of my skin waiting for them to leave, dying to get some answers first from Mr. Valentino and then from what's under Luca's bed. With the Fiat, I'm sure I can easily make it to the school and back without anyone noticing I've even left. I'm sure my conversation with Luca's teacher won't take long.

The Fiat 500, the Topolino, sits in its usual spot on the far side of the house behind the cypress trees. Sal's pride and joy. I can see why he loves it so much—that shiny, smoky-blue metal is something to look at. Sal has never

CHAPTER TWENTY-ONE

allowed me to drive it, parroting one of several of Mussolini's beliefs, which he agrees with, that women belong in the home, not on the road. But it's the 1930s, and lots of women in Italy drive these days.

Sal must have compartmentalized his anger when I stole the Fiat the day I fled for my life. I'm sure he was angry not only because I took the car but also because he became aware that I'd been practicing driving behind his back. Sal doesn't like to not know things.

Over the last few months during school and work days, I've been getting private driving lessons from Giorgio. Giorgio insisted I learn to drive for my safety and for my independence. He's constantly pushing me to stand up for myself and believe in myself. He says I'm missing things that are right in front of me, both the simple things in life and the darker things that could harm me.

Goosebumps ripple through my skin as I slide to the driver's seat, recalling how terrified I felt the last time I drove it away from my family. I think about the shed and the smell and the shoe. My mind repeatedly plays everything that's happened over the last couple weeks, and I feel connected to it all somehow. I want to talk to Greta or Anna or Giorgio about it, but I can't.

The warm summer wind tousles my hair as it blows through the open windows, and I feel a little bit free as the wheels bounce lightly on the lane. The small taste of independence is invigorating and squelches my nerves for a moment. But it's short-lived because, as I slow the car at the intersecting road, I'm pretty sure I see Sal sitting in the passenger seat of another car. One that's not Massimo's. We roll to a slower speed at the same time. Luckily, the three cars in front of me create some distance to obscure Sal's view.

He's busy talking and doesn't notice his Fiat turning left onto a connecting road. I keep my head low, as if seeing his car isn't enough for him to know who's driving it. I turn the steering wheel and glimpse the driver who appears to be, of all things, a woman. No, it can't be.

From the rearview mirror, I watch them go straight in the direction of our house. Calm down. There's no way Sal is taking a strange woman home. Soon I doubt it was even him. No sense going back; if it's him, he'll notice the absence of his car right away, and then it won't matter if I'm gone five minutes or five hours. The outcome will be the same.

When I near a small cemetery, I know I'm just a block from the school. My pulse races as I park near the building. I fix my hair, straighten my dress, and walk to the door.

An older woman rises from a desk as soon as I enter and greets me with a smile. I explain who I am and why I'm here. She says to wait while she gets the principal.

A few minutes later, Mr. Valentino emerges from a door adjacent to the woman's desk. He's wearing a brown tweed suit and shiny shoes. He looks down at me like he's observing a misbehaved child who has been sent to the office for discipline.

I stand so we're eye to eye.

"Signora Perri," he says in a soft voice. "What a surprise." He opens the door to his office. "Come inside." He points to a chair across from his desk and I sit.

"I'm here to check on Luca and see if his behavior has improved since we last spoke," I say. "I'm sorry if he's still giving you trouble. I also came to talk about these." I place the two suspension notes I'd found in Luca's backpack on Mr. Valentino's desk.

"It's nice to see you're putting in some effort to be involved in your son's education. I've spoken with your husband about this and—"

"You spoke with Signore Perri?" I say. "About these?" I slap my hand on the notes.

"Y—yes," he says. "He reassured me he would take care of it as he's always done and—"

"Take care of it?" My left eye begins to twitch. "When did you speak with him? Did you call the house?"

"Not exactly," he says. "I saw Signore Perri outside of school one evening. We ran into each other; we—um—we talked."

"Where?" I say.

"Does it matter where?"

"Why was Luca suspended?"

Mr. Valentino looks at me, studies me, judges me. Then his eyes soften.

CHAPTER TWENTY-ONE

He folds his hands together and rests them on his desk. "I apologize for any confusion. I assumed you knew. This recent incident with Luca was more serious. He fought with one of our underprivileged students—called him names and then punched him and broke his nose. Several students witnessed it. We're sorry we had to suspend him for a couple days."

This doesn't sound like Luca at all. "Were any other boys with Luca at the time this happened? Any of his friends?"

"Yes, there were a couple boys who only watched."

"Was Peter Rossi one of them?"

"I can't tell you that."

"I already know he was," I say. "How do you know it was Luca who got in the fight? Do you have proof that it was him and not someone else? Maybe Luca was blamed for something because he was there." And then I say something I'm not proud of: "You know Peter is in the Turio Detention Center for what happened to those girls, don't you?"

He looks at me, astounded, and I am astounded myself.

"Yes, I am aware of that," he says. "I believe his parents are working to appeal his sentence because they believe in his innocence."

"That makes two of us," I say. "Two parents who believe in their children's innocence."

Mr. Valentino pauses as if to reflect for a moment. "Luca's teacher says he seems angry lately. Keeps more to himself and is less friendly or talkative with his classmates. Two weeks ago, I was called to the classroom because he was arguing with her."

"Arguing with his teacher?"

"Luca accused his classmate, Brianna, of stealing something of his. He wouldn't say what was stolen even after his teacher tried to work through it with him. She spoke with both Luca and Brianna, but Luca was adamant that Brianna had taken something. He told his teacher to mind her own business."

My jaw drops at hearing those familiar words and at hearing Brianna's name, the same name written on the paper in that envelope I'd found. What does it mean?

Mr. Valentino leans in closer to me. "Later in the afternoon, someone heard Luca make a threat against Brianna. Brianna's parents were concerned and pulled her out of school for a few days. Has he ever mentioned Brianna to you before or said he was angry with someone at school?"

I'm stunned. I can't imagine Luca arguing with his teacher or making threats. What could he possibly own that would cause him to be angry enough to threaten someone?

"No, I've never heard him mention her name or anyone specific for that matter. He doesn't talk much about school or his classmates," I say. "Signore, how can you be so confident that all this is true?"

"I know my students," he says. "Every single one."

"You're sure Brianna didn't take something of Luca's by accident? Maybe she didn't know it was his or who it belonged to and took it innocently. I'm not excusing Luca's behavior, but maybe he wasn't lying about who took the item."

"Quite sure," he says with an expression I am not sure how to read.

I want to defend Luca against his teacher, his principal, the rumors. I want to defend him against the wall inside that holds me back. The wall that says to open my eyes and see what's in front of me. The wall that asks, "What if they're right?" Could Brianna be the one he sneaks out to see at night? Boys can sometimes be annoying toward girls they really like because they don't know how to express their admiration.

I'm always defending people I love: Sal's sour mood to our friends and family, Luca's and Franco's behavior to Sal. It's exhausting to love people as much as I do.

"I don't know what to say, Signore Valentino. I'm sorry to hear this."

He doesn't acknowledge my apology. "How is Luca when he's at home? What does he do? How does he behave for you?"

Fine when he's not sneaking out of the house in the middle of the night.

I shift in my chair. "We've had some behavior issues at home as well, but nothing like what I'm hearing from you. Luca works at the marina with his father every day after school and on the weekends. We try to keep him busy."

CHAPTER TWENTY-ONE

"Ah, the marina," he says wistfully. "You've taken great care of that lucrative business of yours. Such a wonderful and enriching part of our town."

"Thank you."

"It's a shame about Julia's body being found so close," he says. "I'm sure that has to bother you."

"Of course it bothers me." I'm appalled at his lack of empathy. I've tried to put aside what happened there and not let it scar the beauty of the marina itself. "It's devastating."

"And still no arrests," he tuts, shaking his head. An awkward pause stands between us. "Well, it's good you're keeping Luca busy," he continues. "I just hope he has enough time to do his homework."

"He does it right after school before he goes to the marina, and sometimes he has to finish before bed." I stretch the truth on this a little.

"Does he listen to you and your husband when you tell him to do something?"

"Usually." Less and less lately.

"What happens when he doesn't do what he's supposed to do?"

"I beg your pardon. Aren't we discussing Luca's behavior at school?"

"Yes," he replies, "but it helps to get a full understanding of a child when we can look at that child's behavior both at school and at home."

I fold my arms at my chest. "We have consequences at home when he doesn't do what he's supposed to do." I won't share Sal's consequences.

Mr. Valentino leans over his desk. "Has there been any sort of trauma he's experienced or perhaps witnessed?"

The trauma he lives with or something else?

This question almost makes me vomit. What is he getting at? Does he know something?

"Not that I'm aware of." It sickens me to say that. I redirect the conversation. "So, how do we help Luca?"

"Well, your husband said he would talk with Luca about it—make him understand how serious this is, take away some privileges. Maybe he shouldn't be allowed to work at the marina for a while."

"I see; yes, that makes sense."

"And I will have to suspend him indefinitely if anything—and I mean anything—happens again. Keep an eye on him, Signora Perri. Observe how he reacts to disappointment, how he interacts with others. See if you notice any patterns. Maybe have him talk to someone."

"Someone . . . like a professional?"

"Perhaps, or another adult you trust and you think he'll trust."

Suddenly I feel the walls are closing in. "Thank you for your time, Signore Valentino," I say, standing. "I will reinforce this message with Luca. I promise he will be better."

"I certainly hope so," he says. "I've known Luca since he started school. It's not like him to behave this way." He extends his hand and we shake. "Thank you for coming in today," he says pleasantly for the first time since we began our conversation.

Instead of going straight to the car, I head to the back of the school where the students go during recess. I stand to the side when I see Luca and watch how he interacts with the other students. One boy tosses him a ball and Luca dives to catch it. He smiles and throws it back. This goes on for a few minutes before a few others join in. I breathe in deeply and walk away. Luca seems okay today.

CHAPTER TWENTY-TWO

Since I'm already out with the car, I take advantage of the opportunity do something I've wanted to do for a couple days. I stop at the corner stand and buy a bouquet of sunflowers to take to Giorgio and Camilla. I want to thank them for dropping everything to take me in that day. I know I can never repay them for their kindness, but flowers might be a good start.

About a mile from their house, I'm pretty sure that the car behind me is the same one that's been there since I left the school. Could someone be following me? I keep thinking about what Giorgio said about Sal and his alleged ties to the 'Ndrangheta. Giorgio doesn't trust Sal and never has. He's always questioned Sal's business connections and his business ventures at the marina. He often uses the words no buono, no good, when talking about him.

But I never questioned anything about Sal and the business. Not until recently, when strange things started happening and I couldn't look away—the long hair on his jacket, the terrible ending to our evening with the Russos followed by their disappearance, and the obscurity around Sal's arrival at the house with Massimo that night.

My eyes flick to the rearview mirror. The car behind me rides dangerously close to my back bumper. Did Sal sent someone to follow me? As soon as I turn into Giorgio's neighborhood, the car swooshes by me fast, nearly sideswiping my door, and then continues straight. My heart races as I watch it disappear down the road. I release the breath I'd been holding.

About halfway down Giorgio's street, several police cars are parked side by side creating a blockade. A police officer turns toward my car and holds out a hand to not come any further. Is there an accident? I'm curious to know what has happened.

From behind the police officer, someone waves their arms and walks toward me. It's Giorgio, and he is visibly distressed. When he gets closer, I can see that his eyes are red and tear-filled with a look of despair. His lips part but nothing comes out.

I throw the car into park, open the door, and step out. The police officer warns me not to come any closer. He stops Giorgio from going past him. A discussion ensues between them and then an understanding. The officer lets him by, and Giorgio rushes to me. I still don't know what's happened, but I sense something terrible, and I immediately sense the anguish, misery, and suffering pouring from Giorgio. His pain vibrates right to me.

"Giorgio, what is it?" I say, searching his eyes. But they're locked, keeping me out, held captive in a state of fear and shock, stuck in their last expression from what they saw. What did he see? "It's okay. I'm here."

An earthy, feral sound escapes his lips and forms a cry. "She's—gone." I wait for him to go on. A tear falls from his left eye and rolls down his cheek. "I was too late. Too late."

"Take your time," I say. "Tell me what happened."

"They were there," he says.

"Who was there?"

"The door was open." He covers his mouth with his hand and stares at the open space between us, like he's there again, reliving the horror he witnessed. His eyes dart in all directions. "I went inside and there was blood—everywhere." His face contorts in pain, and he lets out a silent, desperate moan. "I looked for her but . . . I knew before I saw her—" He gasps. "Oh God! They killed her!"

People who gathered near the road sign snap their heads in our direction. Oh my God. Camilla.

"No!" I yell. "Not Camilla!" I pull Giorgio to me. He sobs into my shoulder.

CHAPTER TWENTY-TWO

I burst into tears and press my lips to contain my vomit. We stay like that for a couple minutes.

I lift my head and, in my peripheral vision, I see something, a car like the one that followed me. It stops and then slows as it passes us. I watch it go by, but the glare on the window conceals the driver.

"Get in the car," I say.

Giorgio opens the passenger door and slides in. "I don't know what to do," he says, distraught.

"Did you see anyone coming from your house? Anyone suspicious?"

"No, nothing. I wasn't paying attention until I saw a car—a white Fiat."

My stomach sinks. Was it the car following closely behind me?

"Did you see where it went? Did you see the driver?" I ask.

"No, it was too fast, too hard to see," he says, glancing at the flowers on the dashboard. "Why are you driving Sal's car? Were you coming by?"

"Giorgio, when you said, 'They were here,' what did you mean? Who was here?"

He comes close to my ear and whispers, "'Ndrangheta."

"How do you know?"

"I know," he says. "It's payback."

This makes my skin crawl. I know he's insinuating that Sal is somehow involved in the attack on Camilla.

"No," I say.

"Iz, it's the truth, trust me. This was payback for letting you stay with us, and for all the scandalous things Sal is convinced happened between us. I feel it. Sal's involved. You shouldn't go home."

"I have nowhere else to go."

"Anna's," he said. "Go to Anna's." He straightens up.

"I can't go to Anna's," I say, "She won't speak to me. I'm not going to burden you right now with why. I have to go home, Giorgio. I'll be fine."

"Keep a knife nearby," he says, "to protect yourself."

"I will, but I'm not going anywhere right now. I'll wait here with you."

"I need to go back with the police, but they won't let you go past that." He points to the line of cars. "You shouldn't be here," he says.

I hug him again. "I'm so sorry." I don't know what else to say.

Giorgio gets out of my car and walks toward the police officer, his body slumped, defeated. I pull out and speed away, my eyes hardly leaving the mirrors, watching for evidence of the white Fiat. I regret leaving Giorgio alone to deal with what has happened to Camilla.

What happened to you, Camilla?

Had Giorgio's connection to La Stampa and his recent run-in with the mafia put them in danger again? Or was Sal somehow connected to it like Giorgio believes?

On the drive home, I recall a conversation between Anna and me. She'd asked me not to repeat what Giuseppe had heard about Luca recently, that he'd been hearing Luca's name come up in several circles, and not in a good way.

It had taken a while to get her to explain what she meant by circles, but finally she spat it out: circles known for crime.

"The mafia?" I said. "There is obviously some mistake."

Then I asked her if she believed any of it and she replied, "Do we really know what our kids or our husbands do when they leave the house?" We didn't speak for a few minutes but then she said, "You need to start asking the right questions—be more vigilant, watchful, prepared."

"Prepared for what?"

"There's always been something I can't quite grasp about Sal. And you still don't know what happened to the Russos. I think Sal knows. You should ask him. We need to start taking things into our own hands. Get some control back. Who knows what we might find."

That's exactly what I'm doing. For all the unanswered questions. For Luca and Franco; for Julia Bernardi and Gia Lovallo; for Giorgio, Camilla, and for me.

CHAPTER TWENTY-THREE

My thoughts are mangled branches after a storm, broken and bent yet tightly woven together. An unruly debate takes place inside my head, prosecuting, defending, examining proof, and determining truth. Twisted and incomprehensible. I can't begin to imagine how to straighten it all out.

Franco enters, breaking my trance. He says hello and gives me a strange look. I expect Luca to follow, but he doesn't.

"Where's your brother?"

"Back there," Franco says, thumbing behind him toward the road. "Got stuck talking to someone."

"Who?"

"Some girl from school."

My heart flips. I poke my head out the front door, but I don't see him. I turn to Franco. "Do you know who she is?"

"No idea," he says. "Seems nice though. Luca's type—pretty."

Brianna?

I'm fidgety and nervous thinking of Luca possibly bothering Brianna or asking her about whatever it was he thinks she took of his. Or threatening her. "Franco, could you please go get your brother and tell him I need to see him right away?"

Franco gives me a look.

"Now!" I yell.

"Okay, Mamá!" He's agitated but stops what he's doing and heads outside to get Luca.

About five minutes later he and Luca return. Luca runs past me to the stairs.

"Luca!" I yell.

He stops mid-step.

"Slow down. What's the rush? Come sit for a minute."

His eyes dart to the top of the stairs and back like he's contemplating or needs to get to something. Then he hangs his head, disappointed, and joins Franco and me at the table.

"Would you like a snack?" I say, pointing to the fresh-baked cookies I'd placed on the table.

He shakes his head.

"How was your day?"

"Fine."

I place a hand on each of theirs and look first at Franco and then at Luca. The words turn in my mind, the ones I'll use to tell them about Camilla. How will I put something so terrible into the right words?

"I have something to tell you both." My eyes jump back and forth between them. "Something very bad has happened." Again. Their anxious faces wait for me to go on. I explain that I'd gone to take flowers to Giorgio and Camilla as a gesture of thanks for letting me stay with them. I briefly describe that the road was blocked and police officers were everywhere, but Giorgio spotted me and came to tell me about Camilla, that she'd been shot and killed. I hardly get the words out before I break down and cry.

Franco's and Luca's faces turn white. They rush to me and wrap their arms around me. Luca whispers, "What about Max? Does he know?"

"Yes, Giorgio is probably with him by now."

"This is terrible, Mamá," Franco says, distraught. "Do they know who did it?"

"Not yet, but they will find out," I say.

"They haven't even found the person who killed Julia and Gia," Luca says. "They'll never catch this guy."

CHAPTER TWENTY-THREE

"They'll catch him," I say. "Sometimes it takes a long time to gather all the evidence."

"Why didn't they have a candlelight service for Gia, like they did for Julia?" Franco asks.

"Gia's parents are overwhelmed. They don't know a lot of people, having only moved here a year ago. If there is anything for Gia it will probably be small and simple with immediate family," I say. "At least that's what I've heard."

I notice Luca's expression change, a slight pop in his eyes like he's suddenly afraid or he's got an idea.

"Did you want to say something, Luca? You look like you have something on your mind. I'm sure you're worried about Max or are perhaps afraid because of what has happened to his mamá? It's normal to be afraid."

"I'm not afraid," Luca says.

"You're—you're not?"

"No." He looks at Franco and me. "People who get hurt easily need to be more careful. I'm always careful, so I'm not afraid of getting hurt."

I squint at Luca. I'm sure he meant it to come out differently, but his response seems calloused, and I don't like it. "Sometimes it doesn't matter how careful you are. Bad things just happen. You can try to make good choices and be aware of your surroundings, but if someone has evil intentions toward you, you might not know until it's too late."

"Because they've probably been watching you for a while," he says.

"What do you mean?"

"Nothing specifically," he continues, "but doesn't that make sense?" He faces Franco. "Don't you think that makes sense, Franco?"

"Yes, when you put it that way, I guess," Franco says. "I've never really given it any thought until now."

"I want you both to be careful wherever you are, whomever you're with, do you understand me?" I say. "And look out for each other."

They both agree and then head in separate directions, Franco to the plantation and Luca to his room.

I step outside for a private word with Franco. He's already halfway to the plantation. I run until we're walking in step.

"Franco, can I ask you a question?"

"Another talk, Mamá?"

"No, just something quick. Stop walking for a second; I won't keep you long."

Franco stops walking and waits.

"Through your eyes, I want you to tell me if you think Luca is okay."

"Okay?"

"Yes. You're his brother; you would know if he's okay or not, right? I see things from the perspective of his mamá, and that's not always accurate."

"He's okay, I guess. Just been a little moody lately. He doesn't tell me anything, Mamá. He keeps to himself more."

"That's what I thought," I say. "I know you have a lot going on right now, too, but I really need your help keeping an eye on Luca. Stop in his room and say hi later. Make a connection with him so he knows you're there for him. I worry about both of you, but I know you'll be okay, Franco. I am confident in that. I don't have the same confidence about Luca, do you understand?" Franco nods. "Luca needs someone who is not his mamá to look after him when I can't. Do you think you can do that as his big brother? It would make me feel a lot better."

"Yes, Mamá."

But I sense a reluctant tone in his voice.

When I return inside, I perceive that something is off. Just watch him. I bolt up the stairs fast and light, slowing to a walk at the top. I tiptoe to Luca's door, which is closed almost all the way. He's rummaging through something, but I can't see what it is.

I stare through the small space in the doorway, preparing to jump out of the way if he comes toward the door. My mind frantically races for reasons as to why I was just about to knock on his door.

For a moment, I lose sight of him, but it's only because he's squatting down near his bed. The top of his head is all I see. He might be looking for something on the floor or under his bed. I remember the strange floorboard I hadn't gotten back to. He's been crawling around in that one area for a few

CHAPTER TWENTY-THREE

minutes. What is he looking for?

His head pops up as if he senses he's being watched. My heart drums wildly in my chest. Slowly he stands and approaches the door. I sprint to my room, closing the door halfway.

While I'm standing slightly behind my door, I peek into the hallway to see if he's left his room. Not more than a minute later, he does leave, closing the door behind him with a quick check of the knob to ensure it's latched. I listen as his footsteps fade, and the front door screeches open and slams.

Then I leave my room and head to his.

Giorgio's words of caution ring loudly in my mind as I enter Luca's room. Just watch him. See what he does. Where he goes. If there is ever a time to heed Giorgio's warning, now is that time.

Luca's room is dark when I walk in. It's strange that he'd close his curtains in the middle of the day. When I pull them back, I notice the window is open a crack. This time it's a pencil keeping it from closing completely, much less noticeable than a book. Unless you're me and you're looking for it.

A quick scan of his room reveals an unusually messy desk of homework papers, books, and an old water glass. I walk past his partially open school bag sitting on his desk chair, but that's not what I'm here for. A quick check in his closet turns up nothing unusual, but that's not where my concern lies most. Watch what he does. Having watched Luca a few minutes ago, he spent quite a bit of time near his bed—near the floor of his bed. So I do the same.

I lift his pillow and look under the covers. Nothing is amiss. Then I squat low near the bed and observe what I can at that level. Finally, I get on my hands and knees and lower myself to the floor to look under the bed. It's hard to see with the small amount of light coming from the window.

But something does catch my eye. I stretch my arm to the spot where I remember seeing something before. Something was odd about one of the wooden planks under Luca's bed. My finger grazes a sharp, jagged piece of wood, and I pull it back at the quick flash of pain. But then I go back because now I've found it. The edge of one plank feels like it's raised slightly higher than the others.

I push the bed out of the way so I can see that partially warped, possibly loose floor plank. I try to lift the jagged edge with my finger, but I can't get a good grasp of it. I tap along the plank and, when I do, something odd happens. When I press on one end, the other end with the jagged edge pops up.

I grab hold of the popped end and pull straight up. It comes away easily, and so does the plank lying next to it. Two planks that weren't nailed down like the rest. A burst of cold air rises to my nose from the dark space below. When I lean closer, something takes my breath away. Something I'm not prepared for.

CHAPTER TWENTY-FOUR

I reach in with both hands, scooping gently beneath, grasping carefully, and pulling straight up. I set it on the floor beside me and peer again into the secret shelter, making sure there's nothing else. I don't know what to make of it: an old, handcrafted, wooden jewelry box with a cross beautifully sculpted into the top. A silver hook clasp fastens it closed. My mother had a jewelry box like this and kept it on her dresser.

When I release the clasp and open the lid, a sulfuric, mildewy smell rises from it, and I cough. Residing in the box are a few odd objects, and I'm curious of their connection and why he keeps them here. One by one I take them out and examine them closely. A small gold ring with a frosted pearl; an old shoelace with frayed ends mixed in a handful of stones and crumbs of dirt; and a barrette with blue sapphires along its length.

A rush of anxiety flies through me like a swarm of bees as I hold the sapphire barrette in the palm of my hand. I shake my head at the thought of her. But there it is, plain as the day I saw it in her hair. The same day I thought, Finally, some nice friends for a change. My heart leaped at the sight of both of my boys happy with their new friends, especially this new friend with the pretty smile. I noticed her long black hair pulled back on one side, tucked behind a beautiful sapphire barrette. It must have been a gift, I'd thought. No, it can't be hers.

All at once, the air escapes my lungs. A broken, raspy moan exits my mouth. Nooooo. This can't belong to Gia.

Quickly I realize I'm no longer aware of my surroundings. I straighten myself and glance around the room.

The trembling in my hands spreads to my whole body. I put everything back into place as best I can. For a second I consider keeping the barrette. I could hide it. Or discard it. But then Luca would know I'm on to him. I place the barrette back inside the jewelry box with the other items, close the lid, fasten the clasp, and put it back inside its cave. I slide the planks on top and move the bed back to its original position.

I jump to my feet, brush my hands against my pants to remove excess dirt, and glance into the hallway. When I'm confident no one is there, I run to the bathroom and vomit into the toilet. Then I sit on the edge of the tub and cry. I have to get it out in order to compose myself in front of my family. I have to think clearly about what to do about this.

When I return to the kitchen, I observe the boys through the window, working together in the yard. Franco is on the top rung of the ladder, plucking the citrus, handing each one to Luca, conversing with one another as they work. Such a normal scene. No one would think anything different.

Perhaps this is the moment Franco will check in with Luca. Would Luca tell Franco what he has under his floorboards? Maybe Franco's known since the beginning and they've both been playing me. What if they're in it together? No, don't think like that. They're good boys; you know it.

My mind sifts through the details and rationalizes what I saw. The barrette could have belonged to anyone. Gia couldn't have been the only one who had a barrette like that. Luca might have found it in the yard or at school, and, because he liked it so much, he kept it.

Even if it was Gia's, it's possible it fell out of her hair the day she was here, and Luca found it with the intention of giving it back to her. But then, of course, he couldn't give it back because she disappeared, so he kept it to remind him of her.

Peter might have known Luca had the barrette and he might have demanded it from Luca. And Luca, being angry and jealous that Gia was with Peter, decided to keep it out of spite.

Regardless of the reason, the fact remains that Luca has a barrette that Gia wore in her hair the last time we saw her, right before she went missing.

CHAPTER TWENTY-FOUR

And the realization that I need to confront him about this sits like a heavy brick in my stomach. I wish I could sink into the earth with it.

I glance out the window again to see Franco has the ladder hoisted over his shoulder, and Luca is adding the last of the citrus to the barrel. A plump barrel of bergamot heads each row of trees. Franco and Luca must have finished the last row faster than I realized, and now they're heading to the shed. The shed.

I should stop them before they see something they're not prepared for. Or I should wait to see if they have a key to get in. I wait and I follow them. When they get to the shed door, they fiddle with the lock and enter with ease. They have a key. But of course they do if they want access to the tools Sal keeps on the unfinished side of the shed. Where someone was hiding. Or kept there. Likely the same person who lost the shoe I now have in my possession.

Another thought interferes: do they know about the person who was in the shed? Did they put her there?

Franco and Luca exit the shed a few minutes later, just enough time to return the tools to their positions and walk out. Not a minute longer to do anything else. They're talking to each other, smiling, sharing an occasional chuckle as they leave. No sign of having smelled something foul as I had the other day. Franco locks the door and drops the key in his pocket.

I retreat to the house so I'm not seen and sit in one of the porch chairs like I sometimes do. I grab the book on the side table and pretend to read. I expect Franco and Luca to arrive only moments later, but they don't. I stand at the porch railing and squint toward the plantation. They've stopped walking and they're facing each other, engaged in what appears to be a serious conversation. Speaking closely, probably not much above a whisper. About what?

Their heads turn at Giorgio's car pulling into the driveway. I insisted Max stay here while Giorgio takes care of funeral arrangements for Camilla. Time escaped fast between the floorboards and now. Max heads in the direction of Franco and Luca; Giorgio comes to the porch.

He's visibly distraught, eyes drawn low at the corners, wrinkled at the edges. His skin is ashen and his hair disheveled, like he's slept in his clothes for a week. He hugs me tightly and still holds firmly even when I let go. I wrap my arms around him again. As soon as he buries his head in my neck, his shoulders begin to shake, and my heart fills with sadness.

He loosens his hold on me and steps back, his face wet and red. "I keep seeing her," he says, "I can't get that image out of my head. She was by the door, she was trying to get away, blood was—" His hand flies to his mouth. "They covered her up on that gurney. I wanted to see her again, just one last time, but they wouldn't let me. Why wouldn't they let me?"

"I'm so sorry, Giorgio."

"I always tried to keep her safe." He glances at the boys still talking near the trees. "Max is devastated. I can't even look at him sometimes—see the emptiness in his eyes. Who would do this?" He raises his eyes to the sky. "I should have protected them more."

"This isn't your fault," I say. "You can't be everywhere at all times. You were a good husband, Giorgio—the best. Camilla knew that. Don't doubt yourself for a second." I stare into his eyes. "She was lucky to be married to you." Heaviness tugs at my heart.

"I should have known it would come to this." Something blazes in his eyes when he says this. "I should have known Sal would be our demise."

I can't pretend not to think this too. I've worried about it for years since that brief moment—indiscretion—with Giorgio, and then when I escaped Sal's grasp and chose Giorgio's for protection. Sal has always been jealous of Giorgio.

Fleeing to Giorgio's was a natural response for me. He represents everything in life that is good, normal, and peaceful. His presence calms me and always has. He's been a safe place for me since we were kids. A kindred soul. The only one who truly understands me, truly knows who I am.

I can't deny the ugly weight in my stomach, the harrowing thoughts in my mind that I believe we both share. Neither one of us wants to say it, that Sal had something to do with Camilla's murder. And because I went to them for protection, I'm the one who brought this to their family. I'm disgusted with myself, with my selfishness.

CHAPTER TWENTY-FOUR

I back away from Giorgio. "This is my fault. If I hadn't—"

"Stop." Giorgio's face is sincere, serious. "You and I both know this is Sal's doing. He probably wants you to think it's because of you so you'll feel guilty and remorseful and you won't leave him." Giorgio reaches for my arm. "He has never liked me or our family."

The boys approach us, and Giorgio waves at Franco and Luca and gives Max a hug. Then he turns to me and hugs me. "Thank you for keeping Max here. It will be good for him."

"Of course," I say.

Giorgio gets in his car and gives one last look before he drives off to plan his wife's funeral.

* * *

While Luca and Max work together on their science project, I begin knitting one of two blankets I plan to give to each of Julia's and Gia's families. The blankets will be a small token of care and compassion in hopes of providing comfort during this sad time in their lives. I wrap a piece of yarn around one needle and feed it through the loop on the other while keeping an ear on Luca's and Max's conversation.

I stop midway at the next purl stitch and listen as Luca goes to answer the door. When I identify one of the voices as Carlos, I place my knitting on the sofa and join Luca at the door. Both Jonathan and Carlos are standing in the doorway.

"Hello, boys," I say. I glance at Luca. "Probably not a good time."

"They're here to work on the project with us," Luca says.

It irritates me immediately. As Carlos and Jonathan walk to the kitchen, I pull Luca aside. "They can stay for one hour and then they have to leave. This is a difficult time for Max, understand?"

Luca nods and then joins the others.

About fifteen minutes later, Luca retreats upstairs. I have half a mind to follow him to make sure he's only using the bathroom and not going to the floorboards under his bed, but instead I seize the opportunity to talk to his friends in his absence.

I take a glass from the cupboard and fill it at the sink. "It's so nice of you to come over and work on this project together."

"No problem, Signora Perri," Jonathan says.

"How are things at school? With all that's happened, I mean?"

Max keeps his head down as he works.

"It's fine," Carlos says. "Not a lot of kids knew Julia as much as Gia."

"Everyone knew Gia," Jonathan adds.

"You mean because she was so sweet?" I say.

Carlos and Jonathan exchange glances.

"Luca was in love with her," Jonathan says.

Max's head pops up.

"No, he wasn't," Carlos says defensively.

Max shoots Jonathan a warning look.

I watch the stairs for Luca.

"Have either of you heard anything about Peter or how he's doing?" I say. "Such a sweet boy."

Another glance between Carlos and Jonathan.

"Peter can be a little . . . intense," Jonathan says.

"Intense? That surprises me. Why do you say that?" I ask.

"He's got a temper," Carlos adds.

"You don't want to get on his bad side," Jonathan says, "kind of like Luca."

"What do you mean?" I try to keep my voice calm.

"Luca and Peter are not a good mix," Carlos says.

Max looks up again. "They hated each other because of Gia."

I'm surprised to hear anything come from Max. "Why?"

"The whole thing got confusing," Jonathan says. "No one knows the whole story, but Peter called Carlos to come over because Luca was—" Jonathan stops. His eyes dart to Carlos and then to the kitchen doorway.

CHAPTER TWENTY-FOUR

We follow his stare, which ends at Luca. How long has he been standing there?

"Luca was what?" Luca says. "Go on, finish it."

"Luca," I turn to him, "we were just catching up a bit while they waited for you."

"Catching up about me?"

Carlos starts to talk but I interrupt. "You probably heard Carlos ask what was taking you so long. Are you okay?"

"I'm fine," he says, looking like he believes me, "and now I'm back."

My blood boils at his dismissive tone. "Good. So now you can get back to work before your time runs out." I glance at the clock purposely, a reminder to Luca of the hour I gave him and an acknowledgement that I have the final say, not him.

CHAPTER TWENTY-FIVE

I crawl into bed exhausted. Every part of my body, even my skin, is heavy and lethargic. The soft, cottony pillow cradles my head, and for a moment I'm in the clouds. A gentle breeze from my window caresses my skin, lulling me to sleep. But as much as my body wants to float to the sky, my mind is tethered to the ground, imprisoned by thoughts of the present and a growing obsession to know what happened between Luca and Peter. I'm convinced that understanding what happened between them might unlock the truth of what happened to Gia.

I don't know what to think about that barrette. It was definitely the one I saw in Gia's hair. After finding it in Luca's hiding spot under his bed, I can't get it out of my mind. The more I think about it, the more I realize Gia didn't have just one; she had two barrettes in her hair, one above the other. So much sparkling blue in that one area, and that's why it caught my eye.

It's possible that Luca might have had a crush on Gia. If Gia was more interested in Peter than Luca, it probably hurt Luca quite a bit. And Luca's pain comes out in anger. It's not unusual for adolescent boys to fight over girls. Luca and Peter might have gotten into a small scuffle, and it could have gotten out of hand. Perhaps Gia tried to break them up, and in the process one of her barrettes fell to the floor. Maybe that's when Luca found Gia's barrette and decided to keep it—not to protect Peter, as I had once thought, but to use it against him.

A terrible thought intrudes, and I don't push it away. What if both barrettes

CHAPTER TWENTY-FIVE

had fallen out of Gia's hair and Luca kept only one? What had he done with the other one? If he'd kept one for himself, he could have given the other to the police. Not directly, but somehow make them find it—an anonymous call or a note. Or maybe he slipped it into Peter's belongings and alerted the police to it. Was that the evidence the police said they'd received which resulted in Peter's arrest?

My head begins to throb. Why am I thinking these terrible thoughts about my son? Of course he wouldn't do something like that. I get out of bed, thankful Sal isn't home yet. I take my medicine and follow it with the glass of water on my table, then I go to the window. The shadows stand bold against the moon's light. I must be the only one awake on this road.

The sweet smell of citrus floats through the window. I glance in the direction of the shed. My skin prickles at the dark monstrosity its shadow projects. The truth about the shoe lies inside.

An unusual noise, like a thud, pulls me from the window. It's in the house, in the hallway. Luca? He should be asleep. I peek into the hallway and, when I see that it's clear, I head in the direction from where I think it came: Luca's room. I open his door about two inches and see him lying in his bed, his head visible on his pillow.

As I begin to pull his door closed, I hear the sound again. A thud, and then another, only this time whatever made that noise now hits the window, causing Luca to stir. Is someone trying to get his attention?

Luca opens his eyes and then sits up and looks toward the window. His eyes brighten, and I witness his excitement and acknowledgement of what's outside his window. He jumps out of bed, gets to the window, and makes some kind of motion with his hands. He's communicating with someone outside. He throws on the shirt and pants he had lying at the end of his bed, slides into his shoes, and jumps to the window again.

I don't stop him.

Just before he climbs out, he checks over his shoulder. My heart races as I press myself against the wall. Luca swipes something from his desk, then he's out the window before it slides down to the pencil and stops. He's gone.

I fly down the stairs two at a time because I don't want to lose sight of him or where he's going. I'm doing as Giorgio said: I'm watching him.

I grab my shoes and jacket and slip out the front door, praying I'll catch a glimpse of him before he's gone. And I do. The moon is on my side tonight, shimmering through the leaves, giving just enough light to see his shadow as I catch my breath on the side of the house. Their shadows. There's two of them.

I follow the sound of their feet in the crunchy grass, staying behind enough but not too much. My nose is runny and my fingers are cold, my warm breath clings to the chilled air. I can make out Luca running toward someone who waits for him in the shrubs.

I get to the Fiat and tuck myself behind, hoping to blend into the shadows. Luca breaks into a run toward the plantation, running between the rows. He's hard to follow, running in a zigzag pattern as if he knows he's being followed. Whoever he's with must be ahead of him. They're easily gaining speed, and the distance widens between us. I'm running faster than I've ever run in my life, and it feels like my heart is going to explode. I can't lose sight of him.

Where the plantation ends, there's a private road that connects to a neighborhood. I remember walking with Franco and Luca when they were younger through the plantation to visit a friend who lives in that neighborhood. The sweet smell of citrus flashes me back to that simpler time. It's also a shortcut I'd sometimes take to see Anna. And it's not far from where Julia Bernardi lived.

My lips and mouth are dry, as is my throat. I stifle a cough that's been tickling my lungs. I need to take a break and catch my breath. All at once, Luca stops running, but my feet continue. It takes all I can to abruptly slow my speed. I jump aside and duck behind a tree just as Luca turns around.

When I crane my neck around the tree, it appears that Luca is talking with the person he followed. Whoever it is, they're slightly taller than Luca, almost the same height difference as Luca and Franco. Franco. No, Franco is in his room asleep. Except I didn't look in his room before I ran down the stairs. I was too afraid I'd lose Luca.

A misty fog begins to settle, making visibility even more difficult. I know

CHAPTER TWENTY-FIVE

we're at the end of the plantation when I hear the clinking of the lock on the gate. Then the gate closes, but they don't lock it, probably for a fast, seamless return home. An occasional streetlight cuts through the fog, illuminating their path. Luca runs swiftly and confidently like a cheetah. He knows where he's going. He's done this before. He slows to a jog and then to a walk. He's headed straight toward one of the houses.

He cuts across the grass in the front yard. What is he doing? As I follow, I pray no one sees either of us. Now we're both trespassing; now we've crossed a line and there's no going back. What kind of mother runs through yards in the middle of the night? Probably only those whose children like to flirt with danger. I stand a few yards behind my son, a traitor to all the mothers in the world.

Luca snaps his head toward his accomplice and nods and then they continue in opposite directions. His accomplice goes left toward an adjoining neighborhood and Luca goes right, continuing through this neighborhood. I follow him as he cuts through one yard to the next. Eventually he stops and stands directly in front of one particular house, all dark except for a blinking front porch light.

He appears contemplative the way he stands, feet apart, hands at his sides, a slight tilt of his head. Is he waiting for someone? About a minute or two later, he walks around the house to the left and enters the backyard.

Now Luca's standing a few feet from one of the bedroom windows. He begins to pace back and forth in front of it. Then he faces the window again and moves slowly, sauntering closer and closer to it until he's just inches away, like a predator preparing to pounce on its prey. My skin crawls as I watch him.

I'm panic-stricken. What's he going to do? Why is he here? I don't know whether to call out his name, turn around and run, or go to the door and alert the owners. My eyes dart from Luca to the grass to the trees to the stony path beneath my feet. I pick up a good-sized stone near my foot and raise it above my head.

CHAPTER TWENTY-SIX

Nausea sweeps through me as the stone exits my hand. The realization of what I'm doing—what my son is doing—overwhelms me.

The stone doesn't even come close. Luca reaches for the window. This time, I'm more committed. I pick up another rock, fixing my aim and throwing it much harder than the first one. It misses him again but falls to the grass next to his foot, diverting his gaze. He returns his attention to the window, both hands now braced against the edges of the window frame. He's going to go inside. Why?

I have to do something. I pick up a handful of stones and hurl them at him one at a time in quick succession. I'm not sure which one hits him, but I hear its soft impact on his jacket. Luca turns around and our eyes lock. He faces me, jaw dropped, motionless, like he's trying to make sense of who he's looking at.

I take one step forward beneath the moonlight, shaking. My heart sinks. "Stop, Luca." My voice quivers and catches. "Whatever you're about to do, don't. Whatever you've been doing, for God's sake, just stop."

Luca remains still, his face darkened by the house's shadow, but I can tell by the way he's standing that he's scared. Slowly he turns his head and looks over his shoulder at the house, then back at me.

And then Luca runs into the woods.

"Luca, wait!" My voice echoes in the night.

CHAPTER TWENTY-SIX

I run after him, but he's got a big lead on me, and it's too hard to see him through the trees. Which way did he go? If I follow him into the woods, I'll risk getting lost. To be safe, I choose to head back in the direction I came. It's possible Luca will try to sneak back in through his window and pretend he never left, unaware that I'd seen him go. Or he might hide in the plantation until morning so he doesn't have to face me.

On my way back, I stop again at the house where Luca almost entered, recalling the vision of him standing at the window, preparing to go inside. What would have happened if I hadn't followed him, if I hadn't distracted him, pulled his attention from the window?

When I finally arrive home, I realize the front door is locked and I hadn't taken a key with me. I glance at the open window next to the door and see Sal standing there, arms crossed at his chest.

He lifts his arms. "What are you doing?"

"Just open the door, Sal. I'll explain when I come in."

"You can explain from there," he says.

My tired body wants to fall to the ground, but rage rises inside me. I pound my fists hard against the door. "Open this door!" I yell. When he doesn't, I take my fists to the window, knowing how worried he is about his precious windows breaking. They rattle with each pounding.

The door swings open fast. "Get in here," he says, grabbing my arm.

I yank it free and move away. The warmth of the house engulfs my cold body.

Sal's face is contorted. The last time I saw his face like that was right before his hands wrapped around my neck. I throw my hand up "Stop! I need to tell you something urgent!"

He takes a step toward me.

"It's Luca!" I yell.

He stops. "What about Luca?" he growls.

"Have you seen him? Has he come back?" Desperation leaks from my voice.

"What do you mean 'back'? He's in bed, asleep!"

"He's not in his bed, Papá," Franco says from the top of the stairs.

"Yes, he is," Sal says. "Mind your own business. Go to bed."

Franco doesn't budge.

I face Sal. "Did you think to look in his bedroom?"

"Watch your tone," he warns.

"We don't have time for this," I say. "Luca left again, and this time I followed him."

"You did what?"

"I wanted to see where he goes when he leaves in the middle of the night. I followed him, and I'm glad I did. He went to the neighborhood behind the plantation. He went to someone's house."

Sal's eyes widen but he doesn't interrupt.

"Do you know what he was about to do? He was about to open a window."

Franco comes down the stairs as I'm talking.

I look at him. "Where have you been?"

He furrows his brow. "In bed."

"Are you sure? You weren't with Luca?"

"How could I be with Luca if I'm here now?"

"Luca was with someone else, and at some point they separated." I study Franco for a minute, size him up; it could have been him. "You could have gotten back here before Luca easily. Are you in this together?"

Franco's jaw drops, appalled.

"All right, that's enough," Sal snaps. "How much medicine did you take tonight?"

I keep my eyes on Franco and ignore Sal. "Did you know what Luca was doing?"

"No," he says. "I don't know anything about this." Franco looks sincere, hurt even, but I'm just not sure anymore.

Sal's face is all screwed up again. He comes in close to me. "You're telling me you went through the plantation and all the way to the next neighborhood in the middle of the night by yourself?"

"Yes. I had to know where Luca was going."

Sal shakes his head, but I'm not sure if it's at me or at Luca.

"Did you know about this? Did you know he was going to that house?" I

CHAPTER TWENTY-SIX

ask Sal.

"Of course not. Don't be stupid," he says with a look of contempt. "Did Luca see you while you were spying on him?"

"I got his attention in time before he could open the window. He saw me and then ran into the woods."

"What the hell? So you just left him there and came home? You didn't go after him? He's probably lost now. Good job."

"Luca knows those woods better than either of us. He has no problem leaving the house to traipse around in the middle of the night, so I wouldn't say I left him there."

I'm surprised at myself, and so is Sal. He seems stuck, like he doesn't know what to say.

"I did go after him at first, but he was too fast, and I lost him. I was hoping he came home."

I turn to the stairs and race to the top. Sal and Franco follow me. I open Luca's door, praying to find him in bed pretending to be asleep, but he's not there. I glance at Sal. "What do we do?"

Sal looks at Franco and me and then goes downstairs without saying a word. We run after him.

"Where are you going?" I say.

"To get my son!" he yells in my face, then slams the door.

I'm shaking, frantic, like I'm losing my mind. I put water in the tea kettle and sit at the table with Franco. For the next two hours, we take turns checking in Luca's room to see if he's finally returned.

Finally, Sal walks in alone, and my heart breaks. He joins us at the table, and we wait in silence.

Sal opens the folded newspaper sitting in the middle of the table. He flips through the pages, but I can tell he isn't reading anything, which makes me think he's actually worried.

Suddenly, Franco's eyes dart to the door and Luca walks in.

Sal pushes back from the table. "Where the hell have you been? Your mother was worried to death about you!"

"I'm sorry, Mamá." Luca's eyes graze me briefly.

Sal cocks his head. "What kind of man has his mother follow him in the middle of the night?" Sal's reaction is confusing. Is he upset for me or embarrassed by Luca?

Luca glances at Franco.

Sal bangs his fist on the table. "Look at me when I'm talking to you! And speak when you're spoken to!"

Luca's eyes dart to me.

"Don't look at her; look at me."

Luca shifts from one foot to the other. His expression is hard to read. He opens his mouth and pauses. "I don't know," he sighs.

"You don't know," Sal mocks. "You better know."

I turn to Luca. "Why did you go to that house, Luca?" Sal glares at me for interfering, but I don't care. "What were you going to do?" I say.

"He'll answer me first," Sal says.

"Who lives there?" I say.

"Damn you," Sal says to me. His fists clench at his sides.

"Papá!" Franco yells.

Sal snaps his head at Franco.

"Stop, Papá!" Luca screams. "It's just a girl from my class!"

All eyes jump to Luca.

"Don't lie," Sal says.

Luca stares at me. "I wasn't going to harm her. I—I just wanted to . . . see her. She—she knew I was coming over."

"She knew you were coming over?" I say. "Are you sure about that? At that hour? Her parents couldn't have known."

Sal faces me. "You blew things out of proportion!"

I ignore Sal completely, which I know makes him angrier. "Luca," I say, "I want to believe you. I do, but—"

"Enough!" Sal's temples bulge. "Apologize to your mother for scaring her and tell her you won't do it again."

"Not yet," I say, and they all look at me bug-eyed. "I need to ask Luca about something first." I head to the stairs.

"Where you going?" Sal shouts.

CHAPTER TWENTY-SIX

"Mamá, wait!" Luca runs after me. He follows me to his room and watches as I shove his bed aside. "What are you doing?" His voice is high.

Franco and Sal appear in the doorway.

I squat to the floor, yank the two floor boards out of place, and put them aside. I dig my hands into the tight space and retrieve the jewelry box.

"What the hell is she doing?" Sal says.

Luca steps forward. "No, stop," he says.

I open the jewelry box and reach inside for the barrette, but it's not in there. I turn the jewelry box over and dump out the contents. Everything else is there except for the barrette. "Where is it, Luca?" I turn to Franco. "Franco?"

"What's she talking about?" Sal says.

"Tell him, Luca," I say.

"I asked you a question." Sal's voice deepens.

Luca hesitates. I see the wheels start to spin. "I don't know what she's talking about," he says. He's denying it. Lying right to our faces.

"Stop lying, Luca. The sapphire barrette," I say. "Gia was wearing one exactly like it in her hair when I met her. I found it in this jewelry box you've been hiding, and now it's gone. Where did you put it? Why are you hiding things?" I jump to my feet and start rummaging through his drawers, looking in his closet, taking his room apart bit by bit.

"Were you snooping around his room?" Sal says.

"Any mother who is worried about her child would do the same. I noticed something odd under his bed when I was cleaning the other day. The floorboard is raised a little and loose. When I was examining it to see how loose it was, it came out." I run my hand over the dumped-out contents on the floor. "But I wasn't expecting what I found under the floor, especially the barrette. Why would he have these things hidden under his floor? Why would he have Gia's barrette? Do you know how this looks?"

"This is ridiculous!" Sal yells.

"Ask him," I say. "Ask him yourself why he had the barrette."

"For God's sake, woman!" Sal's face is crazed. His forehead wrinkled. He glares at Luca. "Do you have or have you ever had this barrette?"

"I found it," Luca blurts. "I mean Peter found it first and gave it to me. I was planning on giving it back to her, but then she—"

"So you were keeping it for Peter," Sal suggests.

"Y—yes," Luca says.

"When was the last time you saw Gia?" I ask.

"The night of the candlelight service when she came back to the house with our other friends."

"That's it?" I say.

"Yes," Luca says, and looks away.

"I remember the day I met Gia for the first time," I say. "She was very sweet and very pretty. We had a pleasant conversation. You and Franco walked her home after the service." I place my hands on my hips. "But that wasn't the last time you saw her, was it?"

Luca shook his head. "Yes, it was." He looks at Franco for support.

Franco's eyes drop to the floor.

"Come to think of it," Luca continues, "it might have been at Peter's party the next day."

"What party?" I say.

"Peter had a few friends over, including Gia, a day or two after the service," Franco says. "Luca wasn't invited, but he showed up anyway."

"Why?" I ask. "Why weren't you invited, and why did you show up?"

"I don't know," Luca says, which I know is a lie.

"Luca," I say, keeping my voice soft, "do you know where Peter is right now?"

"Yes."

"So you know, then, that he's in a juvenile detention center."

Luca nods.

"You probably also know that the only reason he's there and not in jail is because of his age. He's too young to go to jail—right now, anyway. Do you know why he's at the detention center?"

"Because they think he had something to do with Julia's and Gia's deaths."

"Murders," I correct. "Let's call them what they are. Because he was the last one to see Gia alive."

CHAPTER TWENTY-SIX

"Okay," he says.

"Okay," I parrot. "Did you also know that a witness saw you with Gia on the same day Peter was with her, and that was later in the day? The witness isn't clear about where or when, just that you were definitely there."

"What's your point, Isabella?" Sal says after a long silence.

"My point is," I walk right up to Luca, "Peter wasn't the last one to see Gia, was he?"

Luca's face flushes. "What—what do you mean?"

"You were upset that Peter liked Gia," I say. "You told him to stay away from her because you liked her too. Then you found out Gia went to Peter's house later that day, so you went there too."

"Where are you getting this?" Sal says.

"It was one of the girls from the neighborhood who heard Luca and Peter arguing. She knew who you both were, and she saw you punch Peter."

"Yes, I punched Peter!" Luca blurted. "I wanted to hurt him! But I never meant to hurt . . . Gia!"

"So it's true?" Sal swoops in front of me and puts his face within inches of Luca's. "You were there, too, with Peter?"

"Yes," Luca says, stepping back.

"How could you be so stupid?" Sal says. "Do you realize how lucky you are that no one but that girl saw you there? You could be in that detention center!"

I'm dumbfounded at Sal's reaction, like he's coaching Luca on how to stay under the radar. "Wait a minute," I say, stepping next to Sal. "Luca, you said you never meant to hurt Gia."

"Yes."

"Does that mean you did? Hurt her?"

Luca doesn't speak.

"Was there an accident?"

"It doesn't matter anymore," Sal says.

"It matters a lot," I say. "Luca, why were you in Anna's neighborhood when I found you? Were you going to the girl's house?—the one who knew you were with Gia?"

"Why would I do that?" he says.

I don't want to say it, but I do. "To . . . quiet her? Warn her not to say anything?"

"Isabella, you sound insane," Sal says.

"One more question for now, Luca," I say.

He tilts his head.

"That girl you went to see tonight . . . her name wouldn't happen to be Brianna, would it?"

All color drains from Luca's face. He's as white as a ghost.

"Enough!" Sal yells. "Luca, Franco, go to your rooms!"

They turn to go.

"Our boys need help!" I yell. "We are failing as parents!"

"No, you are failing as a parent—and as a wife. Don't think I don't know about you going to Giorgio's."

The air escapes my lungs. It was Sal who was involved in Camilla's murder. I won't discuss this in front of the boys, but I will bring it up again.

I face Luca and Franco, who stare at me, frozen, from the top step after Sal's accusation. Then I look directly at Sal. "If you're not going to help them, I'll do it myself. I don't need your permission."

Sal glances at Luca and Franco. "I said go." After they go, he turns his attention to me. "What did you just say to me?" His voice is a low, monotonous growl.

But something other than fear takes residence in my body, something unusual and exhilarating. I choose to stay silent and not defend myself. I have nothing to defend. Those are my boys, and I will always protect them from people like Sal.

I'll bet I know why he's reacting the way he is: he wants to protect Luca's secret. Whatever the specifics are, he's willing to protect his secret rather than teach Luca to do the right thing. It makes sense coming from Sal, who is full of secrets.

"I don't even know what to say to you right now," he says, pacing. "I don't know who you are anymore! You've lost yourself completely. I don't think there ever was a barrette."

CHAPTER TWENTY-SIX

What's interesting is his tone. It sounds powerless, a tad defeated, less pompous.

I don't engage. I'm confident in what I saw. I pick up my knitting needles and bag of yarn and take them with me to the living room, fully expecting Sal to come firing in, but he doesn't. I glimpse the doorway every few seconds, but even after an hour passes, he still doesn't enter the living room. Where has he gone?

Giving Sal time to cool down is good for both of us. But guilt about what I've discovered weighs me down, as does the decision about where to go from here. I can't stop thinking about Anna, Peter, and their family and what they are going through. Peter might be innocent. How do I reconcile knowing what I know? How do I protect my own son and at the same time do the right thing?

CHAPTER TWENTY-SEVEN

I rise early in the morning like always, brew coffee, make breakfast, and hand lunches to the boys as they head off to school. Sal already left for the marina hours ago. I'm crawling out of my skin with an overwhelming need to get back to Luca's room and to the jewelry box. I practically push Franco and Luca out the door.

I remove my apron, rest it over the back of a kitchen chair, and make for the stairs to Luca's room. I don't have to look very far; I see it as soon as I open his door. The barrette rests on top of a folded piece of paper in the middle of his bed, Mamá written on the front fold. A rush of dread flies through me. I pick up the barrette and open the note.

Mamá,

I am sorry to worry you so much. I know I give you trouble sometimes, but Papá is wrong—you haven't failed as a parent. I'm giving you Gia's barrette because I thought about what you always say about telling the truth. I found it the day she came over, but I didn't take it from her. It must have fallen out of her hair. And you were right, I went to that house last night to see the girl who heard me and Peter fighting. I wanted to find out if she was planning on telling the police when they talk to the neighbors again. I wouldn't have hurt that girl no matter what she said. I only wanted to talk to her, maybe to scare her so she wouldn't say anything. And not because I did anything wrong but only because it looks like I did. I'm sorry I lied to you.

CHAPTER TWENTY-SEVEN

Your son,
Luca

My heart softens at Luca's admission to taking the barrette and about going to the girl's house. I'm relieved, not because he lied but because he admitted to lying and apologized for it.

But a sick feeling returns, and I'm soon doubting him again as I recall a piece of paper I'd found in his school bag with Brianna's name written on it. Luca never confirmed if the girl he went to see was Brianna from his class. I can't help but wonder if it's possible that I was so close to uncovering a revelation even I don't want to face. Is the reason he wrote the note to cover for himself?

If he's being truthful, he did the right thing, but it doesn't excuse his behavior. He needs help, an intervention to steer him from these poor choices he continues to make. I've been blaming his friends this whole time. Although I don't trust his friends, especially Carlos, I know some of Luca's behavior comes from the time he spends with Sal.

I pull my address book from the kitchen drawer, flip to our doctor's number, and leave it open to that page. Perhaps Luca should see a doctor. But what exactly would I tell the doctor? Do I tell him about the barrette? Do I say Luca went to a girl's house last night to either warn her or keep her quiet about what she might know? That she overheard an argument between Luca and Peter about another girl, Gia—he'll know exactly who Gia is—one of two girls murdered in our small town?

The house Luca went to last night was within earshot of Peter's house, where Luca, Peter, and Gia allegedly were at the time she died. This sounds bad, very bad. The more I think about it, the more I realize I can't tell any of this to our doctor. Maybe, instead, Luca should talk to someone like Giorgio or someone else he trusts. Or maybe it's best to bring him to the spiritualista my mother often relied on. If I chose that path, I would have to be cautious and tell no one. I'd have to convince Luca that she was an old friend of mine, not someone who consults the stars.

I was raised to believe honesty is one of the most important traits in a person. How can I expect honesty from my boys when I'm not being honest with myself? I look at the barrette resting in the palm of my hand, possibly the key to everything that's happened.

But instead of choosing to be honest, I'm desperately searching for ways around it. The fact remains that Peter, one of my best friends' sons, is in a detention facility and might not belong there. I scour the corners of my mind, even the darkest ones. The only way to keep both Peter and Luca out of the detention center is to redirect suspicion onto someone else, like Carlos. But then I'd have to somehow get the barrette into Carlos's possession.

Why am I thinking this?

No, I won't stoop that low, and I'm sick that the thought even crossed my mind.

I go to the cupboard and retrieve the box behind the flour. I place it on the counter and remove the lid. My hand brushes over the money. I lift the shoe partly out and place it back inside; next to it I spy the opium, my medicine, in its newest hiding place inside the box. My mouth waters as I hold it between my fingers and imagine taking just a little bit for a much-needed break.

I let it fall from my hand and bury it beneath the shoe. I can't take it if I ever want to leave, get my sons far away from their father. I can't keep doing that. I glance from the barrette in my hand to the box. I grasp it tightly before gently wedging it beneath the money, the opium, and the shoe. I guess Luca isn't the only one with a box of secrets.

* * *

CHAPTER TWENTY-SEVEN

I make one phone call while it's early enough to still catch Giorgio at home during lunch. It's been three days since the funeral for Camilla, a small gathering for only immediate family, no one else—not even close friends of the family, like me. I know he's back to work now and should be home on his lunch break, so I ask him if he'll mind coming by before he returns to work, and he agrees.

A few drops of Sal's whiskey are all I add to my coffee, enough to ease my frayed nerves. The first sip is smooth with a slight burn in my throat. The next two are more like gulps, like I'm gulping down my fears about Luca. My biggest fear—that Luca is becoming just like his father—might destroy me.

Another two sips for my worries about Franco and his possible connections in all this. He's been a bit evasive lately. I recall how he'd come home from school one day looking worried and pensive. If I hadn't dragged it out of him, I don't know if he would have told me that, within the next year or two, he'd be quitting school, an idea he said came from Sal. Damn Sal for always getting what he wants.

It's not uncommon for boys Franco's age to quit school and help with the family farms or businesses. I just had different hopes for Franco. He could have been the one out of all of us to complete his high school education. That could take him far in life.

Franco must have read my face. "Why are you looking at me like that, Mamá?" he said.

"I just hoped you would be able to finish school, that's all," I said.

"Mamá, everyone is doing this. Rico, Jon, Pablo . . . I would be the only one who didn't. I don't need to finish school. You will need my help on the plantation full time. It's the right thing to do. Papá actually smiled when I said I'd do it."

A smile emerging from Sal's lips is like a unicorn emerging from the sky—only reserved for friends, sometimes Luca, and very rarely me. Franco hardly ever does anything right in Sal's eyes. Although Franco sometimes says he hates Sal for the way he treats us, I understand how that one smile is enough for him.

Reluctantly I agreed, but that was only because I wouldn't be the bad guy while Sal got all the glory in this decision. The muscles in Franco's face relaxed immediately. I really didn't have a choice.

Through the window I see Giorgio approach, and I rise from the table to answer the door. He's more put together since the last time I saw him; in fact, I find the stubble on his chin and jawline endearing. We embrace briefly, and he follows me to the kitchen where I fill two cups of coffee, no whiskey this time. We sit across from each other, and he smiles at me, immediately lifting my mood.

I don't know what I would do without Giorgio in my life. I briefly bring him up to speed on everything that happened last night and everything that's happened since finding the shoe in the shed. I even go so far as to show him the box I've kept hidden in the cupboard all this time. He's known about the box of money and my plans to leave Sal, but he's never seen it. No one has.

As I place the box on the table, Giorgio's eyes brighten like a child's first glimpse at the wrapped presents beneath the Christmas tree. I hand him the shoe and he turns it around, studying it closely. Then I take out the barrette and hold it in my open palm. He stares at it and starts to speak, but something else in the box catches his eye.

"What's that?" he says, pointing.

I cover it with my hand. "Nothing—my medicine."

"Your medicine . . . Iz, you didn't tell me you were taking something. Is that opium?"

"Yes, I only take—"

"It doesn't matter how much," he says, his eyebrows pointed. "Do you know how dangerous that is? I know people—men—who have used opium and never stopped."

"I'm not taking it anymore," I say.

"Then why do you still have it?"

"I'm holding onto it . . . in case."

"Let me have that," he says, opening his hand. "I'll keep it for you. If you ever need it, you can get it from me." His expression shifts from anger to concern to affection.

CHAPTER TWENTY-SEVEN

My heart pounds as I take the small bag of opium and squeeze it above Giorgio's open hand. I don't need this. Let it go. I release the bag and watch it fall to his palm. My heart flutters as he puts it in his pocket. I take a deep breath. I don't ask the question in my mind. What if I need it in the middle of the night? I need to let it go and I know it.

I slide the barrette to Giorgio. "I don't know what to think of this," I say. "I don't know what to do."

"Do you really think Luca could have any involvement in Gia's death? Is that what you're saying? That means Peter is innocent, right?"

I'd hoped to avoid that question. I want Giorgio to already know the barrette belongs to Peter because his uncertainty increases mine.

"I don't want to think it," I say. "I'm not saying Peter is completely innocent, but something inside keeps haunting me."

"Are you considering the police? Because you know as well as I do—"

"I know," I admit. "Some members of the police might be paid by the 'Ndrangheta. And I know you believe Sal has connections to them too."

"Look at his father, Iz. It's highly likely. You can't tell me you don't think it by now."

I think it but I can't say it out loud. "Before I make any decisions, I was wondering—hoping—you might have a talk with Luca, not just once but regularly. He needs a strong male role model. He doesn't have one."

"I'd love that, but if I'm to be around Luca more than usual, won't he think it's strange? Won't he tell Sal?"

"We'll have him come to your house more often to spend time with Max," I say. "We'll think of reasons why he needs to be there. Then you can insert your influence on him, show him what a true father-son relationship is really supposed to be. You already have a connection with him, and you'll gain his trust."

Giorgio agrees to talk with Luca and be more involved.

"Thank you," I say. "This means more to me than you could know."

He reaches across the table and holds my hands in a way he's never done before. On instinct, I pull back slightly, but I don't let go. Then I squeeze back and our eyes lock, and my stomach flips. We stay like that for a deeply connected moment that seems to transcend time. I find myself wanting to reach across the table and pull his face to mine, and I wonder if he feels the same. I shake it off, chiding myself for my insensitivity for Camilla.

His eyes jump to the clock, and his hands gently release mine. "I have to go," he says, standing.

I stand too and walk him to the door, enveloped in a warm haze. "Thank you so much, Giorgio," I say as we hug goodbye. His skin has a woodsy scent I hadn't noticed before. I open the door, and as Giorgio steps onto the porch, I think I see someone near the shed. "Is that Massimo?"

Giorgio's eyes follow my stare. "It looks like it. What's he doing here?" He tells me he'll find out who is by the shed and why they're here. He says he'll make sure they leave when he does. But what if they come back later?

CHAPTER TWENTY-EIGHT

Every Saturday morning, Sal and Luca take the private road that leads to the marina, where they'll spend most of the day until sunset. On days like today, when Franco isn't as busy on the plantation, he accompanies me into town. We're taken by surprise when Sal suggests that Franco should drive his Fiat. I hesitate as soon as I hear him say the words, thinking it might be a trap or a test. Sal makes decisions only if it positively affects him, so there must be some benefit I'm not seeing.

Fresh-baked bread and pastries greet us as we're steps away from the ever-popular Pasticceria Callipari, the best bakery in southern Italy. The entire street is a scene out of a painting: tables displaying beautiful floral arrangements surrounded by magnificent baked foods, various ingredients and spices, produce and sweets; smiling vendors eager to help. They know their customers will seek the best of the best inside their stores. On Saturday mornings, Lorenzo displays several delicious samples of his best baked goods on a table outside the entrance to his bakery.

As Franco and I approach the sweets, my skin prickles, and the hairs on my neck rise. I get a distinct feeling we're being followed. I glance over my shoulder across the street from where we came. I scan around us for possible hiding places if needed. My eyes flick to Lorenzo, who is nervously shifting from one foot to the other. He smooths the front of his apron as I come closer and cracks an uncertain smile, making me stop and think twice about proceeding.

Lorenzo's eyes flash wide in warning. Franco and I glance at each other. I pretend I've forgotten something and turn around as if to retrace my steps. Franco points to another store on the opposite side as if that's the one we meant to go to, and we head that way.

We cross to the gastronomia where I'll purchase a few deli meats. I glance again at Lorenzo's display and notice a commotion inside his store. Two men dressed in suits exit the pasticceria and go to the flower stand next door. My heart races. Is it me they're searching for?

The men dart in and out of the next few stands as if they know what they're looking for but haven't found it yet. As they near the gastronomia, Franco and I hide beneath one of two tables in front of the small store and watch their feet go by. The men fly into the gastronomia and bolt out again, nearly knocking over the "Today's Specials" sign as they head out the door. As soon as we stand, the old lady at the tomato display waves me over. I link my arm in Franco's and we turn from her so she doesn't draw attention to us.

"We need to go," I whisper.

Franco nods, and we escape to the car. We pass a newsstand and I grab an issue of La Stampa just before we reach the car.

We lock the doors as soon as we're inside, both visibly shaking.

"What was that?" Franco says.

"I'm not sure," I say, catching my breath, "but I think they were looking for us—for me."

"Why?" Franco asks.

"I can't say exactly. Let's get out of here."

We pull away from our parking spot, and through the back window I swear I see one of the men pointing at our car.

"Go faster, Franco!"

Franco shifts into gear and speeds away.

When I feel we've put enough distance between us, I relax, turn back in my seat, and pick up La Stampa. On the front page, it reads: "Boy charged and sentenced in Bernardi murder, suspected in second murder of Gia Lovallo." My heart sinks. I imagine Peter in that detention home for boys with other

CHAPTER TWENTY-EIGHT

boys around him who are criminals, who actually belong there.

I turn from the guilt that torments my head and makes my heart ache for Peter, away from the fear that forces images of Luca at the detention center instead.

I wonder what, if anything, Franco has observed of Luca lately and ask him about it.

"He's been quiet," Franco says. "A lot more than usual."

"Does he seem upset? How is he besides quiet?"

"Not really a lot of emotion from him," he says, "but he's been late a lot, especially the other night. I asked him why he was so late getting home from the marina to help me on the plantation, and he said he had to make a delivery."

"A delivery for what?"

"For Papá," he says. "He asked Luca to deliver something for him."

"Do you know what he was supposed to deliver or where he was supposed to go?"

"Luca said it was just fishing supplies. I guess Papá was supposed to do it but ran out of time."

"That doesn't sound like Papá," I say. "Why would he have Luca deliver something any of his men could have delivered?"

"I don't know. That's just what he told me."

"Do you believe him?"

"Luca or Papá?"

"I'm talking about Luca," I say. "Do you believe he actually had a delivery to make, or do you think he's making it up?"

"I believe him," he says. His eyes flip to the ceiling as if recalling something.

"What is it?"

"Last night, when I got up to use the toilet, I heard Luca yelling in his sleep. I opened his door. He wasn't yelling, but he was mumbling something about a house. His legs were twitching, he was moving a lot, so I woke him up. He said he was having a nightmare about being stuck in a house or something."

"A house?"

"He said it wasn't our house, but it was a house he knew."

"What do you mean, 'a house he knew'? Like a friend's house?"

"No, not a friend," Franco says. "The more awake he became the less he talked about it. He said that—" Franco stops himself as if he realizes what he's about to say isn't good.

"Said what?" I say, eyeing him.

"It was a house he'd been to with Papá." Franco is jittery and begins shifting his feet.

"Go on," I say.

He rolls his eyes and draws in a breath. "Luca and Papá weren't the only ones at the house." His eyes are serious, and his hesitation says enough for me to know.

"A woman?" I say.

Franco's eyes drop to the floor.

"It's okay, Franco. I had my suspicions." It hurts hearing something I've been wondering about, hearing it confirmed out loud, and from my son. "Have you ever seen this woman? Do you know who she is?"

"No, I've never seen her."

"Has Luca? Did he say if he knew her?"

"He didn't say anything else except that she was there."

I think about the long, dark hair strand I'd found on Sal's jacket. How dare Sal bring this woman around our son? Luca is a young and impressionable young man, struggling enough as it is. Anna would say it's because Sal is a narcissist. He only loves himself and, therefore, only cares about himself. The people he chooses to be with and the things he chooses to do are for his own personal gain.

Anna got to know Sal on a different level. She was interested in politics, and Sal was happy to share his political opinion with anyone who would listen. The worst part of it was when they'd start talking about Mussolini. Whenever they discussed Mussolini or worsening relationships in our country, it made my stomach turn. Sal's views and actions were changing to be much like Mussolini's.

I miss Anna. I'm saddened to think that one of my closest friends no longer wants to see me. How I wish I could talk to her now. I recall our last

CHAPTER TWENTY-EIGHT

moments at the detention center. I wonder if Anna thinks I'm a narcissist too.

Franco places a hand on mine. "I'm sorry, Mamá."

"You have nothing to be sorry for."

"I'm sorry you married Papá."

"Oh, my boy, you don't have to be sorry for me. Don't carry that burden. I'll be okay. I'm stronger than you think." I notice something as soon as I say those words: I didn't flinch when I said them. My body didn't revolt against it. Maybe I'm starting to believe it.

CHAPTER TWENTY-NINE

Sal

It's dark tonight. The cloud-laden sky makes it heavier and darker than it should be. Not even a slice of the moon can be seen. There's a thickness in the air, too, which makes it hard to breathe.

I turn to Luca, who's got his head buried in his hands. "Is there something you want to tell me before I go in there?"

Luca lifts his head and wipes his nose with his sleeve. His eyes are red and swollen.

"How'd you get those?" I say, pointing to the scratches on his right cheek.

Luca doesn't answer. He doesn't need to. He opens his mouth like he wants to say something.

"Well? What is it?"

"I didn't mean for it to go that far, Papá, I promise," he says, beginning to cry again.

I know where this is leading, and I don't want to ask. "Is there someone in the shed, Luca? Answer me now."

Luca nods.

"Girl or boy?" I'm holding my breath.

"Girl," he blurts.

"Is she . . . alive?"

CHAPTER TWENTY-NINE

Luca nods again.

"Did she see you?"

Another nod. Now I know what has to be done.

"Are you gonna help her?" he says. "And then let her go? I think maybe you should."

"Now you listen to me." I get right in his face. "When I get out of the car and start walking to the shed, you get out, too, and you run to the house. Climb back in through your window like you do. You get into bed right away and get to sleep. You better hope your mamá isn't awake. You and I will talk about this after you get up. You hear me?" He's looking at me dumbfounded. "Answer me. Tell me what you're gonna do when I get out of the car." He's lucky he can repeat my orders.

I step out of the car, give a nod to Luca to get on his way, then I walk slowly toward the shed. I listen to the crickets and locusts in the empty night air. When I near the shed I see a thin line of light beneath the door. Luca should have thought to turn off the light. He also didn't lock the door. Sloppy work. I push the door and it swings in. I step inside and immediately I smell it: fear. And not mine.

I see her in the corner: long, dark hair pulled to the side, a tear in her shirt at the neck, probably from the struggle. She's sitting with her knees pulled to her chest, her head resting on top. Thin, probably pretty from what I can see. If I had to guess, she looks mid- to late teens. Probably in Luca's or Franco's classes. One of her shoes is missing.

When she looks up, I'm taken aback at how much she looks like Gianna Russo from next door. If I didn't know any better, I'd think it was her. But that's impossible; the Russos are gone, although I'm not through with Greta. Who is this girl?

She sees me and starts to hyperventilate. Her eyes bug out. She opens her mouth like she's about to scream.

"No, no, no. Shh. It's okay," I say. "I'm not here to hurt you."

She undoubtedly hopes this is true, but I'm sure she senses my lie.

A gust of wind catches at the back door, blowing it open an inch or two. Her eyes widen as she notices her way out. She's going to run. She glances at me and then the door. I see her messing with the ropes tied around her wrists, and her eyes jump from me to the door and back.

All at once she bolts for the door. She's fast, but I'm faster. I block her with my arm. She falls back hard against the wall and slides to the floor. But then she gets right back up. I can't believe what I'm seeing. This girl's got spunk. She evades my grasp and exits the back door. I run after her through the trees, listening for movement in the grass, but she probably stopped to do the same. Dammit.

I call out a few times, try to get her to trust me and come out from where she's hiding, but it doesn't work. I catch a quick glance of her dashing through the plantation, and now there's only one way she can go. I get to the car and tell Massimo where she's headed, but I don't go with him. I stay back for two reasons: one, to make sure Luca makes it to his room, and the other reason is to be ready if she comes back. One way or another, we'll get her.

* * *

It's a busy morning at the marina. I keep looking for signs of Luca, who should have been here twenty minutes ago. He's lucky he was in his bed when I checked after that girl ran off. What a long night.

Finally, Luca rounds the corner and gets busy right away helping a family take out their boat. Occasionally he glances at me but quickly gets back to work. After about an hour, things start to slow down at the marina as they normally do. There are no more boats to prepare, so Luca has no other choice but to come inside.

"Luca," I say when he walks in, "viene qui. Come here." I point to a chair next to mine.

He's standoffish at first but sits. His eyes open wide and serious as if he wants to ask me something. "Did you—is she—"

CHAPTER TWENTY-NINE

"It's taken care of," I say, expecting relief in his tight expression, but there is none.

"Did you convince her not to say anything?" he asks.

"She won't be talking," I say, assuming he knows what I mean. He doesn't ask for clarification, and I give none. "What happened with the girl? What did you do to her?"

"I—I just wanted to see if I could do it," he says. "If I could actually capture someone . . . like you do."

Massimo's head snaps up, and we exchange glances.

I hit Luca upside the head and glance around quickly to see if anyone heard him. "Are you insane? Where'd you hear that?"

"I didn't hear it. I just know."

"You don't just know something out of nowhere."

"I've seen you—at the other house."

"Seen me? What do you mean you've seen me? What house?" What the hell did he see? "You don't know what you're talking about. There's nothing to see. There is no other house. You're sounding more and more like your mother."

"But Papá, you can trust me. I'm—"

"Now you look at me right now," I say, gritting my teeth. When I'm satisfied with his attention, I go on. "You did not see anything. Not last night, not the night before, never. You got that?" Our eyes are locked in an intense stare. Is he backing down or pushing forward? I squint and lean closer. "Do we understand each other? If you want to work with me more often and learn all sides of the family business, then I need to know you'll do as I say when I say it. Capisci? Do you understand?"

Luca nods.

"Say the words."

"I understand, Papá."

I have to make sure I'm in control, which means everyone beneath me needs to be in control as well. People may think I'm calloused, but it's better than having them think I'm weak. Besides, I've got my bosses, too, and they're worse than me. The only time I felt a small twinge of sadness or regret was the day they found Gia Lovallo. Luca and I were together when a farmer found her body in his field, and he was talking about it with someone about it at the marina.

Luca and I were within earshot. I'll never forget the look he gave me—like hatred, sadness, and defeat all wrapped up together and aimed at me. It was the one time we weren't in sync with one another, and it changed a bit for a while after that.

"You got a minute?" Massimo joins me at the small makeshift bar I have at the marina. He pours two glasses of whiskey. "You know who Luca was referring to when he said something about capturing people like you, right?"

"Why you gotta bring that up again?" I say. "I didn't know she was so young. It was a mistake. I thought it was her older sister. I was wrong. Let it go."

"This isn't good," Massimo says. "Nothing good can come of any of this."

I glare at Massimo, throw back my drink, and slam the glass on the table. Then I get up and walk away, counting down the hours 'til closing when I can have my space alone near the water. I glance at the clock. It's just about the time I'd be leaving the marina to see her. I pull my wallet from my pocket, open it, and remove the photograph I keep tucked inside the fold.

The edges are crinkled and worn from the same repeated motions, a ritual since the day they left. My eyes jump to the clock at three forty-five. I retrieve my wallet, remove her picture carefully, and stare, instantly lost in her eyes. And then it's like a hot fire spreading through me, consuming my thoughts with anger.

It wasn't me who sent the Russos out of town. They left on their own accord—their choice, not mine. I've scoured the whole southern part of Italy, sent teams of my men to find them—her—but she's nowhere. They must have gone north to hide in the Tuscan hills.

Massimo thinks they're in the witness protection program. If that's true, then Rocco opened his mouth and said things he shouldn't have. Being friends with the Russos should have had its advantages. Rocco was a cop we could trust. He took care of me; I took care of him.

I knew my instincts were right. I knew he was turning. I felt something

CHAPTER TWENTY-NINE

was off as soon as he stopped giving eye contact. And all that happened before he found out about Greta. Did he think our partnership would be without risk? And if he and his family are safe and sound, tucked away in the Tuscan hills, he better keep looking over his shoulder, because I'm coming for him. And after I take care of him, I'm taking Greta back with me to the house I'm building for her.

Every time I look at this photograph, I'm reminded of what I almost had. I run my thumb over the length of her beautiful, long, dark hair. The way it falls over her shoulders makes my whole body warm with electricity. Her perfect lips and smile. I remember the first time we were together, the first time I felt her skin, I thought I would die right then.

She'd resisted at first, being Isabella's closest friend, but I convinced her that what we had was meant to be—that and her awareness that no one says no to me. But she'd overreacted the night we came over for dinner. She was upset that I'd slipped something into Isabella's wine so she'd pass out. That I'd asked Rocco, who was good with cars, to take a look at my fake failed engine. The kids were entertaining each other in the back room, so I took advantage of the situation.

I wanted to be with Greta. I hadn't seen her in weeks. She gave me one excuse after another. I knew her idea to have us over for dinner was her way of finally seeing me. The fact that she wanted to be with me even if it meant our families were there showed me how much she wanted me, too.

She was washing dishes at the sink when I walked in. I came up behind, pressed against her, and wrapped my arms around her waist.

She stiffened immediately, pushed my arms away, and stepped aside. I assumed she was afraid we'd get caught, so I tried to reassure her we were alone. But that wasn't why she was so standoffish. She said we were through. Done. She wanted nothing to do with me anymore. I tried to tell her that's not how this works. I told her we just needed to go back to the way things used to be between us. She said there never was an "us." I couldn't understand what had happened.

"Is it because of Rocco?" I asked. "Did he tell you to end things?"

"No, it's because this"—she moved her hand from her to me—"isn't right."

Her eyes held such contempt. She said, "You have ruined me—you've ruined my life."

It was a slap in the face after everything I've done for her—for her family. But I could tell that wasn't it. She was hiding something from me.

Rocco came back inside, his face drawn and his eyebrows furrowed like he was annoyed. He'd said he found nothing wrong with the engine, that it was in perfect condition. His doubtful, accusatory tone made my blood boil. But I stayed calm and thanked him anyway.

It must have been the expression on Greta's face that caught his attention. They began a secretive communication, back and forth glances, brief facial expressions. A private conversation right in front of me that I wasn't part of. I was enraged. I'm the guy on the inside, engaging in secret conversations. I make the decisions, I'm in control. I will not be on the outside looking in.

It got heated fast between Rocco and me. He said things he didn't mean, like wanting out of our agreement. He said as of that moment we were done, he didn't want to be connected to me anymore, that it wasn't about the money but about family. Family. That's a laugh. Rocco isn't exactly the family man he pretends to be. He doesn't get to decide when he's done; that's not how this works. He's got balls—big, brass balls.

So I threatened him with his life. "You know what this means, don't you?" I said. "Don't make me do something I don't want to do. You've still got control here; you can make it different. I'm not responsible for what's to come."

At that time, Franco came into the living room and just looked at me. I have no idea how much he heard. All I know is we had to get out of there or I was gonna do something in front of everyone I'd regret.

Greta glared at me. "Really, in front of the kids—and with your wife, my friend who we've all betrayed, the kindest friend I've ever had—right there at the table," she'd pointed. Then she walked off, disgusted, back to the kitchen.

Rocco took a glass of whiskey to the porch. I went after Greta to explain that all of this was for us, for her and I, but she wouldn't listen. I stormed out of the kitchen just as Isabella entered. She looked at both of us, confused.

CHAPTER TWENTY-NINE

I ordered her and the boys to leave with me, and we left.

The next morning they were gone, plucked right from their house in the middle of the night. Not one trace was left behind. That's when I knew they were in some sort of protective custody, and I was screwed. But I won't give up, not until I find her.

The customer bell rings at the counter. Through the window, Massimo is talking to someone on the pier. I slide Greta's picture carefully into my wallet and approach the impatient customer with the angry stare.

CHAPTER THIRTY

Isabella

I head outside through the back door, a full laundry basket hoisted on my hip. I place the basket below the clothesline and hang the first item, one of Sal's shirts, clipping it to the line at each sleeve, moving to the next, without a thought about the clothes, like a well-oiled machine.

The sun's harsh rays scorch the top of my head and shoulders. Even when he's not around, I feel Sal's eyes upon me. I attach the last item and take the basket in to get the next load of clothes. I reach for the doorknob and freeze when I see a folded piece of paper on the doorstep. I glance behind me at the woods and ahead at the road before I bend slowly to retrieve it.

The paper was not here when I first came out. I wouldn't have missed that, would I? That means someone must have put it there while I was hanging the laundry. They were probably watching me the whole time. I shiver at the thought of someone being so close without my awareness.

I step inside the house, close and lock the door, and peer out the window. Who's out there? Are they watching me now? I pull the curtains closed on all the windows on the first floor. Then I sit at the kitchen table and unfold the paper.

You think you know what you're doing but you don't. You have something you

CHAPTER THIRTY

shouldn't have. I tried to warn you, but you're still not listening and you're running out of time. You're protecting the wrong person. You are all in grave danger.

The same handwriting as the other notes—pointed letters and overly scripted Ss. The message is the same, but I am listening. I'm trying to do the right thing. I possess things I shouldn't have—the barrette, the shoe, strands of hair . . . What else?

The phone rings and I run for it, grabbing it quickly. "Yes—hello?" I hear a click from the switchboard operator and then my sister's voice. Alena lives further north in Firenze, Florence, and has been there since she got married. She's one of the lucky ones who found love after marriage. Alena only calls when something's wrong. It's been well over a month since we talked.

"Alena?"

"Izzy? That you?" she says.

"Yes, is something wrong?"

"I've been meaning to call you just to see how you are," she says, "but I don't know where the time goes. I also wanted to ask you something. It's the strangest thing, but have the Russos moved?"

This surprises me. My stomach tenses hearing her say their name. "Why do you ask?"

"Well, about two weeks ago, when I was shopping in Arezzo, I could have sworn I saw Greta and the girls at the Piazza Grande," Alena says. "I wasn't very close, so by the time I got to them they were gone. But I'm telling you it looked exactly like them."

"Really?" I say. "Maybe they were visiting."

"Visiting who?" she says. "From what I remember, Greta doesn't go very far to visit people."

Neither do you.

There's a click on the phone line.

"You still there?" I say.

"Yes, I thought I lost you for a minute," she says.

"You heard that click?"

"Yes."

"Is someone else on the line?" I ask.

The one thing I dislike most about telephones are shared phone lines. Right now there's empty air, like someone's there but they're not speaking and they're not hanging up either. I start to panic. What if someone has been listening to my calls? What if Greta doesn't want to be found, or worse, she's forced to be there because she's hiding?

"If someone is on the line, please hang up and try again in a few minutes."

No one replies, no click to indicate a hang-up.

"Maybe it's just static," Alena says.

"Perhaps." I'm not convinced.

"I might have been wrong thinking it was Greta I saw," she says, "but I know for sure I saw Sal the other night. I had no idea his business takes him Montepulciano."

I swallow hard. "No, it couldn't have been him."

"Oh, but it was. He looked right at me and turned away. He ignored me completely," she says. "I realize Sal and I are not fond of each other, but to ignore me was so disrespectful."

"When was this?"

"It was Monday—no, Tuesday. I saw him near that park I like."

"At a park?"

"He wasn't at the park; he was near the park in a car with an old man. I only heard a little of what they were saying. I think the old man is a builder or a designer or something. Are you looking to come out here finally and live closer to me?"

I don't know why she asks questions like this when she knows we'd never leave the coast to go anywhere except maybe America. Tuesday, Sal came home very late, but there's no way he was all the way in Montepulciano talking to a builder. "No, it wasn't him, Alena."

"I'm telling you, Iz, it was him," she says. "I'd bet my life on it. And you not knowing he was there further supports my view of him. You need to get away from him. He's no good. I don't know how many more times I have to warn you about him."

Had Sal gone to see the woman he's having an affair with? The one in the

CHAPTER THIRTY

house Luca dreamed about? The one Franco told me about? Alena and I finish our conversation and I'm alone again.

My mind wanders to the darkest corners to a deep-seated angst that something is going on right in front of me. The grasp I have on my family, the little world closest to my heart, is starting to loosen. If I delve any deeper, push any harder, it might completely unravel until everything I love is gone.

CHAPTER THIRTY-ONE

The slightest thing will startle me now. A ringing phone, a breeze against the window, a knock at the door. Normal, simple things I didn't used to mind now cause an extreme panic. But today, when I hear the knock at the door, it isn't a friendly-knuckle-tapping-on-wood sort of knock. It's bigger than that—angrier. The banging that ensues on my front door sounds like a thousand fists at once, demanding me to answer.

My heart races as soon as the knocking starts. I have to catch my breath and try to calm myself before I answer the door. I peek out the side window near the door and see the same two officers as before, D'Amico and Parnello. They stand wide, hands on hips, scowling at the door. I open it, trying to smile. I've done nothing wrong.

"Hello officers," I say.

"We'd like to have a few minutes of your time," Officer Parnello says. "We'd like you to come with us to the station to talk about some new developments in the Gia Lovallo case."

"Oh dear." My legs buckle. "Can we talk here?" The officers glance at each other. "I—I have to be here. The boys will be home soon and—"

"That's fine," Officer D'Amico says. "We want to talk with your boys too."

"May I ask why you need to speak with me?" I say, trying to calm my trembling voice.

"There seems to be some discrepancies in your story about the night your sons walked the victim home," Officer D'Amico adds.

CHAPTER THIRTY-ONE

"Discrepancies? I told you what I remember happened."

"It's the timing we're trying to understand," Officer Parnello says. "You see, you said your sons left around ten o'clock to walk her home and that they were home by ten thirty."

"I said to be home by eleven o'clock at the latest, and they were."

"But a witness who knows your sons very well saw one of them walking back toward your house after eleven o'clock, which means he wasn't home by eleven as you previously stated. That's the first discrepancy." Officer Parnello slides his hands into his front pockets. "The other concerns someone who says they heard your son, Luca, fighting with Peter Rossi while in the presence of the victim earlier that same day."

It feels like the ground is shaking, and I can't form a complete thought in my head. He's wrong. I checked my boys' bedrooms and both were in bed.

I clear my throat. "Both boys were in bed when I checked."

"What time was that?" Officer D'Amico asks.

"Eleven o'clock, like I said," but as soon as the words come out, I start to doubt having really looked at the clock that night. Or had I been satisfied that they were in bed when I checked and assumed it was eleven o'clock? It had to be. I would have been worried if they were late.

Officer D'Amico clears his throat and glances at Officer Parnello, who raises his eyebrows and looks at me like he's about to say something. "The timing is concerning, the voices overheard by a neighbor is concerning, but what's most concerning is that we now appear to have a motive."

"Motive?" I say. "How?"

"Luca's voice was overheard during an argument with Peter, which places him at Peter Rossi's house on the day of the candlelight service. Luca was angry that the victim was at Peter's house. Later that evening, the kids met up with one another at the candlelight service, and she came back to your house for a while. Luca walked her home. Timing seems a bit off. The next day, she was missing. Do you see how this looks?"

I walk to the sink and fill a glass with water. "Would you like some?" I ask.

They both agree, so I pull two more glasses from the cupboard, fill them, and set them on the table. Through the window I see Franco and Luca approaching the house.

Before they enter, I blurt, "Luca wasn't the only one who walked Gia home. What you're saying proves nothing."

Franco and Luca enter hesitantly, glancing at each other, then at the officers and then at me.

"Come have a seat, boys," I say. "These nice officers would like to talk with you."

Officer D'Amico says to me, "Would you mind leaving us while we talk with the boys?"

I'm taken aback by this. "Um—I—why can't I stay?"

"We want to talk with them without outside influences or coaching," Officer D'Amico says.

"I beg your pardon," I say, "but they are still children, and I will be present when they speak to you. You don't have to worry about my input during your interrogation."

Officer Parnello pierces me with his eyes like he wishes to say more, but he's biting his tongue. "This is not an interrogation, Signora Perri. If it were, you would have been taken right to the station, possibly even in handcuffs."

I stare right back, but I'm viewing him differently now. I knew he looked familiar when I first met him. I've seen him before any of this started happening.

Had he been the officer in a close conversation with Sal a while back, the time I'd witnessed a small bag exchanged between them? That had to be roughly five years ago. The more I look at Officer Parnello, the more convinced I am that he was the one talking with Sal. He may have had connections at the time with Sal.

I'm pretty confident he and Sal have lost their connection, judging by the way he's advocating to have Luca blamed for these crimes. What would Sal do if he knew his old pal was trying to arrest his son right under his nose? I'm thinking I should share this with Sal tonight when he comes home.

The questions aimed at Franco and Luca are not much different than what the officers had already asked me. The boys have no trouble with their answers, only a little stumbling over their words when asked what time they

CHAPTER THIRTY-ONE

came home the night in question and what Peter and Luca were arguing about.

The officers stare hard at us and then Officer D'Amico steps forward and places one item in the center of the table: Gia's sapphire-studded barrette. I try to relax, keep my eyes soft, but they're twitching like crazy.

I'm watching Luca and Franco, and they're watching me. At first, I think maybe they found the barrette somehow in Luca's possession. But as I examine it closely, I realize it's a trick. The stones on this particular barrette are not all sapphire. The officers are testing us to see how we react. This barrette means something to them, to the case.

Officer D'Amico says, "This barrette was in the victim, Gia Lovallo's, pocket the day she was found." The item in her pocket. My heart races heavy and loud like a freight train through my chest.

Luca's face begins to crack.

Oh my God, I know what this means.

You could hear a pin drop in the silence surrounding us. In no time, the officers put their notepads away, take the barrette, and thank us for our time. They finally leave our home, but they have no idea of the mess they've left behind.

CHAPTER THIRTY-TWO

The truth is right in front of me, but my mind can't process it. The edges of what's real fade, blurring the facade I've been protecting. It happens the moment the police officers leave my house. Although I shouldn't do what I'm going to do, I have no other choice. I'm making a choice similar to the one my mother made when I was little. After she made the choice to see her special friend, the spiritualista, our lives improved.

I don't call the spiritualista, I go to her. I leave right at dawn after Sal heads to the marina. I'll have enough time to get there and back before the boys rise for school. I walk with my eyes peeled in all directions. The lantern provides scant light on the road ahead. Where I'm going isn't far from the marina, but to stay hidden, I'll take the road that winds around the back of the marina to a small tucked-away oxbow that few people even know exists.

Some say, years ago, people of the oxbow community were encouraged to leave due to sanitary restrictions. Others say they were forced out. A handful of families still remain, refusing to abandon their homes. The spiritualista is one of them. Her name is Adelina. She specializes in communicating with ancestors and healing.

I arrive at the back of Adelina's house, as she prefers, and walk through the hanging bells precisely placed to alert the spiritualista before reaching her door. I knock three times with a slight pause between the second and third knock.

A small, slender woman with an odd grin answers the door. She stares at me through round spectacles until recognition flashes through her eyes. "Isabella," she says, fondly. "Well, look at you. How long has it been?"

"I was much younger when I saw you last," I say, thinking back to that terrible day when I came to Adelina as a teenager for advice. I'd witnessed something that stayed with me since the moment it occurred. I'll never forget the terrified look on the face of the girl who was kidnapped right in front of me. We were near the playground, but it was much later after all the children went home from school.

Several of us older teens would gather there every day. On that one day, I was the only one who saw it happen—the kidnapping. A man and a woman got out of their car and approached the girl who was several feet from me and my friends. I thought maybe they were her parents, but the way they interacted with the girl seemed unnatural. They dragged the girl to their car, and it was obvious she not only didn't want to go but she didn't belong to them. As they drove off with her in the back seat, she looked at me through the window with tear-filled eyes and a look of terror.

Before I knew it, they were gone, and I had done nothing about it. I'd been frozen with fear. I could hardly move from where I was standing when it was finally time for everyone to go home. I wished I'd done something, made a fuss, yelled after them, run up and grabbed her, but I couldn't do it. Each of us had been asked about what we may have witnessed, but I was so scared I couldn't speak. That girl's face has haunted me ever since. I was so distraught that my mother brought me to Adelina for healing and advice, the exact same reason I'm here now.

When Julia and Gia were taken, I was immediately brought back to the day of the kidnapping, as if it had just happened. I was overcome with deep fear and sadness at Julia's and Gia's and once again felt the loss of the other girl.

I can't bring back the little girl, and I can't bring back Julia and Gia, but I may have an opportunity to bring justice to this community.

But can I rectify the past without sacrificing my son? That's what I need Adelina for. She can heal Luca. She can tell me what to do and help me bring healing to this town.

"Come in," Adelina says, stepping aside to let me in. Her tiny dwelling consists of one small room with a table and chairs and a sofa. Off to one side is a partial wall with a bed behind it. She clears a dish from the table and gestures toward a chair. We sit across from one another.

"I won't take up too much of your time, Adelina, and I have to get home soon to see the boys off to school, but would it be okay to talk with you for a few moments?"

"It's interesting," she says, "the reason for your visit. Similar in ways to what happened when you were young." Her knowledge of what I have yet to say startles me. "You have a decision to make, and you don't have a lot of time to make it."

"Well, yes, I know, and I need your help. Is there—is there something you can do?"

"Like what? Witchcraft? You know you shouldn't meddle with that."

"No, of course not witchcraft," I say. "But you can heal people, right? You can heal Luca?"

She clicks her tongue and looks up to the ceiling. "It's not just Luca," she says. "Your whole house and everyone in it needs healing, including you. I'm sorry to say that what has happened, Isabella, has already grown exponentially beyond healing."

"What do I do?"

"Do you still plan to leave your husband? I'm getting conflicting information about this," she says, referring to whoever she talks to that I can't see.

"Yes, I—"

"I wish you'd have stayed out of the house when you had the chance. Now that you've gone back, you've created a stronger force around you which will be harder to break. It may even be resistant to the earth's elements—wind, water, fire."

"What if I bring Luca to you? Could you talk to him, get a feel for what he's done, what he needs?"

"I think I'm already aware of that, but if you would like me to see him, you can bring him to me." Adelina tilts her head at me and holds it there. "You

CHAPTER THIRTY-TWO

still haven't asked about the hair."

"The hair?" I say.

"The strands you found on Sal that didn't belong to him."

A slightly eerie sensation sits with me at her awareness.

"You'll look further into that," she says. Then Adelina stands as if to indicate the end of our time together. "Bring him to me. Soon." She walks me to the door and sees me out.

CHAPTER THIRTY-THREE

The clouds float low in the afternoon sky giving the appearance of soggy, white pillows clumped together. No breaks of blue. No streaks of sun. Not even a shadow. The kind of day that's better to stay inside under a warm blanket succumbing to heavy eyelids.

With Sal working late and Franco on a date with Cecelia, I take the opportunity to bring Luca to see Adelina. I tell him he'll be coming with me to visit an old friend. He resists briefly, but after a reminder about the barrette, he concedes.

A black bird swoops to a branch above as we walk to Adelina's house. It cocks its head and stares at us before flying away. The bells chime as the wind follows us and we approach the door.

I introduce Luca to Adelina, and she takes him inside. I am to wait on her porch, which consists of nothing more than a few pieced-together slabs of wood and a chair. Adelina keeps Luca inside for almost an hour, and it drives me crazy not to know exactly what they're talking about.

She pokes her head through the door and says Luca and I will now trade spots. He will sit on the porch while she talks to me. I sit down on her small sofa, and she stares at me with such an intensity.

"He admitted to a few things: the girl at the house where you caught him breaking in; he said he liked Gia, didn't like Peter. But he's keeping more to himself than what you think. A darker secret, Isabella. He wants to let it out, but he's resisting. Luca did share something interesting," Adelina continues. "He says he's been having recurring dreams. Has he told you about them?"

CHAPTER THIRTY-THREE

"Dreams?" I say. "He used to sleepwalk a lot. He hasn't mentioned dreams to me, but he did say something to Franco about a dream that bothered him." I recall the strange way he acted the other night. "There was one night when I found him next to my bed, standing over me in the middle of the night—scared me to death. He was crying, and I assumed it was because of a bad dream."

"Did he say anything about the dream?" Adelina asks.

"No, but he kept saying he was sorry about something, and he repeated more than once, 'I didn't know.' That's all I could get out of him."

Adelina puts her hand on her chin. "He said someone's always after him in his dreams. It's the same person every time, but he can't see their face."

"What do you make of it?" I ask.

"I'm not sure, but he's convinced the house in his dream is the same one every time. It has a basement he's afraid to go into, yet he's forced to go there." Adelina's expression is sincere.

"Do you think Luca is dreaming about a house he's been to before?" I ask.

"I asked him that exact question, and he told me no, he hadn't been there before. But I find that hard to believe, because the clarity in the details he shared about the house was so vivid. I could have drawn a replica just from his descriptions. In fact, I did." Adelina takes a torn piece of paper and hands it to me.

"You drew this from Luca's description of the house?"

"Yes," she says, "and when I showed it to him, he had to look away. I asked him if he knew whose house this was, but he said no. I know that boy is not telling the truth."

"Whose house could it be?" I ask, recalling the homes of everyone we know. But there's nothing quite like it anywhere I've ever been.

"I don't know," Adelina says.

"Are you sure you don't know, Adelina? Is there a way to find out?"

"I will try," she says. "But there's one more thing—Luca says his dreams have always awakened him in the night, driving him out of his bed and out of the house. He says it's the only way to get away from them. He said that's when his sneaking out at night became something else."

"What do you mean?" I say.

"Once he realized he liked being out at night, he began to go on his own, even when he wasn't awakened by his dreams."

"He said that?" I knew it.

Adelina nods. "I also asked if he thought the house he dreamed about might have represented the one Gia was last seen in."

I know it's not. For one thing, the house he was last seen in with Gia was probably ours. And even if it was Peter's house, the drawing looks nothing like those in his neighborhood.

"Luca has considered going back to the house you found him trying to get into, but I think I talked him out of it," Adelina says.

I gasp. "What do you think we should do?"

Her face turns grave. "I don't want to scare you, but you must act fast. This much I know—you must stop him from going to that house again. Your husband is not the only one who brings him there. It is not a place for young men. Luca cannot be alone with these men. You must do something if it's not already too late. The state of his soul is at risk."

His soul.

"Do whatever you can, even if it means destroying it."

"Destroying what? The house? I don't even know where it is. How am I to destroy it? I don't think I can do this. I've never done anything like this before."

"Listen to me," Adelina says. "What has happened to these girls will continue to happen. You need to face everything you've learned in the last few weeks. You need to show some tough love, or your worst fears will be realized."

Adelina, who is facing the door, moves her eyes from me. I turn, and Luca is standing behind me.

"Can we go now?" he asks. He gives no indication that he heard us, but he could be pretending.

CHAPTER THIRTY-THREE

✲ ✲ ✲

Franco and Luca disperse to their usual spots after dinner, but I don't go to the sofa to finish knitting blankets for the Bernardi and Lovallo families. I take advantage of the time Sal is still out.

Upstairs in my room, I close the door, take out my jewelry box, and open it. The barrette lies on top, daring me to do something about it. And I'm ready to. Adelina is rarely wrong about her predictions and her readings on people. She knows me well, and I trust her. I know I must do something I'm not ready to do. Tough love is something I'm not good at. It's not in my nature. But some of my worst fears are being realized, and I think I'm partly to blame.

What am I still doing here?

If I take this barrette to the police, knowing they have its matching pair, this could be very bad for Luca, maybe even Franco. I pick it up and squeeze it in the palm of my hand while my heart crumbles. I place the jewelry box back inside the drawer and, while Luca is working on a project at the kitchen table, I go to his room.

I go to the wobbled floor beneath his bed and move the planks like it's one of my normal routines. Move the bed, pull up the loose plank, retrieve the antique jewelry box. The more I handle the box, the more convinced I am that it belonged to my mother. Luca must have taken it from her trunk after she passed.

After I put things back to the way they were, I take the entire box with me to my room and hide it in my top drawer next to my own jewelry box. Then, with the barrette still in my hand, I go downstairs to make a phone call, a call I've been avoiding for so long. But it must be done. I remove the phone from its cradle and take it with me to the living room. The cord is stretched tight as I sit next to my knitting bag on the sofa.

The operator picks up. I lower my head and tell the operator just above a whisper to connect me with the police department. I explain who I am and that I have something very important to share with them regarding the two—I can hardly say it—murders in our town.

The officer asks me questions I don't want to answer over the phone, like can I tell them what the object is?

"I'm not alone," I whisper.

"Okay, I understand," he says. "Are you in danger, ma'am?"

"No, not at the moment," I say, turning the barrette over in my hand. The light from the table catches perfectly on the dark-blue stones.

"We'll send someone out today," he says.

"No, not today," I say. "Tomorrow is better."

The light dims like there's something between us, and a voice above me says, "Tomorrow is better for what?"

Sal had slipped in quietly, probably on purpose. He must have seen the tight cord and followed it, heard me speaking in hushed tones. He probably sensed something was off, someone was betraying him. He was right.

I tighten my grip on the barrette, attempting to casually conceal it in my pocket, but he's quicker than I am.

"Sure, no problem," I say into the phone, feigning a conversation with a friend. "Thanks for calling." I stand, ready to return the phone to its home on the table, but he blocks me. I stumble over my words. "Um, I . . . was talking to . . . that was Anna."

He has no idea Anna and I aren't speaking. It's normal that we would talk on the phone. I pray he doesn't ask to speak to her, or that the policeman has already hung up. He doesn't ask, probably because he has other things on his mind, like what I'm hiding.

His gaze lingers on my pocket. "What's in your pocket?" he asks.

I'm dumbfounded and tongue-tied, but I have to answer him. "My pocket? A few clothespins. Why?" I lift one out.

"Let me see the rest."

My hand fishes for another clothespin. Luckily, I still had a few from hanging laundry earlier. The barrette holds to one, but I shake it back to the bottom. I hand Sal three clothespins like a guilty child who's stolen a cookie.

CHAPTER THIRTY-THREE

"I think you have something else in your pocket," he says. "Take everything out. I want to see the inside." As he says this, he puts his hands in his pants pockets, and I hear his fingers on something that jingles, like keys.

"Sal, this is silly," I say, moving around him to hang up the phone. "You're treating me like a child. If I tell you I have clothespins in my pocket, that should be good enough. Do you think Giuseppe asks Anna things like this? Would Rocco ask Greta?" His eye twitches when I mention Rocco's and Greta's names. "Do you think Giorgio did that with Camilla?"

"I don't care about them, what they do or what they don't do," he says. "If I think I'm being disrespected—lied to—I'm gonna find out, and I'll ask whatever questions I need to ask."

Desperate for a distraction, I swoop in close to him as if I'm going to give him a hug or a kiss. He shifts back a little, like he's unsure of what to expect, but his dark eyes never leave mine.

I lean my head toward his neck, prepared to act like it's the first time I smell her perfume. But I don't have to act. The sweet scent of musk with light floral notes emanates from his clothes, like the perfume bottle on Greta's dresser. Hundreds of women have that same perfume; it could really be anyone. But my gut refutes that thought.

I sniff. "What's that smell? Like flowers or something sweet."

His face changes from a tyrannical dictator to genuine concern. The lines on his forehead fade, his lips pout as if deeply pondering something. He squints at me, and I'm sure the feeling he's left with isn't a good one. Anger has traded with something of equal value.

"What is it about that smell that is so familiar?" I continue. "I've smelled it before."

"Nonsense," he says. "You're full of nonsense as usual."

"I'm not full of nonsense, Sal, you are."

"Excuse me?"

"You might think I turn my head at the things you do. Had this happened a few months ago, I might have."

His eyes blaze.

"I'm not the same naive, submissive girl you married."

"Oh, yes, you are!"

"No. That girl left you the moment you laid a hand on our children. You might see me standing here, but that's all you have: my physical presence. You'll never have my mind or my heart." My whole body turns hot, and sweat gathers at my neck and on my back. I may appear brave, but there's still a part that's scared.

He furrows his brow. "Why do you do this? It's like you want me to hurt you."

Just then the phone rings once and then stops. We glance at it and then away, and we continue bickering.

"You think I don't know about your other life? You think I don't know there's more to the marina than meets the eye?" My heart flutters. These are the suspicions of Giorgio and Anna that I've only recently come to question.

"You don't know a damn thing you're talking about," he says.

"Don't I? Should we go to the marina now? Better yet, maybe we should go to the shed." I start walking to the door, and he bolts past me, blocking my exit.

"Who do you think you are?" he says through gritted teeth. His temples bulge, and his face reddens. I've gotten to him. I've found the weak spot.

The phone rings again, and like before it stops after one ring, then rings a second time. It's uncomfortable and peculiar.

Something catches his eye. I flinch as he moves from the door to the window facing the Russos' house. I see it too. A light…in the attic. I never thought to check the attic.

"What are you looking at? You're hiding something up there, aren't you?" I say. "Something for her—Greta. She's the one you're having an affair with."

He raises his arm but pulls it down. "Watch your mouth. I'm warning you." He's trying to stay in control.

"I recognize the smell that's on you because it's her perfume—the one she's worn since I've known her. Her whole house smells like it. It's unmistakable."

He starts to speak but I cut him off.

"Don't bother denying it. I saw a few strands of long, dark hair, wavy like Greta's, on your shirts. I suspected something between the two of you but

CHAPTER THIRTY-THREE

threw away the notion. But it was there somewhere in my subconscious." I stare into his eyes, filled with hurt. "Greta of all people? You always take everything good in my life. You can have anything you want. Why her? Why did you have to take her?"

It's not just Sal. I blame Greta, too, but I'm not convinced Sal didn't force her into it, hold something over her to keep her. "What did you do to make the Russos disappear? You did something. Did you send them away? Did you hurt them? Are they even alive?"

He snaps his head at me and clamps his hands on both my arms, predator on prey. "Shut your mouth, woman!"

As he does, a collection of keys on one ring fall from his pocket. Our eyes hit the floor and bounce up.

"Do not touch those." He loosens his grip to pick up the keys.

I reach for the vase holding the flowers he'd recently given me and slam it on the side of his head, probably not hard enough to knock him out but enough to stun him and buy me some time.

I snatch the keys from the floor and run out of the house, past the shed, straight to the Fiat. Luckily, I recognize the key for the Fiat; the others I'm not sure. One of them must belong to the shed.

I rev the engine, back out of the driveway, and head somewhere I should have gone long ago.

CHAPTER THIRTY-FOUR

Anna's house sits back from the road, obscured behind a patch of trees. I park the car, run to her house, and bang my fists on her door.

She whips it open and stares at me in disbelief.

I stare back with the same expression. Anna's body mostly fills the open space, but behind her, Giorgio is talking with someone. What's he doing here?

I crane my neck to get a better view, but Anna moves with me, blocking it. "Isabella, what are you doing here?" she says.

"May I come in?"

Anna stares at me blankly.

When she doesn't answer, I say, "Is that Giorgio?"

Anna hesitates like she wants to say something but doesn't have the words.

Drops of rain begin falling intermittently. I glance at the sky and then at Anna. "Are you going to let me in?" I push into the doorway, and she steps aside.

Giorgio rushes to the door. "Iz, are you okay? What are you doing here?"

I'd like to ask him the same. "No—I don't know," I stutter.

"You look a little peeked," he says. "Come sit down."

Anna's silence is peculiar. I follow Giorgio to the sofa and realize that all Anna's furniture has been replaced by brand-new furniture—beautiful, soft, high-end.

CHAPTER THIRTY-FOUR

"Did you get new furniture?" I ask, thinking how rare it is to purchase something brand new in light of our struggling economy. Giuseppe's income is average at best. Anna has always been frugal and humble in her possessions. I'm awestruck by the nice things she has and confused by it too.

Anna waves it off. "Oh no," she says, sitting beside me on the sofa. "It was a gift—from Giuseppe's parents." She crosses one leg over the other. "So, what brings you here, Iz? Has something happened?"

I try to shake my jealousy, but it's not just jealousy I'm feeling. Although the three of us have been friends since grade school, Giorgio and Anna were often at odds with one another. They fought more like siblings than friends. I was the one who brought us all together. Keeping peace between them was integral to our relationship. Strangely enough, Giorgio wouldn't go to Anna's without me, and it was the same with Anna. They never voiced this; it's just how it was. There was only one time they had gotten together without me. Anna suspected I was having an affair, of all things, and she'd called Giorgio over to discuss what they should do about it. I was hurt that she didn't have the decency to come right out and ask me herself and disappointed that she thought I'd be capable of doing that.

Nervously, I put my hand in my pocket and fiddle with the clothespins and the barrette, rethinking my reason for being here. I haven't seen Anna since the day we visited Peter at the detention center. It feels odd being in her presence now with Giorgio, like I'm on the outside looking in at these people I used to know.

Regardless of this awkward moment, Anna and Giuseppe have a right to know about the barrette I found. Perhaps there's a way to claim Peter's innocence without saying I found the barrette in Luca's possession.

Maybe it's not too late to save them both.

Anna's voice breaks the awkward silence wedged between us. "I invited Giorgio to dinner tonight, seeing that he's alone." She could have told me almost anything else and I would have believed her, but not that.

"Where's Giuseppe?" I ask.

"He's out," she says curtly.

I face Giorgio. "That's so kind of Anna." I put my hand on his arm. "Are you doing okay?"

Surprisingly, he takes my hand. "Thank you, Iz," he says. "It's been very hard. Most days I don't know what to do with myself. I go to work, and when I come home it's just me and Max. Sometimes it feels like there's too much empty space around us. We both need to get out of the house." He squeezes my hand. "Thank you, by the way, for the lasagna. Your cooking is delicious, and knowing it came from you was so . . . comforting." He smiles.

Anna shoots him a look I'm not sure how to read.

"It's nothing. I'm happy to do it," I say, taking back my hand. "I'm glad Max was home to bring the lasagna inside, and I'm happy it made you feel good. I haven't seen much of you lately."

"I've been keeping to myself a lot," he says. "How have you been?"

I nod briefly to avoid a lengthy reply and then I turn to Anna. I can't stop touching the barrette in my pocket. I want to take it out and show her right now, but so many conflicting thoughts stop me.

My head brims with questions and contradictions, but when I face Anna, my eyes fill thinking of the hell she and Giuseppe are going through. Thinking of what I could do to change that.

"Anna," I say, "I'm so sorry for the way we left things at the detention center. I've wanted to come see you so many times since then, but I wasn't sure you wanted me to. The things Peter said, I would never—"

"Yes, I know," she says, glancing around the room. She appears anxious and not attending to what I'm saying. She tucks her shoulder-length hair behind her ear. I hadn't realized how long it's gotten; she usually wears it tied up on top of her head. In fact, she appears slightly disheveled. She twirls the ends of her hair with her finger. "Is that why you came by—to tell me you're sorry?"

"Well, yes, partly."

There's a commotion coming from the other room—people talking, probably Peter's sisters. Anna glances toward the back near the bedrooms. Then she rises quickly and rushes out of the room. Giorgio and I are alone in the living room, my fingers wrapped tightly around the barrette.

"Did you really come here to apologize?" he asks.

CHAPTER THIRTY-FOUR

"Yes, and because I have something to share with Anna and Giuseppe that might give them hope, make things right."

Giorgio tilts his head, eyeing my pocket. "You have something? Like what?"

"Something I found. I'll tell you later." I glance over my shoulder. "Giorgio . . . something's not right here," I whisper. "Even you seem different. What's going on? Why are you really here?"

"For dinner, like Anna said." His eyes drop to the floor.

"Oh my gosh," I say, my voice catching. "You're lying to me. You can't even look me in the eye and be honest with me. Giorgio, look at me. Have I missed something?"

"No, no, it's not like that," he says.

"Do you realize how strange it is to see you here? You've been keeping away from me. Why?" This moment harkens to another in the past just like it.

"It's not what you think," he says.

"What do I think?"

Giorgio shifts in his chair as Anna returns. Something about her is off. As I try to piece together what is happening in front of me, Peter follows behind her.

I jump to my feet. "Peter!"

Giorgio's and Anna's heads snap in Peter's direction. Anna puts her hand to her head. "What did I tell you?" she says to Peter.

"Why shouldn't she know?" Peter snaps.

Everyone faces me. "Peter, you're out of the detention center? Since when?"

"Since yesterday," he says.

"Yesterday?" I say. "I've been worrying and praying and blaming myself, and no one thought to tell me Peter was home?"

"Oh, Iz," Anna says, "everything happened so fast."

"But not too fast to tell Giorgio and celebrate with him at dinner!"

"I'm sorry," Anna says. "I was planning on telling you tomorrow, I really was."

"How? How did this all come about that Peter just got released? Did they find new evidence?"

"Well . . . sort of . . ." Anna stares at Giorgio.

I turn to Peter. "Peter, did they tell you anything?"

"No, they didn't say anything."

I face Anna. "You do know something, don't you?"

Anna's eyes begin to twitch. "No," she says sharply. "And I didn't ask. I just wanted to get Peter out of there."

It's hard not to feel like a stranger in a house I've been to dozens of times. Like I've turned on the radio in the middle of a song with no idea how it started and only guesses to how it will end. I release my sweaty grip on the barrette and pull my empty hand from my pocket. There's no need to tell Anna about it now. I rise from the plush new sofa. Anna and Giorgio do the same.

"I guess I should be going," I say. I hug Giorgio first. "It's good to see you. I'm glad you're not alone."

Giorgio's arms are firmly around me, even when I let go. I can't help but question his motivation for being here and if there's something he wants to tell me.

"I'll be by again to check on you," he says. "I promise."

"You don't need to promise that, and you don't have to check on me. Concentrate on Max." I face Anna. "I came here to apologize. It's been so long since we've talked. I wanted to make sure you knew I hadn't abandoned you. I'm so happy for Peter and your whole family. It's as it should be for you now."

"I'm so glad you did," Anna says, sounding genuine for the first time since I arrived at her house. We embrace briefly and, as we do, I get a strong waft of a floral, musky perfume I know so well. I sniff again to be sure and smell it even stronger. I take a step back.

"What is it?" she says.

"Your perfume smells beautiful. Have you always worn it or is it new?"

"Oh my," she says, grinning. "I've been wearing this since I got married."

"Funny—I never really paid attention to it, but it's very pretty," I say as we

CHAPTER THIRTY-FOUR

walk to the door together.

I step into the fresh, cool breeze wondering if I've just hugged my husband's mistress. Or is his mistress the one no longer living next door to me?

CHAPTER THIRTY-FIVE

Greta

I love the quiet calm at seven o'clock in the morning as I sit on my porch all by myself. The valley still clings to yesterday's warmth, blanketing my skin. A beautiful scene in the Tuscan hills unfolds before me: a lush, green, soft, cashmere blanket spreads across the land; cows graze in a nearby pasture where birds in the trees above them sing.

This is a place I could call home. Except it isn't. There's nothing to dislike about it and so much to love. My real home in southern Tropea waits for me. I wasn't prepared to leave it behind in the middle of the night with only a moment's notice to take what I needed, but Rocco was convinced it was time to go. It was either that or risk the lives of our family at the hands of Salvatore Perri. I knew from the first day I met Sal he was nothing but trouble, but I had no idea just how much trouble he really was.

Our departure was imminent after Rocco was approached by his superior and asked to testify against Sal and his men. They wanted Rocco to disclose information he had about Sal's businesses and side jobs, meaning the crime he was involved in. In return, they offered us money and full protection, full immunity. A fresh start.

But that meant we'd be starting everything over—new names, new homes, new professions, everything new. Rocco wasn't that kind of guy. He didn't

CHAPTER THIRTY-FIVE

want to have to owe anyone anything. He tried hard to make plans for us to leave quietly without the help of the police, but there was one obstacle after another, and usually it was related to Sal. Sal has connections to everything, people from all walks of life committed to being his eyes and ears when he can't do it himself.

The sun's light reflected in an old photograph framed in silver on the end table in the living room. I picked it up and held it to my heart, a reminder of simpler times when we were young.

Rocco burst through the door, startling me so that I nearly dropped it. My heart pounded as he stepped heavy-footed into the room, his face riddled with fear.

His eyes searched mine. "Pack a bag—we have to go." He walked to the window and drew the curtains closed. "Call the girls down here."

I watched him, dumbfounded. "Go?" I said.

His eyes widened, acknowledging an earlier conversation about Sal and the possibility we'd need to leave one day. I didn't think that day would be now. I honestly didn't think it would ever come.

I ran to get the girls and quickly brought them into the living room. We sat closely to Rocco on the rug, curtains closed, lights low. Rocco's face was drawn and serious, his eyes glassy, and he spoke barely above a whisper.

"Pack only what you will absolutely need for the next three days into your pillowcases." He glanced at me. "Greta, add some snacks and sandwiches; water too."

"Papá," Gianna said, eyes wide with fear, "what's happening? Are we unsafe here?"

Sienna and Maria huddled closer.

"It will be okay," he said. "We're safe for now, but we may not be if we don't leave tonight."

"Tonight?" I said.

He shot me a look.

I watched the fear-filled faces of our girls, tears spilling over their cheeks. They had no idea what to think, and neither did I.

Rocco put his arms around us and pulled us close to him. "I promise you have nothing to fear if you trust me and listen to what I say. Can you do that?"

Yes, we said.

Rocco checked his pocket watch. "We need to meet in this exact spot in fifteen minutes."

"What about all this?" Maria said, indicating the living room furniture and the rest of the house.

"We'll have some help getting what we leave behind tonight," Rocco answered.

I had so many questions and objections. If we could just have two minutes alone . . . But while Rocco frantically searched for something in the house, the girls argued in their room. Instead of sorting things out with them, I ran to my bedroom and pulled open a musty old suitcase from the closet.

The clock ticked loudly in the hallway.

I tossed in a few articles of clothing. A shear blue scarf was caught in between, a birthday gift from Isabella.

My worries didn't compare to Isabella's. My sweetest friend was having a terrible time in her marriage. I regretted not having noticed sooner. The kids kept us busy, and I hadn't noticed her well-disguised bruises and random excuses for why she couldn't get together. On the outside, the Perris were a tight-knit family who loved to entertain and be involved in the community. On the outside, everyone thought they were perfect. We had no idea of the ugliness on the inside.

I remembered one time, when it was just Isabella and me, I asked her about the faded purple mark near her chin. She'd looked away and said it was nothing, but I knew. From then on, I watched her closely, and it was evident how much this girl had been crying out for help. I understood why she'd stayed with Sal. His dark reputation and questionable standing meant she would never be able to leave him, at least not alive, and he knew that. I'm sure he loved the power it gave him. She was trapped. I had to do something for her.

I was determined to find something on Sal that I could use to hold over him—blackmail him into promising not to lay a hand on her again. I started

CHAPTER THIRTY-FIVE

spying on him. Many days, after the kids went to school, I'd go to the marina and watch him. How differently he treated the women from the men! Certain women got lots of attention. He was a flirt, charismatic, and seemingly kindhearted to anyone who came to the marina. I discovered a lot about Sal during that time, but I always made sure I was home before my children.

On occasions when Sal ventured to the less desirable, questionable parts of town, or if it was getting too late to stay and watch, I convinced someone else to take over, another friend of Rocco's. I wasn't expecting to learn that Rocco had been working under Sal all this time, that Rocco had become a dirty cop. I confronted him immediately, and he readily admitted it.

Rocco said the small favors he did for Sal grew into complicated dealings, as did Sal's higher-than-normal expectations. Rocco said he looked the other way for robberies and often made charges against Sal disappear. My trust in Rocco diminished quickly. I questioned his promise that he never used the drugs he transferred for Sal.

I gently folded the scarf and placed it in the suitcase. While gathering a few toiletries in my hands, I pick up a pack of matches and was immediately brought back to a dinner party one night with the Perris.

I had met an intriguing gentleman named Massimo, who worked for Sal. Massimo was sweet and charming, but seeing how he was Sal's right-hand man, I didn't trust him at first. He was Sal's shadow, going everywhere Sal went and having all the answers to questions Sal asked.

We were seated together at a beautifully decorated table with crystal glasses and gold flatware. So much money. A book of matches like the ones in my hand were set next to the candle centerpiece. Isabella had gotten overly acquainted with the wine that night, and I was convinced she'd ingested some opium beforehand, a terrible combination and an unfortunate outcome. Isabella quickly grew incoherent, slurring her sentences, hardly able to keep her head up. She did her best to pretend, but her deteriorating condition was obvious. I had tried to cover for her, acting as if I knew what she was saying, but I couldn't keep up with the charade.

She mumbled something I didn't quite hear, but Sal's face had burned crimson red. His jaw cracked, and a hungry rage grew in his eyes. I was about to interject but was stopped short by Massimo, who stood and swooped in just in time before Sal's fury erupted. Massimo ushered Isabella out of the room to a safe place outside where she could get some fresh air.

Sal had put little effort into finding Isabella that night. I personally thought he had assumed Massimo took care of it. He may have, but not in the way Sal expected. Sal acted as if he didn't care in the least how Isabella would get home or if she even did go home. He'd already acquired the attention of Milania, his new goomah and most prized possession. Over the years, Sal had several mistresses, but Milania was the first to be gifted a lavish new home, one he frequented often.

Later, I learned that Massimo had taken Isabella to his house until she was sober enough to know what was happening to her, then he took her home. There were whispers of an affair between Isabella and Massimo, and even Anna questioned it for a while. But I knew there was nothing like that going on. For some reason Massimo had a soft spot for Isabella, and he was only helping her.

I couldn't quite figure out Massimo, though. Was he a good man trapped among evil, or had he been born into evil but was now seeking redemption?

I was getting closer to the truth about Sal, but to do it efficiently meant becoming friendlier with him, and I was terrified to cross that line. Eventually, my overzealous efforts lead Sal to the wrong impression, nearly costing me everything.

Thank God for Anna. She was helpful until she couldn't be. But we needed each other for a while. There was so much to do.

The argument in the girls' bedroom grew louder, snapping me out of my daze. I got to their doorway, and Maria and Gianna each had an arm of a sweater and were pulling in opposite directions. The sweater dropped to the floor when they saw me.

Soon Rocco was at my side. "Five minutes left. You almost ready?"

Gianna stepped toward us. "Papá, I need to talk to Franco. We are supposed to walk to school together tomorrow."

Rocco and I exchanged glances.

CHAPTER THIRTY-FIVE

"I'm sorry, bambolina, little doll," he said, cupping her chin. "We can't tell anyone we're leaving."

"But Papá—"

"We can't, Gianna," he said. "You have to trust me. There's no more to say about this. Go get yourself ready."

Gianna's eyes filled as she looked away, defeated. My heart broke as hope, love, and happiness poured right out of her. I'd had no idea there was more than friendship between her and Franco. I understood Gianna's need to tell Franco what was happening. I wished I could do the same with Isabella. What would Isabella think the next time she came over and found an empty house? Would she worry or would she speculate? Would she think I rudely left her without even saying goodbye? I was tempted to find a way to tell Isabella. Perhaps Gianna was thinking the same about Franco.

Rocco and I were the first to meet in the family room. While we waited for the girls to join us, he whispered the details of his plan.

"It's an offer of full protection our family cannot turn down," he said.

"I thought you said accepting help from the police wasn't necessary," I reminded him. "That we could leave on our own when we wanted to."

"I wanted it to be that way," he said, "I really did. But I think Sal is on to me. I think he knows I've been approached with a plan to trap him. And now it doesn't matter if I turn their offer down; if Sal knows I even thought about it, it's over."

"Why don't we leave in the morning when less people are in the neighborhood and Sal is at work?" I suggested.

"Because it's better to leave with Sal right next door, knowing where he is and not wondering where he is," he said. "Better to not be exposed by daylight but to escape beneath the veil of night."

I didn't like that word—escape.

The phone rang and Rocco picked it up quickly. The conversation on his end was brief and serious, Rocco mostly agreeing with the person on the other end. When he hung up, he told us there'd been a slight change of plans. We would not leave immediately. Instead, we were to leave at one o'clock in the morning, several hours after Sal returned home from work.

We remained in the living room and listened to the radio as the next few hours passed. At one o'clock in the morning, a handful of undercover police stealthily entered our home and loaded their cars with our belongings while our family watched from another car. I trembled as the policemen worked diligently and silently in the night. My eyes were trained on the Perris' house, fearful that Isabella or Sal would awaken and find out what we were doing.

The tension in the car was thick. I laid my head against the window, still watching the Perri house, thinking about the first time we met. It was love at first sight for all of us when the Perri family moved in next door. We fit each other like a well-worn leather glove. Our children were the same ages and played well together, and Isabella and I got on like sisters, an instant connection. We spent almost every day together. It was seamless until we became more acquainted with Sal.

Sal learned early on that Rocco was a police officer, and as soon as he became aware, he latched right onto him. Sal was grooming Rocco to be what he needed. Rocco spent a lot of time with Sal, coming home later every night. I tried to put an end to the friendship, tried to talk to Rocco, but finding time alone with him was almost impossible. Sal or someone else was always present. Sometimes they'd even come to the house to see him, which I did not like at all. I felt Rocco slipping away from me.

I remember how I'd continued to watch our houses as we secretly pulled away. I can still see the last glimpse I had of my house and the Perris' house as we drove into the night.

I brush a tear from my cheek, pull a cigarette from the others, and light it at my lips, looking past the hills of my new home and pondering how we got to this point.

CHAPTER THIRTY-SIX

Anna

When the phone rings, it catches me off guard. I hold the phone to my ear and listen to a series of clicks before a familiar voice begins to speak. It's the chief of police, and he's telling me that new evidence has surfaced in Peter's favor. I nearly drop the phone. Am I hearing him correctly?

"Hello?" he says. "Can you hear me?"

"Yes, I'm so sorry," I say. "I'm not sure if I've heard you right. Did you say there's evidence in Peter's favor?"

"That's correct," he says. "We received a strong tip that proved to be reliable, and, upon further investigation, it was determined that Peter was, in fact, not the last person to have been with Gia Lovallo. Peter is innocent."

My heart nearly bursts. It is exactly what I've been praying for all this time. I'm overcome with emotion so that I can hardly speak. I want to ask him to repeat what he just said. I want to ask who was the last one to be seen with Gia, but only a cry escapes my lips.

"Signora?" he says.

"I'm here," I say. "When can we come and get him?"

"No need," he says. "One of our officers will bring Peter home in the next couple of hours."

The next couple of hours means Peter will be home by dinner time. My knees buckle. I reach for the wall. "Thank you so much, officer—thank you." It's all I can manage without bursting into heaving sobs.

Right away I call Beppe at work, and as soon I as I tell him Peter will be home before dinner, I hear a catch in his voice and a loud tap as if he dropped the phone on the floor. Then he says, "I'm on my way," and hangs up.

When Giuseppe arrives, that's when I let it all out. A cry from the deepest part of me curls its way up and lashes out in full force. It waves through my body, rippling my skin, through my tightly clenched fists and my scrunched-up face. And I hear a sound, raw and feral—the deep, desperate relief of my voice.

Beppe wraps his arms around me, quietly cradling his head in my neck. I embrace him as his whole body shakes. We're overjoyed and relieved, yet shocked at this sudden turn of events. After a few moments, we pull ourselves together and talk about my conversation with the officer.

I notice that Beppe keeps asking me the same question but in different ways. He asks about the officer's voice: Did he sound confident? Did he hesitate at all? I'm confused by his lack of understanding and need for clarification. I can tell in his eyes that he's got some reservations.

"It's so sudden," he says. "Things like this don't happen this fast, not to regular people like us. How do we know they won't come for Peter again?" Beppe's face changes, like he's arrived at an epiphany. His gaze is firmly on me. "It's Sal. He's behind it."

"What do you mean?"

"The visits, the sudden concern—all this." He waves his arms at the new furniture. "He wants something from us. And now . . . we owe him."

"No, it can't be," I say as a sick feeling sits in my stomach. I won't say it out loud, but I fear he's right.

I remember when Sal started coming around to check on us. How silly of me to think he might be doing something good to make up for his bad deeds or those of his family. I was convinced his guilt drove him to it. He'd helped in small ways at first, bringing fruit from a nearby farm stand, stopping in to have a drink with Beppe, little things like that.

CHAPTER THIRTY-SIX

But then there was that one night when Sal stopped over that was different from the others. He and Beppe sat on the sofa, pouring one drink after another. I was so embarrassed when Sal pointed to a hole in the upholstery. The strategically placed blanket had slipped out of position, exposing the hole.

Suddenly the conversation shifted to the condition of the furniture. Sal said he would replace the sofa with a new one. We thought he was just saying it to be nice, but the next thing we knew, he had not only replaced the sofa but he bought a second sofa, a new chair, new tables, rugs; everything in our living room had been replaced with new items. He'd added new decorative items I'd never even dreamed of having.

Then his generosity moved into the kitchen. I should have stopped him. I wanted to, but we'd never had those things before.

Although I felt Sal owed it to us, Beppe was not happy about it. "Sal doesn't give anything for free," he'd said. I should have listened.

While we wait for Peter to arrive, we talk about his release.

Beppe looks at me. "What is it?" he says.

"Maybe the tip was about Luca." My stomach flips at the thought. No matter how angry I am at Isabella, I don't wish ill will on her or her boys.

"I'm just thinking about that day Izzy came with me to the detention center. Peter's accusations—that she was withholding information which could prove his innocence. She was protecting someone, maybe Luca, maybe Sal, maybe herself." I'd never questioned Isabella's honesty or loyalty until that day. But Peter's words created questions, and soon doubts cluttered my mind. I was confused and hurt at the possibility that Isabella would keep something so significant from me. "And now, after the phone call from the chief, I have a feeling the new evidence is related to one of the Perri boys."

"But then Sal wouldn't be behind Peter's release," he says. "Having Peter in jail keeps suspicion off the Perri family. It doesn't make sense. I know he's involved."

I know he's right.

It wasn't until Greta called a few weeks before she and her family disappeared that I had finally started to listen to Beppe—started seeing things differently.

Greta and I had met for coffee after the kids went to school, and Greta revealed all she knew about Sal Perri and the man he really was. She said she'd recently discovered Rocco's involvement in Sal's drug dealing and other crimes. She didn't talk specifics, but what she shared was enough.

My skin prickled as she spoke, especially when she told me about Isabella. I had no idea she was in so much trouble. She never shared anything about her marriage, and not once did she let on that she was struggling in any way. I felt sad that she didn't feel she could share it with me, guilty for not seeing her pain, for not being the friend she needed.

"We have to do something," Greta had said. Her eyes were desperate. "We have to dig deep and find out what Sal's up to, what he's planning. We have to protect our friend."

"How do we do that?" I'd said.

Greta smiled a fearful-hopeful smile. "I may have found something useful," she said. "Something we can use against Sal as leverage. Something that ensures Isabella's safety if she remains with him."

"Why would she even think of staying?" I said.

"She has nowhere to go," Greta said. "Sure, she could stay with us for a while, but how would she support herself and her boys on her own? Then again, she wouldn't want to put us in any kind of danger, so I guess she wouldn't stay with us. It doesn't matter, anyway—when Isabella finds out Sal is considering moving to America in the next couple years, she'll change her mind about leaving him. She won't miss an opportunity to go to America."

"How do you know all this?" I'd asked her.

I remember the intensity of her stare. "That's why I'm here, Anna. You see, I've had Sal followed, and I'm following him myself."

"You what?" I was shocked.

"It had to be done," she said. "That's how I know all this."

"But . . . how did you do it without getting caught?"

"I had to get close to him." Greta's eyes fell to the floor, and I needed no further explanation.

"Oh no, Greta," I said. "You didn't."

CHAPTER THIRTY-SIX

"It's not exactly what you think. We haven't—"

"Oh, thank God. I—"

"But close enough."

Our eyes locked and then drifted away.

And when Greta asked about the new furniture, I'd almost vomited. Sal had given us those things. I remember cringing at the thought of what he might expect in return, especially after what Greta alluded to between her and Sal.

I started re-evaluating Peter's sudden release and everything about Sal's visits and nice gestures.

"What can I do to help—besides getting close to Sal?" I'd said.

"I don't need you to be close to Sal," she'd said. "I need you to get close to Massimo—follow him, see where he goes. He may be the answer we need."

I fan myself with my hands to rid the rising heat in my head. Beppe eyes me.

"What are you thinking about?" he says. "Your face is all scrunched up."

I've never been able to hide my feelings from Beppe. My stomach twists into tight knots just like it was that day with Greta. I'd also been thinking of the unhealthy connection that had grown between Sal and me, one I did not want to deepen.

I shake my head. "Just feeling bad about how I misjudged Isabella. She must think I've abandoned her." I hadn't known about the private hell she'd been going through. Which was why I had agreed to help Greta that day.

Beppe puts his arm around me. "You'll talk to her when the time is right, and she'll understand. She'll forgive you."

I feel guilty for not telling Beppe everything. He doesn't know a thing about what Greta and I did. How we'd arrived at the marina together the next morning before anyone else; that Greta used the key Sal had given her to get in; or that we hid inside the marina watching and listening to everything that went on inside. And when Sal and Massimo left the marina to assist the boaters, we snuck out of the closet to see what they were doing. He had no idea that when they separated, Greta followed Sal and I followed Massimo. We did as much as possible on foot, and when we needed to go farther, we called Giorgio. Since then, I don't remember a time when my body wasn't trembling, my skin not crawling, my mind free.

We sit on the sofa side by side in silence, thoughts running through my head. I'd never shared with Beppe about the time I followed Massimo. Guilt seeps from my pores, recalling how I'd left dinner in the oven and a note on the table for Beppe saying that if I wasn't home for dinner to eat without me. I added that I had gone into town with Greta later than expected, which might result in my later-than-normal return. I remember how my hand shook with the lie I was writing. I imagined the look of surprise on his face, as I was always home for dinner. But it would be easier to explain later rather than getting Beppe's approval before.

Greta had prepared me for the stakeout, sharing who the regulars were as well as the pretty women who frequented for something other than boats or supplies. We stood in wait at the outer edge of the property, just beyond the marina, in a perfectly secluded spot where we witnessed the peculiar workings of the marina.

Greta had been right about a lot of things, including her knowledge that on that particular night, Sal and Massimo would slip out before closing, leaving the marina in the hands of other men. Isabella would not have liked that. Sal and Massimo left almost to the minute of Greta's prediction. My heart nearly burst when the two men headed in different directions, meaning Greta and I would be going our separate ways.

I remember when Greta nodded, and we had to leave our safe hiding spots in favor of the unknown paths ahead. Massimo walked to the unlit and heavily treed area behind the marina. It was difficult to keep up, hard to see with all the brush and overgrown trees, but I did it and, before I knew it, we were deep into the woods. I was terrified, but I knew I had to keep going.

Past the trees, we continued on a well-worn path that ended in a familiar neighborhood: mine. My legs stiffened as I feared his destination was my house. But we weren't in my neighborhood for long and, before I knew it, we were entering the back side of the Perri plantation.

When Massimo picked up speed, I walked faster. When he slowed, I did the same. I never lost sight of him. Not when he unlocked the gate, not

CHAPTER THIRTY-SIX

when he walked through the plantation, or when he made a fast visit to the shed. I kept a keen eye on Massimo, but my heart sank when he stopped just short of the Perris' house.

He stood there for a minute like he was contemplating his next move. Was he there to do something to Isabella or perhaps just watch her? I desperately wanted to warn her, but how? Massimo's head bent as if he were studying something in his hands. And then, slowly, like a prowling cat, he slinked up the porch steps and bent to the door. He took something out of his jacket pocket, something like paper, and slid it under the door.

When he looked over his shoulder, I swear he saw me. He kept himself low, walked down the driveway, turning left onto the road. I hesitated, but I knew better than to alert Isabella to Massimo's secret visit. He'd only slipped a note under the door, that's all. And I had a job to do—follow Massimo wherever he went. Unfortunately, in my slight hesitation, I'd already lost sight of him. I ran to catch up, but he was nowhere to be seen.

I still wonder if he really left the neighborhood that fast, or if he was hiding, knowing I'd seen him. I'd been too afraid to continue after him, fearing he might come out of hiding and attack me. Instead, I went another way home, and on the way, I thought of what I would say to Beppe about my visit in town.

I take Beppe's hand and, when he looks at me, I gaze longingly into his eyes, praying he cannot see my guilt. He'd warned me so many times about the Perri family, told me not to get in the middle of Isabella and Greta's situation, and I'd done the opposite.

A tear escapes my right eye and rolls down my cheek. Beppe's finger catches it. He kisses my forehead and then hugs me.

"Everything will be better when Peter gets home," he says.

I nod. "I hope so," I say and then the doorbell rings.

CHAPTER THIRTY-SEVEN

Sal

Trusting someone doesn't come easily for me. Probably comes from a long line of untrusting men in my family, and with good reason. If we trust you, we're fiercely loyal and protective of you. If we don't—well, you don't want to know. My father taught me how to handle the ones we can't trust.

I've known Massimo almost my entire life. Our families were close since we were children, and both our fathers being in the same kind of business, we grew up together and knew a lot at our young age. We had much common and a camaraderie that was unparalleled to anything else I'd had in a friendship, like brothers. But Massimo didn't need the leadership and power I needed; he was content acting more as an assistant to me. He'd do anything I asked.

In our younger days, he'd get his hands dirty, but as we've gotten older, he's preferred to be more of the cleanup man than the one causing the mess. And that was okay with me.

Until recently.

I'm not exactly sure when it happened, but somewhere along the line, Massimo started to have soft spots for people, particularly my boys and Isabella.

CHAPTER THIRTY-SEVEN

He began to question my decisions regarding my family. Started telling me I was too hard on Isabella—Isabella of all people. How I treat my wife is no business of his. His concern for them started before the last dinner party, when he suddenly became protective of Isabella. I guess it could have been part of his coverup for me, smoothing things over, obscuring the chaos I'd created as usual. But I wasn't totally convinced of that. Massimo was appearing weak, and that feeling unnerved me.

I asked him to check the shed to make sure there was nothing left behind from that girl, Gia. He said he'd examined it thoroughly and found nothing, but I found myself going there the next day to be sure.

I was sure the increased traffic at the marina would draw unwanted attention from the police. That added to Luca's inconsistent behavior at school and Franco's whining about the injustices of the world made for too many unknowns in my personal life. I couldn't have that. I asked Massimo to watch my family and report on anything he found.

I wasn't expecting Isabella to stop taking her medicine. I'd hoped to continue using that against her, keep her mind dull so she wouldn't ask questions. I ordered Massimo to add the opium she'd been taking into her teas. He said he'd done it, but Isabella didn't become incoherent—she became present and sharper than ever.

I wanted him to watch Giorgio because I didn't trust Giorgio at all, especially around Isabella. I'm not stupid. Even his wife, Camilla, could see he was in love with Isabella. What happened to Camilla wasn't meant for her. It was supposed to happen to Giorgio. Camilla was in the wrong place at the wrong time. And because Massimo wanted no involvement in Giorgio's disposal, I had to use someone else. Needless to say, that individual is no longer with me.

People like me are always prepared. I needed to start grooming someone else who was close to my family in case Massimo didn't work out. Giuseppe and Anna were perfect for that. I saw Giuseppe's need for attention and Anna's recent anger at Isabella as their weak spots and took full advantage of it. But even after spending night after painful night in thoughtless conversation with Giuseppe, and even after all the money I spent redecorating their pathetic home, it still wasn't enough. Giuseppe must have felt like he had the privilege of asking me questions about things I needed to stay quiet. Questions that turned the blame for what happened to Julia and Gia away from Peter. I felt like he started pointing a finger at me. I couldn't have that.

Rocco was no longer able to help me with things like this, but I had others. I met with a few of them, paid them well, and they promised to get Peter out of the detention center. That eliminated Giuseppe's need to keep questioning things and kept attention off me, at least for now.

The last thing I want to do is frame my own sons. Others have done it to their family members, but I have my standards. Plus, I still need them.

But a couple nights have passed, and I think I've waited long enough. Time to make a visit to the happy family. I purposely arrive early because I only want Anna to be there, and I don't want her to prepare for my arrival. It's better to catch people off guard; then you'll know if they're being honest with you.

I can tell right away that Anna is keeping something from me. She opens the door and immediately starts looking around like she's paranoid. I step inside their recently beautified home, thanks to me. Anna appears dumbfounded, like she doesn't know what to say or how to behave around me. It makes me uncomfortable.

"Mind if I have a drink?" I say.

"Of course," she says, leading me to the living room. She leaves for a moment and quickly returns with a glass of Cutty Sark. She hands it to me, her hand shaking.

"Where's yours?" I say. "You're not gonna make me drink alone, are you?"

Anna glances at the clock, probably thinking it's too early for a drink, but says nothing of it as she retrieves another glass of whiskey.

"Sit down. Relax," I say. "You're making me nervous with your hovering."

Anna sits in the chair next to me and takes a sip from her glass. "Beppe won't be home for another half hour," she says.

"Where are the kids?"

"In their rooms."

CHAPTER THIRTY-SEVEN

I smile. "Are you enjoying all your new furniture?"

"Yes, very much, but we plan to pay you back as soon as possible," she says.

"No need." I throw my drink back and give a nod to indicate I'm ready for another. Anna hesitates but then pours more whiskey into my glass. "How's Peter?" I continue. "I bet it's great to have him home again. Here's to your family," I raise my glass before slamming it back again. I let out a heavy sigh. "I'm glad it all worked out. It was a little sketchy at times, but in the end—"

"What—what do you mean?" she says. "Are you saying you had . . . something to do with Peter's release?"

"Let's just say they consulted with me first."

"Who's 'they'?" she says.

"You know, the department—chief of police, a few others."

Anna's otherwise pleasant face turns sour.

"Why are you looking at me like that?" I say. She doesn't answer. "I haven't always had a voice in matters like this if you're wondering. It only happened recently with the new evidence, which I helped them with."

"So you know what the evidence is?" she says.

"I'm not at liberty to say. And, by the way, you won't breathe a word of this to Beppe, right?"

"Y—yes. Right," she says, just as Beppe walks through the door.

"You started without me," Beppe grins. "Pour me one. I'll be right in." Beppe removes his coat and leaves his shoes by the door.

I watch Anna pour a third glass of whiskey. I know she feels my eyes on her. I want her to. I want her to know I have control, so if she gets any ideas, she'll think twice or suffer the consequences.

I can get Peter out of the detention center, and I can put him right back in.

About an hour or so later and after a fourth glass of whiskey, I decide it's time to leave. I can tell by Beppe's and Anna's awkwardness that they understand who's in charge. I accomplished what I came here for.

CHAPTER THIRTY-EIGHT

Greta

Gianna steps onto the porch, the sun sparkling through the golden highlights in her hair. Although only two years younger than her sister, Sienna, everyone thought they were twins. I see it more and more each year. Both girls resemble me, while Maria takes on more of Rocco's features.

"I thought you stopped smoking, Mamá," she says.

"I have," I say. "I'm just pensive today."

"Pensive?"

"Filled with thought."

"What's wrong?"

"I can't burden you with these kinds of things," I say. "You already have so much to get used to." We hold each other's stare. "I'm sorry you didn't get to say goodbye to Franco."

Gianna's eyes fill and she blinks away the tears.

"Maybe someday it will be different," I say, "but for now, we have to do what your papá thinks is best."

"You really think we'll go home again someday?" She asks with so much hope in her eyes. I can't bear to crush it.

"You never know," is all I say.

I watch Gianna as she stares out at the hills. How much she's grown. I recognize the fire inside her. I see it in her eyes and in the old soul of her personality. She's just like me. We're both survivors. Fighters. She'll find her way in the world and be incredible at anything she sets her mind to. I do feel confident in that.

In my mind a new plan emerges, a way to get word to Isabella to let her know I'm okay and to tell her what Anna and I have discovered about Sal. A way for her to stay in her life but no longer be afraid.

Maria went to the house once before to try to find my journal, and she got all the way back. Of course, I hadn't known that at the time and did not approve, but it showed me that, if done carefully, it could be done. I could send Maria again, but the thought of it makes me nervous. Maria is easily distracted, which can get her into danger. Yes, she was successful, and secretly I'm proud of her for doing what she did, but the reality is I was lucky she wasn't caught.

Gianna, on the other hand, has more common sense and just the right amount of bravery. I can trust Gianna to get my message to Isabella before Isabella tries to leave Sal.

It doesn't take much to convince Gianna. She readily agrees to go.

"I'm trusting you, Gianna," I say. "I know it will be extremely tempting to be so close to Franco, but you cannot let him see you, not for a second. I have to trust you on this. It could cost us our safety. You understand what I'm saying, right? This is risky. Your father doesn't even know."

"Yes, Mamá. I promise. You can trust me."

I prepare Gianna for the short trip she'll take first thing in the morning. She'll wear some of Beppe's old clothes, disguised as a boy with her hair tucked beneath a cap. I give her enough money for the train to Tropea and then for the driver to take her from the station to our old house. She'll make sure no one is around. She'll carry a box and pretend she's delivering a package. She'll enter through the unlocked back door.

Once she's inside our house, she'll go straight to my bedroom, which faces Isabella's house, and place the note on top of the jewelry box on my dresser. While she's watching through the window, she'll use the bedroom phone and dial Isabella's number, letting it ring once and hanging up. Then she'll

CHAPTER THIRTY-EIGHT

call again and let it ring a second time before hanging up again.

Hopefully it will alert Isabella and remind her of the signal she and I used sometimes when we wanted to talk about something but not over the phone. Whichever one of us received the signal would return the call in the same way, confirming the signal had been received. Usually, our reasons for meeting were related to one of our children and sometimes our husbands.

But tonight's signal will be for a different reason. I pray to God it works.

I explain to Gianna that when she receives the return signal, she is to leave immediately with the driver and come back to Tuscany. If, after a few attempts, she gets no reply, she will have to leave the note in the next best place—inside the book Isabella keeps on her small porch table. But what if she doesn't have a book out there like she usually does? What if Gianna's caught placing the note in the book? I truly hope she doesn't have to resort to that.

The last thing Gianna must do before she leaves our old house is go to the attic and find my journal. It will be inside an old box labeled with my name on it. I've directed her not to read it and will have to trust that she'll respect my wishes, as the entries inside the journal contain things she wouldn't understand right now.

This has to work. Gianna is my only hope at connecting with Isabella and possibly saving her life.

CHAPTER THIRTY-NINE

Isabella

I pull the car slowly into its home behind the trees, cutting the engine just before I park for a noiseless entry. The shed's light signifies Sal's presence. I cringe at the thought of the vase hitting him as I left with his keys and his car.

But his presence in the shed means none of the other keys that clung to the Fiat's belonged to the shed. Or it could be that he has more than one key to the shed.

And because he's in there and not out searching for me, it leads me to believe he was more concerned I'd find a way into the shed than he was about me taking his car.

I recall our last few moments prior to my quick grasp on the vase: his eyes drawn up to the Russos' lighted attic, my accusations of his involvement in their sudden evacuation.

And then it hits me at once—the phone ringing in the middle of our heated conversation. It rang once and then stopped. A slight pause followed before it rang a second time. And then nothing. Sal and I continued to argue, and we were interrupted by the same ring pattern again.

Greta and I used to signal each other just like that when we wanted to talk in secret. Whichever of us received the ringing pattern was to ring back in the same way. Then we'd meet on one of our porches to talk.

A rush of worry flies through me. I hold my stomach, sick at the thought that Greta had finally tried to make contact and I'd missed it. I hadn't paid attention, I hadn't returned the signal. And now it was probably too late. She probably had only a small window of opportunity to contact me.

Instead of going inside my house, I run to Greta's and let myself in through the back door. I take the stairs two at a time to Greta's bedroom, stopping and slowing down just as I enter her room. All is as it was when I left it a few days ago. Nothing different to indicate anyone was here. I've missed her. I've missed my opportunity. But then I recall the light in the attic.

When I step inside, it's cold and musty in the attic, and right away I'm frightened of what, if anything, is hiding behind the boxes. But there's nothing to see among the old packed up boxes of storage. How can that be? Someone was here. The attic light was on—Sal and I both saw it. And now it's off. Who was here and why? There has to be something I'm not seeing.

Think. What would Greta do if she couldn't reach me with a signal?

Disheartened, I take one last look through the attic and then, reluctantly, I decide to leave. But a bright-white, freshly torn piece of paper catches my attention just before I descend the steps. I don't know how I missed it other than the possibility I was looking for a person and not something so small and seemingly insignificant.

I snatch it up and read the one word written in the middle: porch.

I race down the steps and practically fly down the stairs and out the door. I slow my steps again trying to seem normal so as not to draw attention to myself. Then I walk out the door to Greta's porch, my heart racing, pounding out of my chest.

But there's nothing on her porch except for two chairs, one for her and the other usually reserved for me. An empty table sits between them. It's obvious there is nothing on her front porch.

That's because it has to be on my front porch.

I get to my porch fast, keeping an eye on the shed light. It must stay on just a little longer.

On my porch I examine everything, the chairs, the table, the floor.

CHAPTER THIRTY-NINE

Nothing.

I pick up the book lying on my table. I always keep one there. Greta knows this. I open the book and the pages naturally fall apart, giving way to the folded paper inside. My name is neatly written in Greta's handwriting on the front. It smells like her, too, and I'm not sure how I feel about that.

My pulse quickens as I take the note in my shaky hands and unfold it.

Izzy,

I'm so sorry I didn't say goodbye. I had no idea we were leaving until the moment we did. I cannot say anything about where I am, only that we're safe. I sent Gianna with this note, and I pray it's you reading it right now and no one else.

I'm sorry I didn't know you were going through so much with Sal. I should have been more aware. So much has happened. Please understand that I can't give you details about how I've come to know things, but you must believe me when I say that there is nothing between Sal and me. Some may say otherwise, but, although I did go behind your back, I did it for your safety. It was the least I could do to make up for my ignorance.

This is the truth, Iz. You're right about Sal's plans to go to America in a few years. He plans to bring the entire family. I've found a way to keep you with your family but not have to endure anymore pain or fear from Sal.

Sal is not who you thought he was. He's not even who he thought he was. Sal is the illegitimate child of his mother and another man she fell in love with. He is not his father's son. He should not be the leader of the 'Ndrangheta because he is not the heir—his brother is. Sal will do anything to keep this quiet. Anything. He wants to be the legal heir to his father's fortune and his legacy. It is integral to his whole being.

I've taken the liberty to inform Massimo. Don't worry, you can trust him. He has already told Sal he is being blackmailed with this information and he has proof. If Sal wants to keep this quiet, he cannot lay a finger on you or the boys or even threaten to. He's been told that someone is watching him, and they will know if he breaks his promise.

Sal cannot hurt you anymore. You're free, Iz.

I miss you so much, my friend. I probably will not see you again for many years; sadly, maybe never. It's how it must be. But I know you can be strong, and I know you will be okay!

All my love,

Greta

As I read the note, everything around me fades away. No awareness of the house, the cars going by, the wind rustling the leaves on the trees, even the planks of wood I stand on. I momentarily drift away, absorbing every word of the closest friend I'll never have again. I read it again three more times before I fold it and tuck it into my pocket.

It's starting to make a little sense. Sal hasn't been rough with me lately, and I've stood up to him more than I ever have. I don't know when exactly Sal found out about his illegitimacy. It had to have been right before he tried to strangle me. After I kicked him in the groin and left with his car, he welcomed me back with flowers. And just now, after hitting him in the head with the vase and taking his car again, I'd expected him to be waiting for me at the door or on the porch, but he was working in the shed. So, when was it he learned of this? I'll probably never know.

I feel slightly lighter now. Only slightly.

I glance to the end of the driveway and see the two officers from before returning. They park at the end and walk the rest of the way to the porch where I'm standing, still absorbing the freshness of Greta's letter. Their blank faces are hard to read.

"Hello, officers D'Amico"—I say, pointing to one—"and Parnello, right?" I point to the other. They acknowledge my guesses with nods and smiles. "To what do I owe the pleasure of your visit today?"

"We're letting neighbors know that both the Bernardi and Lovallo cases are open again."

I feign confusion.

Officer D'Amico continues. "I'm surprised you haven't heard by now, but Peter Rossi has been released. He is no longer a suspect."

I place my hand to my heart. "Oh my goodness, that's wonderful news for

CHAPTER THIRTY-NINE

Peter! But . . . that means the person responsible is . . . still out there?"

"Unfortunately, yes," Officer Parnello says.

"No leads at all?"

"Not at this time, but don't worry, we'll find the person responsible," Officer Parnello says confidently.

"We're so close," Officer D'Amico says. "We're still looking for one more thing."

Officer Parnello shoots D'Amico a hard stare and then puts his attention back to me. "Is your husband here?"

I glance at the house to keep my eyes from wandering to the shed. "No, he's not at home right now," I say. Not entirely a lie. He isn't in our home. I'm not exactly sure why I don't disclose that Sal is in the shed. Julia Bernardi's and Gia Lovallo's families deserve justice. I'm just not so sure the justice they need comes from my family.

I'm so tired.

But my guilt takes over. "He might be working in his office," I say, pointing to the shed. "Why do you need to talk to Sal?"

"Just want to make sure we tell everyone face to face," Officer D'Amico says.

"And to apologize for any misconceptions or miscalculations we may have had in the investigation," Parnello adds.

"Misconceptions?" I say.

"Your husband—and your boys, for that matter—were strongly considered as possible suspects," D'Amico says.

Parnello glances at D'Amico. "Although we're not supposed to tell you that."

"Understood," I say, feeling a swirl of emotion stirring inside me. "You're welcome to go to his office and tell him."

The officers tip their hats and turn toward the shed. I watch as Sal answers the door and lets them in. And then I let myself into our home and close the door, for the first time feeling slight relief. But my mind and body remain cautious, ready for a new spike of emotion, prepared to fight or flee.

***

It's almost midnight. Sal is snoring, confirming a deep sleep. The boys have been in their beds for a couple of hours.

I slip from my bed and go to my dresser. I remove both jewelry boxes from my top drawer and carry them close to my chest, down the hallway, down the stairs, and to the kitchen.

I place them on the counter and go to the cupboard to retrieve the shoe. I carry these items to the porch and look at each item one last time under the porch light: the warning notes I'd received, the barrette I'd taken from Luca's possession, and the second one he finally surrendered; I turn the shoe around and study it once more—the shoe from the shed that shouldn't have been there.

I open Luca's jewelry box, the one I think he may have stolen from my mother's belongings after she died. The other items inside have no meaning to me, but their presence leaves an uneasy feeling inside.

Just off the porch is the small pit we sometimes use for burning trash. Before I went up to bed, I prepared the pit with the right-sized pieces of wood and a few fallen branches. I stuffed crumpled paper in between the wood.

The stars sparkle brightly in the sky. It is a clear night with hardly a breeze, so when I strike the match against the porch post it lights instantly. I throw it into the sticks and paper and light another and then another. The flames stretch and fold into one another, blending and lengthening as the towering fire licks the sky.

I throw the notes in first, one by one, and watch them disappear into the flames. Then I toss in both barrettes. I tip my mother's jewelry box over the flames and watch the contents fall to their fiery death.

Lastly, I hold the shoe in my hands—a shoe that will never find its match, never rest on the foot it was meant for. It is the hardest thing to part with, and my heart aches as it fights with my head to let it go. I hold it above the

CHAPTER THIRTY-NINE

scorching fire and release it. I wave at the smoke with my hands and add more paper to keep the fire burning for a while.

I look on as the items that once held my mind captive blacken and crumble in the flames, and I remain beside the fire as it warms me first on the outside and then on the inside. I'm not fully convinced this is the right thing to do, but the police no longer think the men in my family are connected to the crimes in our town. So, there is no need to keep these items which have only caused misunderstanding and confusion. We all need a fresh start. These items no longer have power over us.

And no one has power over me.

II

Sneak Peek: Moment of Truth Book 4

CHAPTER ONE

Mona

His eyes won't let me go.
    I'm standing next in line at the café counter when a strange sensation pulses at my temples, my vision fading fast to a narrow, feathery line. What remains are his eyes—penetrating, piercing. His unrelenting eyes won't let me go.

But I escape his gaze. Somehow, in my mind, I've slipped away, and now I'm a young girl again, sitting at my desk at school with friends I haven't seen in years. They fix their expressionless faces and impenetrable stares on a dark hole in the upper right-hand corner of the chalkboard.

Our teacher, Miss Olivia, glides about the classroom, and I'm mesmerized by her singsong voice, flowing through a radiant smile. But she stops fast when she sees me, and she shoots an icy stare as she climbs, cold and rigid, through the rows of desks toward me. As she continues to speak, her voice morphs into deep, dreary tones, forced through a tight grin.

I desperately attempt to make eye contact with my friends to see if they notice what's happening with Miss Olivia. But they concentrate their gaze on that dark hole in the chalkboard. I squint to make out what they're watching so intently. I gasp when I see it: it's me standing in line in the café when the man walks in. He's watching me, waiting for me, but I don't know it yet. Then he's suddenly upon me. I feel my breath escape now as it did then.

I want to know more, but Miss Olivia has finally caught their attention, taken it from that hole in the chalkboard. Taken it from me. They're enchanted by her. Spellbound. Lost.

I wipe my brow and pull at my shirt collar as the room, now devoid of air, leaves me breathless. I'm alone except for Miss Olivia, who approaches me uncomfortably closely. Face to face, peering into my eyes, mere inches apart.

All at once, the doors fly open for recess, and I'm whisked away with my classmates. We spill out onto the playground, releasing a collective sigh of relief. Shoulders and brows relax in the fresh air, and we disperse to our accustomed spots on the playground.

I float from one conversation to another, not adding anything of value and strangely unbothered by it. But as I pay more attention, I hear a difference in the surrounding chatter.

I can't explain the restless nervousness that pervades the conversations among my classmates. They seem to choose their words carefully, as if they are all on the edge of slipping and revealing something they were forbidden to say. Something everyone knows but me. I sense a build-up of emotion about to unravel.

I open my mouth to speak, but I can't form the words. And without warning, the chatter fades and the playground disappears. The day is over.

We burst through the front door as the last bell rings, our pace much quicker than usual. Katarina and Leah lead the way, muttering something I can't understand. Mia and Anna trail slightly behind, whispering to each other. I have to run to keep up with my friends, and the farther we get from the school, the tighter the knot in my stomach becomes.

"Come on," Katarina says, craning her neck toward us.

"Kat, please slow down," I say.

"We're going to miss it," Leah yells.

One small drop of rain falls on my nose. I pull my coat around me to keep the chill from finding its way inside. We're practically running, but then Katarina stops suddenly, perhaps because she forgot something at school. But when Leah stretches an arm around Katarina, and Anna and Mia flank

CHAPTER ONE

either side of them, I realize it's not that.

"What's wrong?" I say. "Kat, are you okay?"

Others gather behind and around us, and together, we resume a slow, deliberate walk straight ahead. I place my hand against my burning chest as we draw closer to each other and then stop. All eyes except mine fixate on that same direction. A confusing mix of anger, frustration, and dread falls upon me as the close-knit crowd blocks my view.

In a small, open space on the right, I slip away and observe the grim expressions of my classmates, their eyes burdened with something terrible. I need to know what they see, but I'm petrified at the same time. Slowly, I maneuver my way to the front where Katarina stands. Her expression mirrors the sad faces of the crowd. A tear escapes the corner of her eye as she draws her hand to her mouth. As something erupts inside of me, fiery and strong, I reach for her. It presses down on me like a waterlogged blanket and squeezes out every breath. I place both hands on my chest and lift my head to the sky, trying to gulp in the tiny amounts of air available. I desperately search for someone to help me, and that's when I notice Father Anthony.

He's standing at the center where I shouldn't be looking. His outstretched hands come together, folded in prayer. Familiar faces draw close to him and a troubled young couple. I soon realize I know them. They're my parents, only younger. My father stares at the crowd with bloodshot eyes, dazed. His cheeks are wet and shiny. My father wraps his arm around my mother as she pleads for help through broken sobs.

Father Anthony motions for all of us to come closer. He speaks in an unfamiliar language, but everyone nods in agreement. I try to get his attention, but his eyes are on my parents and the space before them. I wave my hand to interrupt his gaze and to ask him one simple question.

His head snaps up. He sees me, and I am jolted by his piercing, unrelenting eyes. Those same dark eyes from the café. That's when I know I must look in the one place I'd been fighting not to look. The place on the ground where they're all staring empathetically. My stomach flips as I cast my eyes on a colorful scattering of my favorite flowers: tulips, roses, and peonies. A few small trinkets lie peppered among the flowers, and a framed photograph that looks like me, taken on my fifteenth birthday.

But I'm not fifteen; I'm twenty-five.

Notes lie among the flowers, some neatly folded, others open wide, exposing words of sorrow and encouragement. Notes all written with the same name at the top.

My name.

Mona.

I cup my hand to my mouth and swallow the scream-filled bile rising. An overwhelming scent of roses saturates the air, and all at once a sharp, painful piercing slices into my chest and then again at my side.

I look down, horrified at my dress, which is now covered in blood, and then I fall to the flowers below me, exposing my truth.

The café. Those eyes.

They all think I'm gone.

But I'm not gone. I'm alive.

I'm very much alive.

CHAPTER TWO

Ella

F ear and guilt are always present now, along with an incessant need to protect my family. Fear's powerful grip paralyzes me, confining me to my bed. My limbs weighed down, my mind swirling clouds of nothing. It dominates my dreams, my thoughts, my life. I am helpless under its spell, always looking over my shoulder, constantly calling to check on my family.

On the days I can get out of bed, dark, persistent thoughts plague my mind: Will Luca be back to exact his revenge today? Will it be tomorrow? Maybe I'll open my front door one day and he'll be on the doorstep waiting for me with a crooked, victorious smile at finding me. Or worse, he'll show up at the wedding. I shudder at the thought, and every thought about Luca, my ex-favorite uncle, wanted for the kidnapping and attempted murder of Gianna, his brother and my Poppy's lover. Wanted for kidnapping and murder of other women. Wanted for ruining our lives.

When fear is at bay, guilt kicks in, and guilt on its own is just as bad. There's no rest, no relief, no respite. Worrisome thoughts, dark and heavy, grab hold and squeeze tight. An active spirit of defeat, rendering my psyche to harm. My mind is trapped in a never-ending loop of thoughts about the past, replaying what I could have done differently. Questions I ask myself, knowing I won't find the answer.

If I hadn't gone to Italy and brought to light the darkness in our family, maybe we would still be whole. Imagine if I never found the storage unit packed with women's clothes and personal items. Had I not forced Luca at gunpoint to dig behind the vineyard for Gianna's body, a body I desperately didn't want to be there, we'd never have known she was alive.

To our surprise, Gianna, a grandmother I never knew existed, wasn't dead in the shallow grave as we had all expected. That was when we also learned about Grace, my mother's twin sister. Because Gianna's mother couldn't accept the idea of her unwed daughter having two babies, she had deliberately separated them at birth. Both Gianna and Grace had been kept from us all this time.

If only I hadn't pushed Luca to confess his sins against our family, shattering us like glass, cutting us deeply, irreparably.

But then I think I *should* bear the burden of these feelings because it's all my fault. I was the one who unraveled the tightly knotted, well-kept secret. What if I hadn't done that?

I'd still have my favorite uncle, and I'd still have my best friend, Jamie. Life would be simple, predictable, normal. We'd be living in blissful ignorance among the lies, protected from the shameful truth threatening to expose our shameful history.

That's when Poppy's voice comes to me, soft, soulful, reassuring, and I know that I did what I had to do. It was for Poppy, my beautiful grandfather; his last request. He needed answers to the parts of his story that were missing, answers he ran out of time to find. He needed me to release the dirty secrets. Rid them from our family, wash them clean so we could be free to live in the truth. He'd trusted only me with his secret. And, of course, I listened, although it was one of the hardest things I've ever done, but I would do anything for Poppy.

I'd struggled with it—the truth. It wounded us in ways I can't explain and damaged us beyond recognition. Exposing our family's secrets brought people I once loved and trusted into a light I never wanted to see. It complicated our relationships so that we are still trying to find our way back to each other.

"Sometimes doing what's right is the hardest thing to do," Poppy would say.

CHAPTER TWO

He was so right about that. But exposing the truth isn't the only difficult challenge. When everything was out in the open and we were reeling from the fallout, I quickly learned that the most challenging task ahead was to keep my family safe and pull us all together again. Like the frayed edges of an old, well-loved blanket, we were falling apart.

And I don't care what anyone says—not my mother, not even Nico. It absolutely *is* my job to put us back together. It's up to me to make sure we're safe. I can't wait around any longer. I need to uncover Luca's whereabouts somehow before he hurts us or someone else. There's got to be a way to move forward in our lives and at the same time find out where he is. Poppy would want that. "You can't stop living," he'd say. I do think I've stopped living the way I'm supposed to be living, and I'm trying hard not to do that.

I want to believe we can move on and everything will be okay. That's why Nico and I postponed the wedding. The happiest day of my life—postponed! Nico is one of the good outcomes of this tragedy. Had I never sought the truth, I'd never have found him.

My mother tries to reassure me it's different now. She says this time the police know about Luca, and thanks to Sienna, another good outcome, they're looking for him. He can't continue hiding. He doesn't have Aunt Lena anymore to protect him. Poor Aunt Lena—how devastated she was when she learned her husband had another wife.

Eventually, he'll have to come out of hiding.

But what if they never find him? What if the evidence that Luca left behind isn't enough, or worse, what if the evidence is gone by the time the police get around to finding it? Luca undoubtedly still has reach into the police force, to certain members who can make evidence disappear.

I push myself through the rest of the morning, sipping my coffee, brushing my teeth, running a comb through my hair, anticipating the next few hours ahead. Before I step out the front door, I check all the windows and the back door three times each. Then I give Hercules, my sweet, fluffy, three-year-old lab, a kiss on the head, toss him a treat, and grab my purse.

On my way to the door, I look through the window, and only when I see the empty doorstep do I open the door and step outside. I scan the street and houses and then lock the door behind me, checking it twice before walking away, ignoring the powerful urge to check again.

I slide into my car, close and lock the door, and quickly fire up the engine.

* * *

I'm waiting to see Luca appear on the front porch of Grace's beautiful Tuscan home when I arrive. My mother pulls in after me. It reminds me of the first day we finally came here to meet the parts of our family that were kept from us. My true biological grandmother, Gianna, and her sister, Sienna. My mother's lost twin, Grace, and her daughter, Emily. All hidden and unknown because of one man. The extension of love, history, and culture I had missed out on for so long. I embraced it all, at every chance, including Gianna and Grace shopping for wedding dresses with my mother and me. Having dinner together. I made sure to include them in my life at every opportunity I could, because life is short and nothing is guaranteed.

The same fear exists now, just as it did then. Luca must already be here, hiding inside the house, waiting to punish us and take us down together. A perfect opportunity. I glimpse the side of the house and almost see him emerging from the shore, walking on the sand to the deck where my mother and I will gather with our new family members. Our guard will be down, rendering us vulnerable.

I force him from my mind like so many times before. I won't let him take this moment from me. But there is no way to shut him out completely. Someone has to be on guard. Because no matter what I do, I know he can't be far.

Even in the long, arduous hours at the hospital, spending time with my patients, I sense Luca's presence behind the curtain. He's with me in the elevator, follows me to the help desk, and out into the parking lot. And even on the drive to my home with Nico, I sense his car trailing slowly behind me, headlights popping into the night, keeping far enough behind to predict my next turn. Headlights that follow me to my street. I drive past and they follow, turning where I turn, stopping when I stop. And I question

CHAPTER TWO

myself—the validity of these moments. Am I imagining it? Is it just another car driving a similar path, and my mind is playing tricks again?

I don't think so. The intense fear within me as I pull the key from the ignition and place my hand on the door overwhelms me. I throw it open, jump out, and hug my mother. Then, without words, I pull her along with me up the porch steps because I think I see someone behind the cypress trees, and I can't get into the house fast enough.

Would you recommend this book?

Dear Readers,

Thank you for choosing to read *Lies That Bind,* the prequel to the Ella Perri Mystery Series. Perhaps you started with the first book in the Ella Perri Mysteries series, *Buried Secrets,* or maybe you began with the second book, *One Last Secret.* Now the mystery is mostly complete and hopefully you've arrived at a satisfying ending. In this book, I've taken a closer look at the Perri family to provide a deeper understanding of what happened before *Buried Secrets.* Captured mostly through Luca's mother, Isabella's perspective, *Lies That Bind* provides insight into the evolving dysfunction of the Perri family.

If you enjoy reading *Lies That Bind,* please consider leaving a brief review on Amazon or as a post on my Facebook page. I always love hearing from my readers.

To learn more about my upcoming book or to receive free mysteries and thrillers, visit my website and subscribe to my mailing list. You may unsubscribe at any time.

With gratitude,
Krissy Baccaro
krissybaccaro.com

About the Author

KRISSY is an Award-Winning Finalist of the 2023 Page Turner Awards for Best Mystery/Cozy Mystery and the 2022 Wishing Shelf Book Awards in Adult Fiction, and she was shortlisted for The Page Turner Best Cover Award in 2022 for her debut mystery novel *Buried Secrets*.

Krissy was born and raised in Upstate New York in the charming town of Fairport, where she has taught for over 25 years. She and her husband live in Fairport, New York, and Venice, Florida.

Krissy remembers her love of reading as a young child and how she couldn't get enough of great books such as The Chronicles of Narnia, Lord of the Rings, and The Hobbit. Her love of mystery was first revealed within the pages of From The Mixed-Up Files of Mrs. Basil E. Frankweiler by E.L. Konigsburg and Nancy Drew's mystery series. She mostly reads mystery, suspense, and thriller novels but also enjoys fantasy and historical fiction. Some of her favorite suspense/thriller authors are Janelle Brown, Karin Slaughter, Lisa Jewel, and Mary Kubica.

Krissy is a proud member of Sisters in Crime, Mystery Writers of America, and several online writing communities.

Krissy is currently teaching writing and reading to 5th-grade students and thoroughly enjoys sharing her love of writing and reading with her students.. When the school day ends, the writing begins, and there is never enough time for that. Krissy resides in upstate New York, not far from Skaneateles, where the Ella Perri Mysteries began.

You can connect with me on:
- https://krissybaccaro.com

Also by Krissy Baccaro

ELLA PERRI MYSTERY SERIES
  Buried Secrets
  One Last Secret
  Lies That Bind
  Moment of Truth

SHORT FICTION
  Luca
  Psychological Thrillers Box Set

ANTHOLOGIES
  Once Upon a Story
  The Rearview Mirror

COMING SOON! Moment of Truth Book 4
Blood runs thicker than water—***but revenge runs deeper than both***.

As Ella Perri's vengeful uncle hunts his own family and his psychological warfare intensifies, Ella plunges into a relentless game of survival. With every dark secret she uncovers, the stakes rise and she faces a chilling truth—she must outwit him before it's too late and he destroys them all.

www.ingramcontent.com/pod-product-compliance
Lightning Source LLC
LaVergne TN
LVHW041625060526
838200LV00040B/1437